A

Splitting

Splitting

a novel by

Fay Weldon

THE ATLANTIC MONTHLY PRESS
NEW YORK

Printed in the United States of America

FIRST PAPERBACK EDITION

Library of Congress Cataloging-in-Publication Data

Weldon, Fay.
Splitting: a novel / by Fay Weldon. — 1st ed.
ISBN 0-87113-636-8 (pbk.)
I. Title.
PR6073.E374S67   1995   823'.914—dc20   95-1685

The Atlantic Monthly Press
841 Broadway
New York, NY 10003

10 9 8 7 6 5 4 3 2 1

Part One

A House Divided

(1)
Edwin's Divorce Petition

Sir Edwin Rice was divorcing Lady Angelica Rice. Sir Edwin alleged in his affidavit to the Court—a document which the lawyer Brian Moss was now dictating to his secretary Jelly White—that Lady Angelica had behaved intolerably. And would the Court therefore put the couple asunder.

Jelly White's hand trembled as she wrote. It was a pale, pretty, competent hand. Brian Moss liked it.

Angelica Rice, the document claimed, had committed adultery on many occasions with one Lambert Plaidy. Lady Rice had been discovered *in flagrante delicto* by Sir Edwin, and, what was more, in the Rice family four-poster bed. The housekeeper, a Mrs. MacArthur, would bear witness to this. Such behavior, typical of much similar behavior on the part of Angelica Rice, was unreasonable and intolerable to Sir Edwin.

Jelly White swallowed. Her throat was smooth and soft. Brian Moss liked that as well, and he very much liked the way she dressed: usually a neat knee-length skirt, pale cashmere sweater, a single row of pearls. He could see she was old-fashioned but he liked that too. The pearls were sufficiently translucent and uneven to be real.

Yes, it was intolerable for Edwin Rice to live with Angelica Rice: his health, his happiness were at risk.

Jelly White licked her pink perfect understated lips with a very red basic tongue. Brian Moss resolved not to become involved with her. He had a perfectly good wife at home. Jelly White was an ordinarily pretty blonde girl, of the two-a-penny kind, and too competent a secretary to risk losing.

The Petitioner, Edwin Rice, claimed that his spouse had acted in various other ways unacceptable to him: that she had been abusive and violent, pinching him while he brushed his teeth and otherwise molesting him; he alleged that her kissing of the family dogs amounted to bestiality, and her embracing of female guests to lesbianism. He petitioned the Court to let him go free of her.

Brian Moss heard Jelly White take in a whistle of outrage between her perfect little teeth, but her face remained peaceful and her hand was steady again as it continued to race across the sheet. He went on dictating.

The Petitioner claimed that Lady Angelica made excessive sexual demands on him; that she refused to have children; that she had dirty habits; that she was drunken, and took drugs; that she failed to provide proper food for his guests, thus humiliating Sir Edwin. And that, all in all, her behavior has been intolerable and unreasonable, and he wanted a divorce. Now.

"Goodness me!" said Jelly White, looking up from her shorthand pad. "I'm not accustomed to divorce work, but to me this smacks of overkill."

"How well you put it," said Brian Moss. "But overkill is our stock-in-trade. Here at Catterwall & Moss we prefer to offer the Court offenses in all available categories of unreasonable matrimonial behavior. Offer the minimum, as many firms do to avoid unnecessary trauma to the couple involved, and all you do is risk the Court's rejection of the petition. What pretty white fingers you have!" And his strong brown fingers—or so he saw them—slid over her pale, slim ones, and Jelly White let them stay. Brian Moss did not, in any case, interfere with her right hand, only with the left, which was not observably making him money.

Brian Moss was a short, stocky, good-looking, quick-moving man with a well-developed jaw and an impetuous nature.

"Lady Rice seems to have been a perfectly dreadful wife," remarked Jelly, "if this document is to be believed."
"The Court will certainly believe it," said Brian Moss. "It's true I had some trouble finding an example of physical assault. We had to make do with the bottom pinching."
"But Sir Edwin was happy enough to allege it?" enquired Jelly. "Knowing it was a lie?"
"In my experience," said Brian Moss, "a man very quickly comes to believe his own lies, especially in matters of divorce and if there is a new lady in his life."
"And is there a new lady in his life?" asked Jelly White.
"That is an improper question," said Brian Moss, "and confidential. But since in your new job you will have full access to all my relevant files, I suppose it hardly matters. Lady Anthea Box came along with Sir Edwin to our last meeting."

Jelly White made a hiccoughing little murmur and excused herself rather rapidly. Brian Moss thought it must be for some intimate female reason it was best not to enquire into. Jelly White had been working for Catterwall & Moss for a week—first in the secretarial pool but now, at his request, solely for Brian Moss. She had come through the Acme Agency and her references were impeccable. It had already been mooted that she should stay on as a permanent employee. She was competent, alert and interested in her work. Jelly White returned after a minute or so from the powder-room, composed and co-operative, as ever. Whatever the trouble had been, she had dealt with it effectively and swiftly. He liked that.

"Bestiality stays on the books as a major matrimonial offense," said Brian Moss, "though it's rarely used. It was on Lady Anthea's insistence that the kissing of the dogs is included in the petition."

"Won't Lady Rice just deny it?" asked Jelly White.

"Lady Rice has Barney Evans as her lawyer," said Brian Moss, "so it doesn't make much difference what she does or doesn't do, he'll bungle it. And once a thing is said, it stays in the mind, no matter who un-says it. Lady Anthea strikes me as a far shrewder person than her new boyfriend, if less agreeable."

"I see," said Jelly White, and then she asked, "Does truth and justice come into it?" but Brian Moss just laughed and chucked her under her perfect chin and said, "I hope I'm not going to get accused of sexual harassment," and Jelly White said, "I wasn't cut out to be a feminist, don't worry, Mr. Moss."

"Call me Brian in here," said Brian Moss, "but Mr. Moss everywhere else."

"Very well, Brian," said Jelly White.

Brian Moss invited Jelly White to join him in a glass of sherry.

"It's perfectly possible," said Brian Moss, "that Lady Anthea has been on the scene longer than Sir Edwin cares to admit. He was in here almost a year ago asking me about the parameters of divorce, matrimonial offense, division of property and so forth. He hasn't put a foot wrong. I don't think the wife will get a penny. It was she who walked out on him, vacated the matrimonial home; he even managed to discover her *in flagrante* first. The wealthy know how to look after themselves."

"That's why they stay wealthy, I suppose," put in Jelly White, with an attempt at lightness, but she was pale, very pale. "You mean the bastard just set her up?"

"In my experience," said Brian Moss, "men prefer the next wife to be in place before they get rid of the last. But no doubt the present wife will pick up her life well enough where it left off. She may even be well out of it. To all accounts it was a most unsuitable match. Lady Angelica strikes me as a woman without depth or complexity. Just rather passive, and very stupid not to have noticed what was going on. I hope you can get this document in the post today?"

"Of course," said Jelly White, but it was two days before she did, and even then she put the wrong postal code on the envelope, so it was four days before the document reached Barney Evans. Those four days gave Lady Rice time to present her own petition, thus giving herself some minor advantage in the game that is divorce. Brian Moss swore when he found out, and blamed the post. The Rice couple, he could see, would not be the kind to wait peaceably for a "no fault, no blame" arrangement. Fault there was, blame there was, and fault and blame they'd have. Well, all the more money for him.

Lady Angelica Rice lay naked in her soft bed at The Claremont, an hotel just a stone's throw from Claridges, where she had taken up residence, and appeared to talk to herself, as these days she so often did.

"It is my belief that we are suffering from a perforated personality," said Angelica. "We must expect some confusion while we sort ourselves out."

"I feel perfectly whole and sensible," said Jelly. "Nothing the matter with me. What do you mean by perforated?"

"I mean we haven't quite split," said Angelica, "but if there's any more trauma, by God we will. We won't know any more what the other ones are up to; we won't have to act by consensus; we'll just own the body in turns. Or take over unfairly when the others aren't looking. That's what happens when a personality splits. And, like as not, we'll get ourselves into even worse trouble."

"I have more of a right to this body, than any of you," said Jelly. "Most of the time I can't hear you anyway."

"They're fucking disgusting clothes," said a stranger.

"You see what I mean?" asked Angelica. "It's happening already. There might even be others of us in here. Oh, Jesus! Lady Rice, where are you?"

"I'm so tired, so sad," moaned Lady Rice. "I can't really take any interest in any of you. I just want to be alone."

"Jesus!" said Angelica again, and blocked them all off and took over. She ordered rosehip tea from Room Service, did her yoga exercises, took her Vitamin C and went to sleep.

This is the formal and official account, written by Jelly at a later date, when her narrative skills had been sufficiently honed, of how Angelica had come to be in such a pretty pass.

Chomsky argues that language is inherited, not learned: that all the languages of the world exist in the mind of the pre-verbal child; the skills of a particular language being triggered off by the environment that the child finds itself in. In the same way, Jelly believes, any number of possible personalities exist in the minds of all of us: normally only one is allowed to surface, but in some individuals, in some circumstances, a handful of others will become apparent. We may be conscious of these only as murmur of internalised conversation, of conflicting opinions, warring responses in the head: just sometimes their personalities are such there is simply no keeping them down.

Part Two

A House Restored

(1)
Angelica First Brings Edwin Home

"Mum," said Angelica from a phone box, "I've met this man. I'm bringing him home."

Home was a modest house in the English countryside, outside the village of Barley. Here, on this small estate, teachers, social workers and such like lived; people with good hearts and low incomes. As for the farmworkers, they'd been eased out altogether by falling wages and rising prices. Who wanted farmworkers anyway? Houses grew more profitably than ever did cereal crops.

"You're too young," said Angelica's mother at once. But too young for what, she didn't say. Edwin was twenty-one to Angelica's seventeen.

"You don't trust me," said Angelica. "You never have. You treat me like a child." She'd been saying that since she was twelve, when a film company had moved into the village to make Hardy's *Tess of the D'Urbervilles*. Nothing had been the same after that.
"You are a child!" said Mrs. Lavender White. "For all the rings you have in your nose." Angelica at that time had twelve in each ear as well as the two in each nostril, but Mrs. White had got used to those. It was the rings in the nose she worried about: they might result in disfigurement. And where else did her daughter have them? It didn't bear thinking about. "If it interests you, I've met a man, too, just like you."
"But Dad's only been dead a year," said Angelica, upset.

Widows are meant to fade away; they should keep a low profile for the sake of their kids. That way everyone knows who's where.

"Your father wouldn't mind," said Mrs. White, pleasantly. "He always wanted me to be happy." The man she was living with was married, the father of Angelica's schoolfriend Mary. His name was Gerald Hatherley. He'd been on the PTA with Mr. White, now in his grave. The two men had got on well enough, Angelica had to concede, during Mr. White's lifetime, before he had left his wife a widow and in need of looking after.

"I don't believe this," said Angelica. No one likes to be upstaged. Here the daughter was, bringing home what she'd thought was the catch of the season, only to find the mother already sporting in the water with dolphins.

The public phone box was arguably the prettiest in the whole country. Special permission had been obtained by environmentalists to paint it green, avoiding the traditionalist's scarlet, so that the box did not disturb an eye adjusted to the delights of its surroundings. For three successive years Barley had won a prize as the most charming village in the country—with its well-tended, cosily gardened stone cottages, all hollyhocks and buzzing bees in the summer, the white-painted, brown-beamed medieval houses which leaned into one another for support; its central copper-spired church: the village green, the ducking pond, the ancient market, and the coach park just beyond the village limits especially for the tourists. And even these latter did not disturb Barley's serenity too much, for the Parish Council allowed only one souvenir shop, and made few amenities available for the tourists' convenience, so news got round and the coach parties, on the whole, stayed away from so boring a place.

Edwin and Angelica, having warned Mrs. White, came on round to see her. They drove up in a red MG: two bright young things.

Edwin wore a tweed jacket and a knotted scarf. She wore leather. "That's a nice car," said Mrs. White.

"It's a red MG," said Edwin defensively. "A lot of chaps have them."

The humble housing estate where Angelica's mother lived with her lover was discreetly surrounded by trees, so its existence did not worry the Barleans, as they liked to call themselves. These days Barley proper is occupied by wealthy people who needed to travel to the city only a couple of times a week (if that) for Board Meetings. In the smaller, damper cottages, a few of the original villagers remained—old men who gave local color in the pub and would applaud the incomers' dart matches in return for a glass of beer; their wives cleaned others' houses, or staffed the few village shops.

Barley was a happy village: everyone agreed, and so of course an artists' colony had come to flourish here, in buildings converted from their original use, since current generations had no need of them. Former schoolhouses, chapels, a dozen barns, the old railway station—the rail link had long since gone—now gave the space and style required by the creative spirit.

Writers, potters, weavers, sculptors, architects came to Barley in the hope of encouraging and supporting one another, and having some-one to talk to: though what it came to in the end, so typically, was that spouses got betrayed and swapped, and the group eventually collapsed beneath a weight of bitter gossip, spite and envy, only to rise again, talent and hope renewed.

For this purpose, for this rebirth, a sacrifice is normally required: Angelica was to find herself the living sacrifice, but that was in the future. This was now.

"Most chaps who have little MGs aren't as well-built as you," Mrs. White remarked. "How do you fit into it?"
Edwin was six four and weighed 210 pounds. Angelica's mother looked him up and down appreciatively.
"Well, everyone has them anyway," said Edwin vaguely.
Angelica nudged Edwin and tried to explain that on the estate everyone had practical Ford Fiestas or got on the bus. Edwin looked puzzled and said he could remember Angelica very well driving a Lamborghini, unlicensed and under-age, what was she talking about? Angelica said that was different and Mrs. White said she could see they had a stormy relationship, and Edwin said on the contrary. Mrs. White said trust Angelica to bring home an argumentative man.

Edwin, by chance, for the young couple had met in London, lived single and unappreciated in Barley's dilapidated manor house, Rice Court; he was a scion of Barley's even greater stately home, a further two miles deeper into the Great Park, into the Green Forest, Cowarth Castle. Here Lord Cowarth, Edwin's father, lived. Though perhaps it should not be said "by chance," for how many people do not travel far and wide in search of adventure and distraction to discover that the one they set their hat at, the one who so occupies the erotic imagination, in fact comes from the same town, the next street, even the house next door or the apartment down below. Escape from one's origins, it so often seems, is out of the question, barred by fate.

"At least," said Mrs. White, "you're not on illegal drugs like all the rest or you'd be thinner. Or are you the kind who says alcohol is the worst substance of them all?"
"Am I undergoing some kind of character test?" asked Edwin. You could push him so far and no further.
"Yes," Mrs. White said promptly. "If you mean to marry my daughter you'll have to go through one or two."
"I never said I was going to marry her," he said, alarmed.

Angelica burst into tears and went and sat in her father's study, where her mother had never gone. But now her mother followed her in. Everything at home had changed. Angelica's tears grew noisier.

"Don't embarrass me," said Mrs. White.

"But you embarrassed me," said Angelica, accustomed to having the moral upper hand in these family matters.

"And you're supposed to be so tough," said Mrs. White, looking her daughter up and down. Angelica was a rock-and-roll star. She wore boots up to her thighs and a fringed leather shirt down to her knees, and her hair was canary yellow. If she couldn't look after herself by now it was time she did.

"No one's said anything about marriage," said Angelica. "We haven't even been to bed together."

"Then keep out of it," said Mrs. White. "That way he'll stay around."

Mrs. White had been to bed with Gerald Hatherley, and his wife was now divorcing him. That was different: they were grown-up people. These two were children: Angelica was having a difficult adolescence; an archetypal Billy Bunter, the fat schoolboy, still looked out of Sir Edwin's eyes. And Alice in Wonderland could still be seen in Angelica's, for all she'd earned two-thirds of a million pounds from a single entitled "Kinky Virgin": a sum sensibly put away in a Savings and Loan.

"You don't think I'm some sort of pervert?" asked Angelica. "I just don't like the thought of actual sex. It seems rather disgusting to me. I'd much rather just sing about it."

"I'm sure it's not my fault," said Mrs. White. "Sex disgusting? I never put that idea into your head. I can't have."

Angelica stayed out of Edwin's bed, and soon he asked her to marry him, on the old fashioned premise that that was the only way he'd get her into it. That was sixteen years ago, when marriage was still quite popular, and hit singles happened and made millions for innocents.

And that was when Angelica was still one person or at any rate, if you'd asked her, would have said she was. If you have a name like Angelica, it's asking for trouble. For one thing you have the kind of parents who give you such a name, and for another it's all too easy to split. Angel, Geli (or Jelly), Angela: she got called them all. Worse, if you know about A, J and A, and add an X for an unknown extra, you end up with Ajax. The strong, stubborn, stupid Hero of Ancient Greece, Ulysses' friend. All women have a male within their female, a yang within the yin, but seem nervous of encouraging it. Though men seem happy enough searching their psyches for the hidden female part of themselves—no shame for the yin to contain the yang—what woman wants to inspect themselves and discover Ajax? Naturally Angelica eschewed too much introspection. She skated along on the surface of things, as long as she possibly could.

But that comes after. This is now.

(2)

How They Told Edwin's Father

"We're going to get married," said Edwin to Lord Cowarth, his father. His mother had drunk herself to death long ago. Edwin was the youngest son so no-one took much notice of him. He was allowed to live in Rice Court, the crumbling Elizabethan mansion, if only to keep the damp and moth away.

Lord Cowarth looked Angelica up and down. They were in Cowarth Castle, in the Great Library, where a Caxton Bible was kept beneath glass. At Edwin's request, Angelica was wearing a white sweater and a black wool skirt. Her hair was dyed brown, and she had removed the rings from her nose. The scars were healing, the holes filling in. She looked conventional enough and easily shocked and she spoke with the slapdash incoherence of her generation. Lord Cowarth wore a dressing gown thin with age which fell apart to show skinny shanks and a tiny member.

"Has she got any money?" the father asked. He carried a cleaver wherever he went. He was short, rubicund and savage; thin in parts, fat in others.
"A few hundred thousand," said Edwin proudly.
Lord Cowarth grunted.
"I always thought you had your eye on that bint Anthea," he said. "Plain as a pikestaff but just right for you, the fat boy of the form. Can't abide a fat child," he said, and Angelica thought she saw Edwin wince. Mostly Edwin kept his face friendly and still, accustomed as he was to paternal rebuffs and insults. "Most of my chil-

dren were thin. Perhaps you're not my child at all. When I think of that tart of a woman I married"—Lord Cowarth's eyes narrowed—"it wouldn't surprise me." He spun Angelica round with fingers that clawed into her neck.

"What's your game?" he asked. "What are you after? A title, a house, or an education for your children?"

Angelica took hold of Edwin's hand, but her fiancé seemed incapable of helping her get free. All the strength had drained from him. So much old stags can always do to such progeny as rashly stay around.

Lord Cowarth balanced the cleaver in his hand, letting go of Angelica the better to do so. The cleaver was made of rusty old iron, solid old wood.

"I think he likes you," said Edwin softly.
"What are you whispering about? What are you plotting?" The old man had a front tooth missing. He struck the blunt back of the hilt against his lips. Soon another tooth would go. One way or another there would be blood in his mouth next time he opened it. A useful trick. When Lord Cowarth went to the House of Lords, for a Coronation or the investment of a relative, he would dress in finery: otherwise he kept to his dressing gown, and liked to have a bloody mouth. He seldom left his apartments: he could run the Rice Estate well enough from the Castle.
"I love your son," said Angelica. "That's what I was whispering. Sweet nothings, you know?"
That silenced him.

At least the old man did not forbid the wedding. Edwin could not have stood out against his father, and Angelica would not have expected him to. But now she had a chance to save him, build up his self-confidence, help him recognize and accept himself. She was brimming with good intentions.

"Will your brothers come to the wedding?" asked Angelica.
"Doubt it," said Edwin, stoically. He and she would marry quietly. She wanted to make him happy. She had not understood how anxious family life could make a man, riddling him with the expectation of rejection, of failure. His elder brothers, twins, twenty years older than he, now lived in warmer climes, in the Southern Seas; they had beautiful brown wives. One twin kept a restaurant; the other a marina. The Rice Estate kept both businesses in efficient managers: fish swam up, the yachts slid in: money flowed: titles entranced everyone. The languid tones of the English upper class travel well, though these days they grate upon the domestic ear.

The Kinky Virgin band would, of course, have none of Edwin: of his tweed jacket and knotted scarf, so Angelica would now have none of them.
"I'm giving music up," she said. "All that was only a flash in the pan. I haven't any real talent."
Now she'd seen her mother in a mini skirt, she'd lost her appetite for excess. Now she'd perceived the depths of Edwin's woes, the exhilarations of the rock stadium seemed distasteful. Besides, her father had died and who was there left to shock? Her mother had become unshockable; family friends had come to appreciate her, inasmuch as she put their own young into a better light. It was time to give up and grow up.

Angelica's arms were so skinny Edwin could close his hand right round where her biceps would be, were she to body-build. He liked that. Who these days could win a virgin bride? He felt marrying such a one would make the crops grow, and the dry rot recede: his breaking of the hymen, his staining of the marriage sheets, would bring good fortune and sanity to a land ruled by that mad old man, his father.

Someone had to be responsible: his twin brothers had left him behind to be just that; had run out on him. He had seen his life as a sacrifice: terrible girls had wooed him in spite of his looks, in spite of the veil of fat which protected him in his early years, making his penis seem tiny, his sufferings absurd; they had wooed him and bedded him for the sake of his title, his landed state, his patrician accents, never mind he would never properly inherit wealth, only a fearful responsibility and inevitable rejection: would, like as not, inherit madness from his father, but never have his father's power. Little by little Lord Cowarth had devolved that power to Robert Jellico, his Land Agent, and Robert Jellico, as well as being unerringly competent, was a powerful, sensible man, not given to evident emotion or the recognition of the financial duty that kinship imposes. Edwin complained that Robert Jellico looked at him strangely.

"He's gay," said Angelica simply. "That's all. That's why he looks at you the way he does. He's going to hate me. He's a man who rises at seven and doesn't understand the way you stay in bed till noon."

Edwin loved Angelica because she reduced terrible and complex things to such simple and graceful components, and seemed threatened by no one, except her mother, the only one who could make her cry. But those tears were the tears of the child, confident of love and the eventual pleasures of reconciliation and consolation.

She had not yet split.

(3)
The Wedding

Everyone came to the wedding, including the ghost of Edwin's mother. She was seen at the top of the narrow, ugly Jacobean stairs in a white dress, angrily waving a bottle, with a kind of miasmic mist floating from her: it left a damp coating on the bannisters which Mrs. MacArthur, the housekeeper, pretended was mould. Staff scrubbed and rubbed away at it but it kept returning; you couldn't get a shine on the wood, no matter what.

"Your mother's not angry with you," said Angelica to Edwin, "but I expect she's angry with your father. I'm sure she loved you very much."
"Why?" he asked, gloomily.
"Because you're loveable," she replied, and he looked at her in gratified astonishment, and kissed her chastely. Edwin had got accustomed to doing that. He didn't quite see how on a marriage night the habit of chastity was meant to change to the habit of uxorious sexuality, but if it had for his forefathers (as Angelica had assured him was the case—they had to marry virgins so as to keep the line of inheritance clear) no doubt it would for him.

"Why should my mother be angry with my father?" he asked. He took his father's behavior for granted, as sons will; as the father sees the world to be, so it is: daughters are often more critical.
"Your father is a monster," Angelica explained to Edwin and Edwin seemed quite surprised.
"That's just how he is," said Edwin, and only reluctantly conceded

what his mother had come to know so clearly: that his father was unpleasant beyond normality, even for the upper classes.

Pippi and Harry, Kinky Virgin's violinist and drummer, had seen the apparition.
"A cloud of fucking sperm," Pippi complained, "floating down the stairs. This old lady, following behind, waving a bottle. Was that your mother-in-law?"
"I hadn't even had a smoke," said Harry, "nor a sniff, nor a jab, and still I saw it. Unfair!"

None of Angelica's friends wanted her to marry Edwin: snobby twerp, nerd, cunt: from the posh end of yuppie-dom, who'd given the band, with its foul-mouthed, intelligent cacophony, a passing popularity and been the more resented for it. And rightly, Sloaning and boning its drugs; drawling through the early hours, slamming car doors in the dawn to wake up the babies of the boring, toiling classes, the drears who worried about mortgages and children who failed exams and how to crawl out of the pit of necessity, the miasma of need, which shortened lives and narrowed hope; the steady, frightened classes who included Kinky Virgin in the things most wrong with the world today. Thus the careless and the crude, the wealthy and the wilfully distressed, joined forces in the clubs, each despising the other, but despising the rest more.

Edwin and Angelica declared their engagement, joined hands across a chasm of custom and class, and nasty phantoms leapt up out of the depths to snap and snarl and make them break apart if they could; but at the time the lovers, or lovers-in-waiting, scarcely noticed their enemies; just felt surprised their match was so unpopular. All the world, which was meant to love a lover, plainly didn't.

"Is it wise to marry for money, darling?" enquired Boffy Dee of Edwin at the wedding. Boffy Dee had bedded Edwin once or twice,

he later found for a dare; she'd reported back to his circle, for reasons best known to herself, that his member was minuscule. He had
found himself hurt and humiliated by this: he'd had much comfort
from Boffy Dee, in a warmly dark and confident way; he'd believed
in her affection, trusted her pleasure and his own. Boffy Dee was
wearing a tight orange dress and a cartwheel hat, which made her
ugly: he hated her.

"I'm marrying Angelica because I love her," said Edwin, with a sim-
plicity which opened the way for yet more scorn. He thought it was
his bulk which made them all believe he was slow-witted and gave
him his reputation for clumsiness. Rice Court was a mass of small,
dark rooms and twisted staircases, which would open out into large,
panelled, cold, unliveable-in halls, a few open to the public and
therefore not home; everything crumbled and rotted. If you were a
large person and moved quickly or impulsively you'd put your foot
through the floor or break off some piece of wooden carving which
turned out to be historic and valuable, and cause hysterics. The
Elizabethan and Jacobean builders of Rice Court had been absurdly fine-boned and small-footed. Edwin had got quite accustomed to moving around with caution, but tales of his clumsiness
still got round. Fortunately Angelica had known him only in his
later days: she found him graceful enough.
Anthea Box, Edwin's cousin, was wearing Laura Ashley sprigs
which did nothing for her horsy looks, but made him feel affection-
ate towards her. She was the only one who seemed to have a good
word to say for Angelica.
"I expect the holes in her nose will heal up with time," said Anthea,
"now the rings are out."

Angelica settled down into being one person, un-split. Love is a
great sealer-over of seams.

(4)

Lady Rice, One Year into Her Marriage

"I'm not interested in money," said Lady Rice. "I'm not one bit materialistic." Which was just as well because within weeks of the wedding Robert Jellico suggested she use her funds to buy into the Rice Estate: with the money so released Rice Court could be refurbished.

Lady Angelica Rice gained the title on marriage. She and Edwin lived quietly in Rice Court; they spent a great deal of time entwined in bed; not with great passion, but with considerable affection, secure in each other's loving commitment. Angelica didn't see her friends: Edwin didn't see his. They smoked a great deal of dope. They went into the town for a late lunch, or dinner, often to McDonald's. Both relived, and recovered from, their childhoods.

They were not disturbed. Rice Court had been closed to the public of late; an ornate plaster ceiling had fallen and injured a visitor. Insurance had paid but everyone had had a nasty shock. Robert Jellico's perfect shirt had been seen awry and his smooth skin had sweated slightly. Now he worried that money was being lost while the young couple idled and slept.

The only disrupting energy was Mrs. MacArthur, who complained she had to act as nanny. To Edwin and Angelica she seemed merely vengeful, changing the sheets on the fourposter bed once a day, practically shaking them out of it; rattling empty coke tins into black plastic sacks, hoovering up roaches and snipped bits of this and that, broken matches and Rizla papers, throwing out baked beans on plates cracked because Edwin or Angelica had stepped on them by mistake.

"She gets paid, doesn't she?" said Edwin. "Why does she get in such a state?"

Lady Rice wrote Robert Jellico a check for the amount the cash machine said she had in her current account, minus one thousand pounds: £832,000.

"All that money in your current account!" said Robert Jellico, dazedly. "Not a high interest account, not even a building society? What was your mother thinking about?"

Mrs. White was busy thinking about Gerald Hatherley mostly, and wondering why his wife Audrey was being so difficult, and why Gerald's daughter Mary, who once was such a good friend of Angelica's, cut her dead on the street. It seemed strange to Mrs. White, as it did to her daughter, that the world was so full of people who simply didn't want you to be happy.

"Take the money," said Angelica grandly to everyone. "Money is of no importance. Invest it in Rice Court, if that's what you want. The Rice family is my family now, and that includes you, Robert." And indeed Robert Jellico, with his flat face, his overhanging eyelids, his Cardinal's mien, his grey eminence, seemed the old-worldly yet contemporary expression of the determined Rice soul. He it was who kept the balls of the whole business juggling in the air. For all his complicated love for Edwin, his evident disparagement of Angelica, they knew Robert Jellico was trustworthy enough. Robert knew money and property must be looked after. If Angelica's money went into the tenderest, most vulnerable, most simply sacrificed, last-in-first-out enterprises of the Rice Estate, the crumple zone of the commercial juggernaut, then that was the tax Angelica had to pay because she had no presentable family, and no social status; only money and a recent marriage. Robert Jellico made sure Angelica's money did not go directly towards the rebuilding of Rice Court, in case of future litigation, and any claim that might be made alleging the place to be the matrimonial home. He was not so stupid and she did not notice. Who, lately married, ever anticipates divorce?

The day the money disappeared into Rice Estate coffers, Angelica sat up in bed and said, "Edwin, we have to stop this now. We've recovered from the past, which was an illness. I shall smoke no more dope."

And nor she did, and presently he lost the habit too. They looked around and saw what they had, and it seemed full of promise, and why should Angelica split? She could cope as she was; she needed no allies.

(5)

Lady Rice, Three Years into Her Marriage

—spent a lot of time trying to get pregnant. That is to say, now in bed with Edwin only some twelve hours out of every twenty-four, she failed to take contraceptive precautions. If you didn't smoke dope, you had to do something. She could see it would be nice to be two people enclosed in one and carry that one around inside her: the thought made her dozy and warm. If there was a baby, the twelve waking, walking hours would flow easily and naturally: unedgily, undriven. The warm, milky smell and soft feel of babies, the slippery, honey scent of Johnson's Baby Oil would drift the days together, make day like night, summer like winter, bed and waking hours the same: she would be universally approved; her mother would think of Angelica for a change, not of her lover Gerald Hatherley and the ensuing Nasty Divorce (Audrey was still causing trouble): *Hello* would come and take photographs of Angelica and Edwin leaning into each other and a baby in a long, white christening robe in her arms. Angelica herself had never been christened: her name, she felt, had been the more variable.

"In my time," she told Edwin, "I've been called Jelly, Angel and Angela. People find Angelica too long and peculiar a name for comfort."
"I love it," said Edwin. "I've always loved it. The pale green strips on the icing of the cake. That's why I married you."
Edwin always used her full name, carefully and lovingly separating the syllables, the better to appreciate each one. An-gel-i-ca. She liked that. When her own baby was christened, she felt she would

come properly into her own name. She would allow no one to shorten it, and, as for the baby, it would have a name impossible to diminish.

"*Hello* would be very nice," said Edwin, "and they'd pay us, because we have titles, but the camera would get dust in it. The photos wouldn't come out. Everything round here is crumbling." Edwin, all agreed, tended to look on the gloomy side of things; to expect very little of the material world. From his point of view, if he was disappointed before he began, then failure could be interpreted as success in at least one thing—that he had been right all along. But Angelica encouraged her husband in good cheer, and indeed he was cheering up.

Edwin began cautiously to take up his axe, to chop down a rotten tree or so on the Estate, to tear away the odd beam made flaky by woodworm before it actually fell, whether on to the dining room table or the bed; he learned to trace the tap-tap-tap of the death-watch beetle, to pare away wood and reach the devouring little insect family, remove them carefully, at Angelica's behest, to one of the stables where they would do less harm. Such was her power over him, at the beginning: Angelica, who was tender-hearted towards all living creatures, though they demolish her house, eat away at her inheritance.

Every month with the moon, Angelica bled. Dr. Bleasdale said it took a long time for marihuana to clear itself out of the system, and the drug, even though Edwin and Angelica insisted they scarcely used it now, did impair fertility.
"It's not a drug," said Edwin to Angelica, "it's a leaf. And it doesn't impair fertility. That's just a story put about by the forces of law and order."
After a year, the doctor went further and attributed Angelica's inability to conceive to Edwin's sperm count, lowered, he claimed, by

drug-taking in the past. Edwin refused a test and Angelica did not blame him. The process involved sounded disgusting to both of them.

"Jealous of a simple jar!" said Edwin. "Fancy you!"
"Yes," said Angelica, "I am. Fancy me!"

They started going to the younger, female partner at the surgery, a Dr. Rosamund Plaidy, who said don't worry, there was lots of time. They were both young. Babies came when parents were ready for them. That felt better, and anyway Angelica became less and less sure that she was ready to be a parent. The convictions of youth diminished; the doubts of maturity deepened. If you weren't ever going to be able to have a baby, why bother wanting one? Pretend you didn't want enough, and the pretence would come true: keep the Johnson's Baby Oil for its proper purpose—sex.
"You are still trying, aren't you?" asked Edwin, noticing that the arrival of her period was no longer cause for tears.
"Of course," said Angelica, but she wasn't really.
"You're at your most fertile this week," he'd complain, "and all you do is sleep."

Angelica loved Edwin as much as ever but sometimes sleep seemed more attractive than sex. Or so a voice in her head would tell her, when she turned over in bed towards Edwin's caresses: "Do what you want, for God's sake—not what he wants," and she'd turn back again, away from him. It was Jelly's voice, impatient and imperious, but she thought it was her own.

Disappointment, and it is oddly disappointing to find one does not get pregnant at the first drop of an egg, the next available inrush of sperm, when one had assumed one would, can sharpen the ear to internal voices. They're always there, muttering away, but complacency is an excellent baffle-board.

(6)

Angelica, Five Years into the Marriage

These days Lady Rice would follow her husband out into the fields to watch him sawing branches, or fencing off public footpaths, or lighting bonfires. Edwin was developing muscles: a broad shoulder, a strong back. Things were pretty good, thought Angelica, and, if she did nothing in particular, would stay that way.

Robert Jellico reported back to Lord Cowarth, at Cowarth Castle, five miles up the road, that his youngest son was showing signs of reformation; that, surprisingly, the marriage was holding. Angelica's money had now been taken by the official Receivers of Rice Estate Fungi (Continental) — which had served as the year's most effective tax loss for Rice Estates. Jellico took some credit for the unexpected stability of the youngest son's marriage. Women without funds made better wives than women with funds, being more dependent. "Why aren't they breeding?" asked Lord Cowarth. "What's the matter with them?"

Lord Cowarth's disposition had improved over the previous three years. Infections had given him abscesses under his remaining teeth — six left from a once full set, mostly towards the back — and pain had finally driven him to the doctor. He had been given Prozac, a fashionable new anti-depressant, by Dr. Rosamund Plaidy.

Within six weeks of the first dose, Lord Cowarth married a blonde and leather-booted woman in her mid-fifties, now Ventura Lady Cowarth. (The wife of a youngest son and the wife of a full-blooded, propertied Earl are accorded the same title, or so Lavender White, who studied these matters, told her daughter. "Lady" covers all degrees of honor, saving only "Princess," "Countess," "Duchess" and "Queen." Angelica had become Lady Angelica Rice, but scraped in; Ventura became Ventura Lady Cowarth and had a whole lot of rank to spare.)

Ventura drank a great deal of whisky, but was kind, buxom and efficient, and liked Angelica, with whom she shared a common taste for leather; though Lady Rice, little by little, was taking to jeans and sweaters, neat skirts, little collars and long sleeves buttoned at the wrist.

"She may be a bit 'other ranks,' " said Ventura to her husband, "but at least she's a local and at least she's on hand!" Unlike, by inference, Edwin's elder brothers, the twins who had simply run out on the whole Cowarth caboodle.

Lord Cowarth had lately found the tie to his dressing gown. If it did still occasionally fall apart, it was to reveal skinny parts more robust than heretofore, and fleshy parts less hideous.

One day Edwin and Angelica were lying in the sun on a grassy mound where Cromwell the Protector was reputed to have single-handedly chopped down a maypole. Lord Cowarth's ancestor, Cromwell's friend, had had an ascetic nature and a grudging temperament, and had welcomed the coming of the Roundheads and the politics of the common man: his descendants since had specialized in debauchery, excess and dramatics, as if to make up for the sheer meanness of the man who had founded their fortune by personally shaving the ringlets off Royalist neighbors and seizing their estates.

Even as Sir Edwin and Lady Rice lay on the grass hand in hand, bodies touching, they watched a bird alight gracefully on a chimney. They saw the high brick erection crumble and fall through the tiled roof, heard the debris rumble down through the attic floor, the bedroom floor, to the library below, whence a puff of dust blew out through open latticed windows and dispersed. Of such events are the memories of marriage made.

Ashes to dust.

"Rice Court does need money spent on it, dear," Ventura said to her husband, "in fact as well as theory: brick by brick, not just a business plan!" and her husband had a word with Robert Jellico, who released half a million pounds to that end. The falling of the chimney had impressed everyone. A further half million, it was inferred, would follow when Angelica produced a child.

"I had no idea," said Angelica, distressed, as Edwin made constant efforts, night and day, to impregnate her, she by now having completely gone off the idea of babies, "that there were families left who behaved like this. Your father's worse sane than he was mad."

"There is no such thing," said Edwin, his great, consoling bulk heaving over her, "as a free title," and Angelica laughed, but she was hurt. Edwin would do this for money, but not for love? For Rice Court, not for her?

If Edwin wanted a baby for his family's sake, not for hers, not as a celebration of their love, that clinched the matter: she would rather not have an heir at all, or at any rate not yet. Better to live in a rose-covered cottage, however humble, abrim with domestic love, to have children as an outcome of that love, clustering around the knee, than to live in a mansion, have nannies, and be expected to breed for the sake of a line, in the interests of a family who thought themselves better than others for no good reason, especially since, so far as Angelica could see, that line was now more connected to commerce than to the land. And supposing the baby inherited its grandfather's madness? Its grandmother's alcoholism, its father's idleness? She loved Edwin dearly but without a doubt he was idle. And had not the early Rice forebears been robber barons, the organized criminals of the Middle Ages? The more she thought about it, the worse it seemed. Her side of the family might be mildly eccentric, but surely dwelt within the bounds of decent ordinariness: what could truly be said of the humble was that they tried to be good, if only from lack of energy to be otherwise. The Rice family had no problem being bad.

If Edwin showed signs of wanting a baby for his wife's sake, murmured a voice in Angelica's head, or, better still, saw a baby as the natural outcome of a great and enduring love, no doubt these worries would be quickly swept away in a wave of wanting—but until this happened, until Edwin grew up a bit, stopped trying to placate and gratify his awful family, Angelica would not risk the change in status that the having of a baby entailed.
"Better and safer to be the wife Edwin insanely loved," she would wake up thinking, "than the mother of a Rice child." Through history such mothers found themselves driven to drink, or pushed downstairs, or walled up, or just left at home and thoroughly neglected, once their purpose was served. They'd been allowed to dress up in their tiaras and produced at coronations, or state funerals, or victory parades to keep them quiet, but that was all.

Angelica dug out forgotten family portraits from the cellars and brought down monographs from the attics: restored, dusted, framed them all, and found in the family history more than enough proof for her suppositions. Beautiful girls made miserable mothers.
"There!" said the voice. "Right, wasn't I?"

And so to everyone's surprise Angelica didn't get pregnant. In fact, she had prudently asked at the surgery, before it was too late, for a contraceptive implant, one of a new kind which lasted for a whole five years, and young Dr. Rosamund Plaidy had obliged, tucked it under the skin of Angelica's buttocks with a deft incision of knife and needle. Gently, day by day, the implant leaked oestrogen into her system, keeping her rounded and placid and gentle. The more fertile she looked, the less fertile she was, and no giveaway card of pills either, hanging around to be found.

"You won't tell anyone about this?" Angelica implored Dr. Rosamund Plaidy, who at once looked both shocked and hurt at the notion that she might. "I wouldn't want it to get back to my father-in-law."
"Everything that goes on in here is totally confidential," said Rosamund Plaidy, as the knowing voice in Angelica's head had told her she would.
Dr. Rosamund Plaidy was thirty-four, wholesome, pleasant and well-informed, and was married to Lambert Plaidy, the writer. She had had her own first child at twenty-six and naturally believed that to be the optimum age for procreation. She saw nothing wrong or complicated, at least at the time, in standing between Angelica and her putative progeny. It did not occur to her that Angelica had not consulted with her husband before taking the quite drastic contraceptive measures, more suited to women living in the hot remote Sahara or the dank fastnesses of the Rain Forest, than in rural England. Though sometimes Angelica felt, as one verdant day drifted into another, and nothing much happened, she might as well have been living at the ends of the earth, as one hundred miles from London.

(7)

Angelica, Six Years into the Marriage

Robert Jellico had started a steady relationship with one Andy Pack, a jockey, and had become positively pleasant. He was prepared to exchange a non-acrimonious word with Angelica, and an un-neurotic one with Edwin. Robert, in a flush of generosity, even inflation-indexed the young couple's allowance. The Estate paid staff wages and household bills; Edwin and Angelica had to pay only for food and entertainment, and since their entertainment was still by and large each other, they could even make savings on what came in. Angelica saw fit to send her mother £50 a week: Gerald Hatherley was retired now and it was difficult for couple to pay so much as their heating bills. Gerald and Audrey were finally divorced; Gerald and Lavender married. Audrey had most of the savings. Lavender was finally talking to Angelica again, after Angelica suddenly developed flu on the morning of the wedding.

"Don't you have each other to keep each other warm?" Angelica asked when her mother complained about the heating bills, but clearly everyone's habits were different. The younger generation kept to its bed, if it possibly could: the older you got the easier you felt out of it, until old age set in, when there you'd be, under the covers again.

Robert Jellico said it was unreasonable that Rice Estate money should go to Edwin's mother-in-law, whose husband's duty it surely was to provide for her, and said as much to Edwin. And Edwin said to Angelica words to this effect—"The fifty pounds a week you give

your mother out of our housekeeping would be better spent on the
fabric of this house, on Rentokil and rat catchers. The medieval
drains are collapsing, and you don't even seem to notice."

"You should never have let that archaeologist in," said Angelica, "if
you didn't want them to collapse. I knew he'd be trouble." The actual restoration of Rice Court had still not begun; slowly, plans went
forward. As with a film in its pre-production stage, nothing seems to
happen and nothing seems to happen, and no one even gets paid,
except the director.

A representative from the University of Birmingham's Department
of Mediaeval Studies had turned up to photograph the brick sewer
system and, though asked to touch nothing, had removed for study
some critical piece of figured brickwork and thereby started a general collapse of a system which otherwise would have lasted another
couple of hundred years. If Lord Cowarth fired shotguns at all com-
ers, whether vagrants, gypsies, academics or social workers, Edwin
began to understand why. As he got older, the forces of law and
order seemed more and more attractive to him.

"There you go again," said Edwin, "trying to blame me for a failing
in yourself. Your heart's too kind."
"But my mother needs the money," said Angelica. "She'll be cold
and hungry without it," and Edwin, after complaining that she over-
stated her case, fretted and frowned and put it to his wife that surely
she saw the importance of the present. That surely it was time she
put her old life behind her: why should Angelica help Gerald Hatherley, the betrayer of Angelica's one-time best friend Mary's mother,
out of a fix? Why not? enquired Angelica. The difference caused a
slight coldness between them: a frisson, perhaps, of differences to
come, like wind tinged with ice because it's passed over the snow of
a mountain range, chilling the slumbering foothills.

Nothing to do with the voices, the internal war between self-help and self-destruct; just a kind of cold wind which happened to be blowing at the time, and affected all kinds of people in Barley. It must have, or what was to happen could never have happened.

(8)
More Troubles

"Think of all that money I gave the Rice Estate," Angelica would say, fretting about being expected not to give her mother money. "Surely something's due to me from that?" But one of the rules of the Rice Estate was that money swallowed was money swallowed, buried in earth, as hillsides were moved at Robert Jellico's direction. Roads were driven; river courses changed; estates developed and others torn down to make way for artificial grouse moors or ski slopes: mud everywhere, and gaping holes all around, grand canyons, yawning to receive the gift of other people's money in exchange for which the Rice organism could spew out money neatly and in deliberate fashion, all but unobserved, to interested parties amongst whom it did not include a youngest son's first wife. The Rice Estate knew when to waste, and when to save. Robert Jellico saw to all that: saw to it that the Estate sucked up millions, while shitting out tidy, tax-resistant cash pellets. The more that trust was put in Robert Jellico, the more smoothly the operation would run: that was the general understanding.

"I don't even have a receipt," Angelica would worry sometimes. "And work hasn't even started here; what *happened* to the money?" And she wondered why it was that water still drained from the hand basin before she even had time to wash her hands, so badly had it cracked; why there was so little comfort in her daily life. Mrs. MacArthur, who enjoyed threadbareness, who liked the job, who liked nothing better than a domestic emergency, who loved making do and mending, just said, "Four inches of water is more than enough for anyone to wash their hands in, my girl. The crack starts four and a quarter inches up. Don't be so greedy."

(9)

Angelica, Eight Years into the Marriage

—gave dinner parties. Lady Rice had made a circle of friends. Rice Court was open to the public again, and the great Hall and bedrooms had been roped and annotated—here Oliver Cromwell dined; on this spot the first Lord Cowarth fell, poisoned; here the bed in which he recovered, alas; see here the priest-hole in which the priest was walled up alive and died; this the Chinese vase presented by Queen Victoria; here the love couch on which King Edward VIII sat entwined with Mrs. Simpson; and so forth—but the back of the house, which faced south in any case and caught the last light, could be run as the more ordinary but still splendid home of a comparatively ordinary young couple. Ceilings and chimneys no longer collapsed, doors fitted, windows opened: in the kitchens ancient iron pots had been replaced with stainless steel saucepans; ceramic hobs now ran on electricity rather than hotplates on coal and coke. Mrs. MacArthur seemed ten years younger than once she had. Her hair had been permed, and ringed her dour face in girlish fashion. Mr. MacArthur had been made redundant from his job as a bodywork welder up at the auto factory. His wife was now the family breadwinner and there was no hope of Angelica firing her. But she allowed her employer her head when it came to running the visitor trade.

It was acknowledged, even by Lord Cowarth, that Lady Rice was efficient when she put her mind to it: had a gift for knowing what took the visitors' fancy, why they would prefer cream to butter on their scones, why they would buy fudge but not mints, why they gawped at Mrs. Simpson's love seat but didn't care for Lord Cowarth's collection of arrowheads.

And after the last visitor had gone, when the money had been accounted for and sent off to swell the Rice Estate coffers, and she had earned the approval of Robert Jellico, what could be more pleasant than to have friends round? To prepare meals, using the cookery books brought home by Edwin, who shared the cooking with her, trying out dishes from everywhere, from Afghanistan to Georgia to Iran—places at that time not so riven by violence, cruelty and war as to make their very food suspect, too potentially full of grief for enjoyment.

Edwin and Angelica, Rosamund and Lambert, Susan and Humphrey, were the central couples: others around, espoused or as singles, performed a dance of delicate social balance; creating their own precise etiquette. Friends, acquaintances, colleagues flitted in and out of focus round the table; each knowing their place; smiling faces breaking bread, providing advice, entertainment, common cause. Edwin and Angelica offered the most eccentric yet the grandest table of the group. Though the power and prestige Rice Court represented was now seen as fit only for tourists, even peasant food tasted good on a refectory table large enough to seat twelve and with lots of elbow room. Rosamund, the doctor, responsible, kindly and steady, and Lambert her husband, a writer, wild-eyed, wild-haired, made up in skills and talent for anything they lacked in style: a double act and a crowded table in a book-lined room, down the corridor from the kitchen. Susan, the potter from Minnesota, rosy, exotic and sexy, with her bubbling enthusiasms, her fair shiny hair, her attractive naïveté, a basket-full of English garden flowers or chutneys, Easter gifts or winter comforts somehow always on her arm, forever bearing gifts, her adoring, plump, good, mournful, clumsy husband Humphrey, the architect, served food Japanese fashion, on the carpeted floor, amongst cushions. Rosamund had two children, Susan had one, Angelica had none. Edwin still took that amiss.

"Perhaps I should have had a sperm count," said Edwin one night at Susan's. "What do men *do* when they're not fathers?"
And everyone laughed.
"Love their wives," said Angelica, and realized with alarm to what degree she counted on Rosamund not to tell about the implant. Too late to tell Edwin herself: why had she not when first Rosamund tucked it under her skin? She could hardly remember. Time enough, time enough, as Rosamund averred. A 5 percent increase in visitors this season: there was so much for Angelica to do, and Edwin too if he wanted, but he didn't. Edwin merely seemed to potter and brood; he began to have a puzzled look, as did Humphrey, whose architectural practice was failing. It is a terrible thing to have to search for occupation. Lambert, too, was in financial difficulty. His publishers dropped him from their list; his agent was too busy to speak to him. He was misunderstood. He spent more time with the children, leaving Rosamund free to do night duty; indeed obliged to do so, if bills were to be met.

Angelica, the youngest in the group, saw her task as learning, and learn she did; over the dinner table. She could talk now about abstract matters: what justice was, and injustice; understood better when to confide, when to stay quiet; had opinions about what art was, who really ran the country and so on. Whether agents-provocateurs let off bombs, or terrorists.
From Susan she learned a kind of sophisticated feminine response; things her mother had never taught her. She learned that flowers need to be arranged, not just plonked in a vase; that their leaves had to be stripped, stems crushed. Sensual pleasures, Susan implied, were the same. The more you postponed, the more you enjoyed. This apparently went for sex, too, and suited Angelica very well. Or, as Susan said, "Gosh, your English men are so bad at, like, wooing. This is certainly no red-rose culture you have over here!" Though,

heaven knew, Humphrey circled Susan with bouquets, took her for romantic weekends to Vienna, had her portrait painted, personally manicured her strong potter's hands in a manner most un-English.

Susan took it as her due. She had previously been married to Alan Adliss, the now famous landscape painter. She'd run off with Humphrey, taking him away from Helen, his fat, faithless and insensitive wife—or so everyone described her, taking Susan's word for it. No one of the circle had actually ever met Helen, of course, nor wished to—she belonged to some other world layered behind this one, its sufferings incomprehensible, irrelevant: whining voices on answerphones demanding consideration, remembrance, the money second wives saw as their due. Unloved women, those in the past, should simply fade away, as should widowed mothers. At least there was no one like this in Edwin's past: she was his first wife, his only wife. These emotional and marital difficulties were for others, not for Angelica. Yes, she was conceited, and foolish.

Angelica assumed she was the nicest person in the world: there was not even any internal discussion about the possibility of this not necessarily being the case. How could there be? She was the heroine of her own life. Her lack of response to her father's death puzzled her. The event had scarcely marked her. Why? It was as if he had been some kind of prop, not a person at all. Surely this must be a failing in him, not in her? All the same, she could see her non-grief at his death as being some kind of time-bomb somewhere in her persona, as the oestrogen implant was a time-bomb in her body, antipathetical to the very origins of life.

Back in the Sixties, Lavender Lamb, aged seventeen, married Stephen White, aged fifty-two, and gave birth soon thereafter to a little girl they named Angelica, who was both dutiful and ambitious, cute and swift. Sometimes they called her Jelly, for short—in affection and dismissal, "Oh, Jelly, you are being a pain; what husband will put up with you?"—and occasionally they called her Angel, as in "Angel, dearest, fetch me this; Angel, dearest, fetch me that. Angel, dearest, put pennies on your poor dead father's eyes. He, too, is an angel now. If only you hadn't chosen to sing that rock-and-roll stuff, if only you'd stuck to Handel's *Messiah*, you could have risen to soprano lead and your father might not have got so upset and died. Not that I'm blaming you, my Angel, both our Angel, indeed you were your father's Angel, with a voice that carolled like a lark, in whatever mode you chose, and at least he didn't live to have to listen to 'Kinky Virgin.' At least you preserved your virginity, for his sake, until he croaked, pegged it, passed over, fell off the perch. It was only to be expected, he being thirty-five years older than me, but I can tell you expecting makes no difference. It's still an outrage to be left without a husband."

Larks and lambs, and pure white rice: add a soupçon of barley; all good things. Why do they go wrong? Nothing's ever over, that's the answer, not even the giving of names. They should have called her Jane: it is a name scarcely open to division, perforating, or outright splitting. Angelica was just asking for trouble.

More and more Angelica turned away from Edwin in bed; fastidiousness could tire you out: sleep could become the greater desire. Or was it that the potential of pregnancy, framing sex with light, was what kept sex interesting, as the sun behind a dark cloud will frill it with brilliance? She could almost believe now, in any case, that the implant was imaginary. The Rosamund she'd met for the first time in the surgery had been a stranger: now she was a friend. Everything was different, why not this too? Better not to enquire. Perhaps anyway such implants had been proved not to work: how could anything keep working for so long; and who was to say whether it was actually this pellet of artificially deposited hormone which kept

Edwin's and her destined child out of the world, or an act of God? If Rosamund had made no mention of the implant the first time Edwin had said over dinner, "We're not too hot in the fertility stakes, Angelica and I," or however he'd put it, in his offhand, English way, perhaps it was because there was indeed nothing to mention. Years drifted by and the events of one year were lost in the dramas of the next.

She wished Edwin were more like Humphrey; more adoring, more romantic, less companionable.

She made herself go and sit by her father's grave: the Rice Estate was digging up the churchyard cemetery overflow, where her father's body lay, to build an extension to a new sports center. She knew if she didn't visit now she never could, and even this sense of his corporeal, albeit disintegrating reality, be lost to her. But still she could not bring Stephen White properly to mind: he had been too elderly, too amiable, too vague to be quite real. Someone who had failed to elicit strong passions in her, who had lived in the past, but whose time had overlapped hers; whose enthusiasms had been alien to hers, making her feel a changeling.

She felt dull. Edwin's former clubbing friends would turn up at the new, improved Rice Court from time to time, or friends from the ex–hunting and shooting, now property-developing, junk-bonding set, observe just how very, very dull country life could be, and depart. Angelica's ex-music-biz friends would arrive to gaze at the country moon under the influence of one substance or another, deplore what marriage and maturity could do to a girl, even leaving babies out of it, and depart.

Sometimes Anthea came to dinner, and Edwin would yawn and say, "She thinks of nothing but horses: keep her away from me, though she is my cousin. Do you realize, if I'd been a girl and she'd been a boy, she'd have had my title!"

Or Boffy Dee would turn up for a heart to heart and a glass of gin. She was marrying a racing driver who'd had so many knocks to the head he couldn't speak without slurring, but Boffy Dee did not see brain damage as an impediment to marital happiness. On the contrary.

(10)
Trouble in the Group

Rosamund called Angelica one evening and said, "Angelica, this is terrible: we have to *do* something. I think Susan is having an affair with Clive Rappaport. I keep seeing his car and hers parked in strange places when I'm out on my calls, and nobody in either of them." It was summer and the grass was green.

Clive Rappaport was a solicitor, one of the outer circle of friends: quiet, serious, romantic; very much married to Natalie, plump, dark, effervescent.

"That's completely out of the question," said Angelica.
"Why?" demanded Rosamund. And Angelica reminded her that only a couple of weeks back, at a picnic on the old railway track—Susan and Humphrey lived in a charmingly converted railway station—Natalie had confided, half-joking, half-serious, as women will amongst friends, that Clive had gone off her, lost sexual interest.
"What do I do?" Natalie had asked. "We've never had trouble like this before."
"Wear black lingerie," Susan had replied. "Lace and garters, high heels. Parade up and down. That always works." And everyone had laughed, a little awkwardly. Because it had seemed a strange thing to say, in a group so dedicated to the notion that sex was to do with love, not lust.

"If Susan was having an affair with Clive," said Angelica to Rosamund now, "she couldn't possibly have said a thing like that."

Which just showed, in retrospect, how little Angelica knew about anything.

"Oh yes she could," said Rosamund, "if she was secure enough, conceited enough, knew absolutely certainly that no amount of black underwear could ever get Clive happy in bed with Natalie again and was trying to cover her tracks."
"She's not like that," said Angelica, shocked. "Not Susan."

At least until now she had supposed not. It was true men became animated when Susan came into a room: with her bony, slightly gawky figure, the thick bell of blonde hair swinging; but so did women: it was obvious Humphrey adored Susan, Susan adored Humphrey. Angelica gave the matter minimal thought and put it out of her mind. Rosamund was overworked: mildly paranoid. She was having a hard time with Lambert, who would put her down in company, lament the minimal size of her breasts, her concern for everyone in the world but him, and Rosamund responded, no doubt, by seeing trouble everywhere but at home. She reported to Edwin what Rosamund had said and Edwin replied, "What on earth would Susan see in Clive Rappaport: he's dull as ditch water," which was not quite the response Angelica would have expected, but then more and more things these days were unexpected.

Unexpected, too, when the next week Lambert, Rosamund's husband, came to Angelica and said, "Angelica, I think Susan and Edwin are having an affair," and Angelica said, "Lambert, you are absurd, and what would it have to do with you if they were, anyway, which they aren't? Are you having a breakdown? Why do you look so dreadful?" Lambert did: he wore track suit bottoms, an old army shirt untucked in, and had not had a shave for a week or a haircut for three months.

"You should never have had that contraceptive implant," said Lambert. "Rosamund told you so at the time but you wouldn't listen. Look at the trouble it got everyone into. You're Edwin's wife. You should have given him a baby."

"What?" enquired Angelica. "What? Who said I wouldn't give Edwin a baby?"

"It's in your file at the surgery," said Lambert, and declined to say more. Angelica's concerns were none of his. But if Lambert told Susan, and Susan told Edwin—no, it was beyond belief. Lambert was, in any case, out of his mind.

"Rosamund," said Angelica, going round after surgery, finding Rosamund rubber-gloved amongst blood samples and card indices, busy with the tragedies of others, "Rosamund, what are we to do about Lambert?"

"We?" enquired Rosamund. Her hair was curlier than ever with sweat and exhaustion. Her honest, bright face was pale: her freckles stood out. She was loveable, Angelica realized, and admirable, but she was worthy, and would never be glamorous.

"Friends," said Angelica. "We're all friends," and Angelica gave Rosamund the gist of Lambert's lament, as one would relate the tale of a madman to those most concerned with his welfare.

"There is all kinds of stuff here," said Angelica, "that could really upset people. Doesn't Lambert realize that?"

"Angelica," said Rosamund, "of course he does. It is naïve of you to suppose that people will avoid doing harm if they understand what harm is. Some people like doing harm."

"But not Lambert," said Angelica. "Not anyone we *know*."

Rosamund raised her eyebrows and busied herself emptying test tubes down the sink.

"Isn't there anyone else to do that?" asked Angelica.

"If I pay them," said Rosamund, shortly.

"Rosamund," said Angelica, "this is important."

"It's not life and death," said Rosamund. "Mrs. Anna Wesley has too much protein in her urine. That's important. Lambert has told me that Susan's little Roland is his child, that Humphrey isn't the father. I've looked in their files. The blood types correlate. Humphrey has a really low sperm count, as it happens.'

"Lambert's insane," said Angelica.

"Lambert's been in love with Susan for years, apparently," said Rosamund. "He stayed with me for the children's sake—not mine, he tells me: I don't somehow enter into the equation. Poor Susan. Poor Humphrey. Poor Lambert. Me, I just do the work round here and earn the living. And now Susan says she's pregnant, so Lambert's convinced it's Edwin's."

"But why?"

"Because you won't give Edwin a baby, and Susan's so kind and soft-hearted," said Rosamund, adding, with savagery, "fucking little slut."

Angelica stared.

"You can't keep implants secret," said Rosamund. "Lambert looks through the files for material for his stories. Everyone knows, except you. You did know but you seem to have forgotten. You're very peculiar, Angelica. Sometimes I think you sleepwalk through your life. I'd never suggest Prozac for you: you're enough of a Pollyanna as it is, rising cheerful and positive to each day."

"I don't believe any of this," said Angelica. But when she thought about it, it was true that Lambert and Roland had the same wide-spaced, prominent, wild brown eyes: now the thought was in the head, the evidence was there. Just as the understanding that the continents have drifted apart, over the aeons, from the one original land mass, became evident and obvious to anyone who looked at a globe post-1926, when the notion was first floated, but simply didn't occur to the generations before.

"I don't believe Lambert's in love with Susan," said Angelica, hope-lessly. "You two are too good together. You go together. Why should Lambert love Susan when he's got you?"

"Because I'm boring," observed Rosamund calmly, "and Susan's not. I only speak when I've something to say and Susan babbles ceaselessly on. I work regular hours and wear myself out toiling for humanity, while Susan is full of artistic sensibility. Lambert's a writer, Susan's a potter. Creative, you know? They need the likes of Humphrey and myself to earn their livings, but we're not exactly sources of powerful emotion, are we? We can't expect to stay the course."

"And if Susan's having an affair with anyone," said Angelica, "it's Clive Rappaport, not Edwin. You said so yourself. And Susan would never do a thing like that to me. I'm her best friend. Lambert must stop saying these things. He's insane."

"I'd rather it was Edwin than Clive," said Rosamund. "Because if it's Clive, poor Natalie will have to get to know, and poor Hum-phrey as well—"

"Well, thank you very much," said Angelica. "You don't think it matters about poor me?"

"Oh, Angelica," said Rosamund in dismissal, "you're like me, you can look after yourself," which surprised Angelica very much. It had never been her intention to turn out sensible, good-natured and en-during: the kind of woman who would put up with a husband's in-fidelities for the sake of the greater good.

"And, anyway," Rosamund added, "you don't have any children so it's hardly important." Which made Angelica see why Lambert might well have set his face against Rosamund, might well prefer Susan. Angelica was almost convinced, but not quite. As for Edwin fathering some putative child of Susan's, that was simply not possi-ble. Edwin was too responsible, too lordly, ever to take Susan seri-ously. They liked her, but she was lightweight.

Angelica called Susan to say perhaps she'd better come round and talk a few things over. Humphrey picked up the telephone; someone tried to snatch it away. All kinds of noises came from the other end of the line: bangings, batterings, little Roland crying, then finally screaming; an unknown voice saying, "Humphrey, don't speak to anyone. I forbid it. See a solicitor first." More breathings, and then Humphrey was in charge of the instrument. Humphrey said, with unwonted passion, "Is that you, Angelica? You bitch! You've been conniving with Susan; you knew all about it; she took her lead from you; she's told me about you and Lambert." And Humphrey put the phone down.

Angelica laughed. She could not help it. Edwin came into the room.
"What's funny?" asked Edwin.
"Susan's having an affair with (a) Clive Rappaport, (b) Lambert, (c) you. I'm having an affair with Lambert: you and/or Clive Rappaport are fathering Susan's baby. This is village life."
"I don't think that's funny," said Edwin, but he seemed unsurprised. "Why do you laugh at other people's troubles?"
"Well," said Angelica, "if it was true, it would be my trouble, too."
"So you're denying it?" asked Edwin. "Susan says it's true."

Angelica cannot believe it of Susan, that she should tell such lies to get out of trouble, as if everyone were back at school. A clear sky is suddenly swept by clouds: black ones, layering, level upon level, and a different storm swells up between each layer, each feeding upon its fellows. Lightning cracks the sky; thunder blasts; the tempest pours. Angelica no longer stands pure, untroubled, shone upon by the sun of love and good fortune. The ground she stands upon trembles. The best she can hope for now is not to be utterly cast down. It is all too sudden.
Edwin turns on the television as if nothing was happening.

"Edwin," says Angelica to her husband, "something extraordinary is going on at Railway Cottage. Aren't you interested?"

"No," says Edwin, "it really has very little to do with us."

He has found a documentary on Northern Ireland. He does not take his eyes from the screen.

"I think it has," says Angelica.

"I knew you'd try to make a meal of it," says Edwin. "It's not a good idea to turn private matters into public gossip."

"But Susan is my friend," says Angelica. "She's in trouble—"

"You have hardly behaved like a friend to her," says Edwin.

"If she's telling lies about Rosamund's husband and myself—," says Angelica.

"I think she worries about your plans for her own husband, forget Rosamund's."

"This is bizarre," says Angelica.

She would shake her husband, except he has turned into a stranger, and a hostile one at that.

"Do you have no loyalty to me?" asks Angelica. "You'll listen to any old gossip."

"You're the one who asked it into the house," remarks Edwin. "You're the one who wanted a social life. Susan called me yesterday. She wanted my advice."

And he told Angelica that Susan had been on the phone to Clive, discussing some work project. Natalie had picked up the extension, listened in, misunderstood and become hysterical.

"Though Natalie's own conduct," says Edwin, "scarcely gives her leave to object to whatever Clive chooses or does not choose to do, but when were women ever reasonable? Their idea of justice is very one-sided. Susan was afraid Natalie might cause trouble by calling Humphrey, so she called me. That's all."

"Why you?" asks Angelica.

"I suppose," says Edwin, "because I'm her friend and the only one she can rely on not to gossip or make a drama and a meal of some-

thing so important. Could all this wait till the program has ended?"
"How dare he!" says a voice in Angelica's head. "How dare he!"
Another one says "don't rock the boat," another one says "take him
upstairs and fuck him," and Angelica shakes her head to be rid of
them, which works.

Angelica switches the TV off. Edwin sighs.
"I do not believe Susan has ever had the slightest suspicion about
me and Humphrey," says Angelica, regaining her composure.
"Humphrey is old enough to be my father. Shouldn't we investigate
this? Perhaps it's Humphrey's fantasy? That I'm after him? I'm sorry
I switched off the TV. It was rude of me."
"That's all right," says Edwin, quite cheerfully. "I expect Susan is
over-sensitive. She worries so about growing old. I told her she was
being silly."
"How do you know?" asks Angelica. "How do you know things
about Susan I don't? You sound so close to her."
"When you're busy with the Heritage Shop," says Edwin, "Susan
and I sometimes go for walks. She's interested in all kinds of things
you aren't. English wild flowers, for example."
"The bitch!" says Angelica finally.
"Susan says she thinks there's some kind of lesbian element in your
attitude to her," says Edwin. "It makes her uneasy. She thinks you
may prefer women to men but can't face it."
"And what do you think?' asked Angelica.
"I don't know," said Edwin. "You're not exactly all over me these
days."

Angelica paced, and thought, and thought, and paced, while Edwin
stroked and patted the dogs, Labradors, one of whom lay in his lap
and the other over his feet, large, soothing, fleshy golden creatures.
Edwin turned the television back on. But the program on Northern
Ireland was finished. He sighed again.

"He doesn't love you anymore," one of the voices told her. "He's waiting for you to vanish," but Angelica dismissed that as malicious scaremongering.

"What advice did you give Susan?" Angelica asked Edwin, finally. It was as if she were allowed only one question, as in some child's game, so that question had better be good.

"I said that since Natalie was both vindictive and possessive, her first step would be to get in touch with Humphrey. So Susan had better get in first, and tell her husband herself before the balloon went up. Okay?"

"Edwin," said Angelica, "that was very strange advice. What are you trying to do? Blow things apart? The only thing Susan should have done was to deny everything, everything."

"My dear," said Edwin, "she consulted me, not you."

"Edwin's been having an affair with Susan," said the voice, "and he too has only just now discovered about Susan fucking Clive, and that's indeed what he wants to do: blow the whole thing apart."

"Shut up!" shrieked Angelica internally, and the voice said sulkily, "Don't say I didn't warn you," and fell silent.

There was a kind of scraping at the door, a sound half way between a scrabble and a tap, and Edwin opened the door to Susan, weeping, swollen-faced, shivering with cold and barefooted. There was snow on the ground outside. Her toes were blue. Susan sat in an armchair while Angelica fetched blankets and Edwin took Susan's feet in his hands and rubbed and patted to restore their blood supply.

"Humphrey threw me out of the house," wept Susan. "My own house. I did everything you told me, Edwin. I waited for a good moment and told him how silly and stupid I'd been over Clive: I told him it meant nothing. I told them Natalie was over-reacting. I told them the last thing on my mind was to hurt Natalie: how could I? She's my friend. I told Humphrey he'd been so caught up lately with business matters, he could hardly be surprised if some other man attracted my attention. I'm younger than him, after all. I told him how Clive and I have this fantastic intellectual and artistic rapport—but sex hardly enters into it at all. We just sometimes meet on our own, the way you and I do, Edwin. Edwin and I go on nature walks sometimes, Angelica. I told Humphrey he should learn from this incident and realize his marriage might be in danger so he'd better work harder at it; neglecting me wasn't going to work. And all he did was turn into a primitive Victorian in front of my eyes. Oh shit! He threw me out of the house, literally, physically, without giving me time even to put on my shoes, and locked the door so I couldn't get back in. I went next door and called Clive from there but he was no help at all. He said Natalie had taken an overdose of sleeping pills and he was waiting for the doctor, so he couldn't talk now. He called her 'his wife' as if it was some kind of magic. She mattered and I didn't. She has him totally under her thumb. She's such a mean, trouble-making bitch." Susan caught Angelica's arm. "This is an appalling time for me! You won't let me down, will you, Angelica?"

"Of course not," said Angelica.

"Because you're my friend and you're civilized and you understand these things. You and Lambert are very close, aren't you, and Edwin doesn't make a stupid fuss, let alone lock you out in the snow."

Angelica listened for comments from the voices but there were none. She was on her own. She unhooked herself from Susan's hand. Edwin went to fetch a dry towel for Susan's feet. Whether or not he had caught the gist of Susan's remark regarding Lambert Angelica could not be sure. Perhaps these insane statements just washed over him: some men never listened to conversations between women at the best of times; and if the conversations became emotionally loaded men could become suddenly altogether deaf.

"Susan," Angelica said, all the same, "because you go round having affairs with your best friends' husbands does not mean everyone does. I certainly don't. What do you mean, me and Lambert?"
Susan laughed harshly and said that all she ever got from the English were pious platitudes and no understanding at all of love or its imperatives. All the subtlety of her relationship with Clive, all the power, the passion, the throbbing soul of it, reduced to the glibness of Angelica's phrase—"having an affair."
To which Angelica said, "Bet you didn't say all that 'throbbing soul' bit to Humphrey, unless of course you're sick of Humphrey, which I would understand."

"Why?" enquired Susan, displaying a sudden and mean vulgarity. "Because you'd like to get your sticky little fingers on him?"

Angelica did not think that worth responding to.

Edwin returned. Susan's cold foot now pressed against his cheek, as he rubbed it with the towel.
"I do so badly need someone to look after me," said Susan, "especially now."
"Poor Susan," said Edwin. "Of course we'll look after you, won't we, Angelica?"
"Why especially now?" asked Angelica.
"Susan's pregnant," said Edwin.
"Three months, Angelica," said Susan.

There was a flurry of voices in Angelica's head: she tried to make sense of them: they were calling warnings, giggling told-you-so's; others were swear-wording, fucking and cunting; then out of the cacophony came a silence: then a consensus. "Angelica can't cope. She's no use to us. Get rid of her."

"Angelica, did you hear me?" asked Edwin.
To which Angelica replied, inanely enough, "Don't call me Angelica any more, call me Lady Rice."

And having said it, Angelica, that anxious young woman of many parts and an interesting past, fled without warning into the fastnesses of herself, as abruptly and rashly as people flee to escape rocket attack, earthquake, forest fire, in the interest of survival itself, leaving a mere Lady Rice behind, to cope as best she could.

"I'm sorry," said Lady Rice, the too-sudden transition confusing her as well, "I don't feel very well."

Lady Rice was always sorry and seldom well. She was a loving, drooping, companionable creature, but now stood alone, like some eighteenth-century face mask, the kind worn at balls, behind which a series of others hid; some blonde, some dark; some young, some old; all at the moment deathly still, all terrified—only Jelly, perhaps, craning a little this way or that, just visible, showed flickers of life, of intent. None of the other souls had yet, of course, introduced themselves to Lady Rice. She perceived no difference in herself. As did Angelica, she just suffered from voices in the head.

Lady Rice fainted. As she fell into the black and sickly swirl of a consciousness deprived suddenly both of oxygen—for a moment she had stopped breathing—and of familiar identity, she heard Edwin say:
"Poor Susan! But you did the right thing. We all have to try and do the right thing."

Lady Rice had to ease herself to sit against the edge of the sofa, had to scramble to her feet unaided. Edwin was helping poor, shook-up Susan to the one spare bedroom available, at the top of the house. The decorators were at the time in all but this one.

Thus it was that Angelica's personality perforated, allowing her to resign, if only temporarily, from life; she was lucky: there was some-one pacing about in the wings of her soul, waiting to take over. Angelica could just simply and suddenly resign, subject as she was to too much upset. It could happen in anyone's head. A trauma, a shock, a faint, a word out of place, evidence of betrayal, a bang on the head, any assault on the identity and who's to know who you'll be when you recover? And if you have too many names to begin with, and a title added to confuse others' views of you, who are you to know who you were in the first place? Too many internal personae in search of a cohesive identity, and not enough body to go round!

Lady Rice went to bed, where Edwin presently followed her. He said he hoped she was feeling better but she should try not to steal Susan's limelight. It had been absurd, pretending to faint like that. Everyone knew she was as strong as a horse.

Haltingly, Lady Rice apologized and tried to persuade her husband it was simply not so about herself and Humphrey, not so about her-self and Lambert, but all Edwin said was do be quiet, what does any of that matter, women always deny everything anyway, you told me that yourself only this evening. Lady Rice thought she'd better be quiet.

"Poor me, poor me, poor me," sighed Susan, now a house guest, through Rice Court. Poor Susan, all echoed. Locked out of her house, separated from her child. Those few in the Humphrey party—his parents, Rosamund, and a handful of comparative strangers: for example, the man in the Post Office who hated all women, the hedger and ditcher who believed in UFOs—urged Humphrey to go to his rival's house and beat Clive up, but Humphrey, though he raged against women, against Susan, Natalie, Rosamund and Lady Rice, as all in one way or another party to the legitimization of his wife's whorishness—they'd encouraged it, sanctioned it—did not ever meet his cuckolder face to face. Even in such circumstances, Rosamund complained, men stick together. The faithless wife gets murdered; her lover is left unharmed, and often unpunished.

"Get that woman out of here," Mrs. MacArthur implored. "She's trouble!" but Lady Rice had become so vague in her dealings with the world, and so forgetful—perhaps she'd bumped her head when she fell?—she could envisage only the horrors consequent upon false accusation and looked warily not trustingly at Mrs. MacArthur thereafter. If Lady Rice and Edwin could help Susan in any way, they would.

Susan was being sweet, and tearful, and full of confidences; Lady Rice took her to the Rice lawyers—four weeks later Susan was still locked out, still separated from her little Roland, Humphrey still holed up in Railway Cottage, and if you tried to get him on the phone you heard this terrible, harsh voice saying "Bitch! Cunt!" over and over. He had taken leave of his senses, everyone agreed. He was going through some kind of fugue. It was assumed he would recover. Rosamund said he might if she could keep the psychiatrists off his back. She thought little Roland was in no danger; his grandparents Molly and Jack had moved in to be with Humphrey, sometimes gently removing the receiver from his hand, replacing it, with a "sorry, caller."

But the Rice lawyers, summoned by Edwin, were clever: injunctions were served, Humphrey was given no time to recover: he was ejected from the home, Susan re-installed, with little Roland back in her care, within six weeks. Clive and Natalie attempted a reconciliation: they stayed under the same roof but Natalie could not stop crying; not even Rosamund's Prozac helped.

The upset had lost Susan her baby (though Mrs. MacArthur claimed it was too much gin and a purposefully too hot bath that did it). Humphrey was blamed by everyone for his insane jealousy, for murdering the unborn child by so upsetting the mother. No one blamed Susan. It was clear to everyone that Humphrey had driven Susan to infidelity. He was obviously unstable. Susan was too open, too innocent, too charming, too impetuous to have the marriage-breaking instincts which Natalie, Rosamund, and Humphrey claimed she had; these three had come to regard Susan an obsessive hater of wives, rather than a lover of men. Natalie, in the meantime, was said by everyone, except Rosamund (who had access to her medical records but wasn't in a position to talk about her patient) to have a long history of infidelity, culminating in her current affair with a colleague at work. Clive too was to be pitied, not blamed. If only Clive and Susan could get together! Mad Humphrey, possessive Natalie, the story went, stood in the way of true love.

Before Susan left the shelter of Rice Court, she said to Lady Rice, earnestly, "Don't ever think Edwin isn't safe with me: you are my friend, after all," but there was a look behind a look, a smile behind a smile which made Lady Rice then later say to Edwin, in bed, for once not rolling away from him but towards him—Lady Rice was more obliging than Angelica and had more regard for others' feelings than her own—
"Did you and Susan ever—?"
And Edwin looked astonished and said, "Good heavens, Susan's

like some kind of sister to me. I'm very fond of her, Angelica. Angelica is such a long word. Couldn't we shorten it? Anglia, perhaps?" and he laughed heartily and Lady Rice felt bad. It was the kind of name you'd choose for someone at a distance.

It was with distaste that Edwin reported home one day that he'd encountered Humphrey in the street, and that Humphrey had spat at him. Spat! In the circles in which Edwin had been reared, infidelities were commonplace, but no one minded much, no one went around with long faces, everyone kept a stiff upper lip and no one *spat*. Lady Rice felt herself excluded from desirable circles, and indeed responsible for Humphrey's bad behavior. The friends she had found for her husband turned out to be scarcely worth the candle of his acquaintance. Boffy Dee came over once or twice: Anthea decided the dogs were putting on too much weight, and persuaded Edwin out on long hearty walks. Edwin went so reluctantly Lady Rice did not believe for a moment there was more to it than Anthea's passion for healthy animals. Not happy animals—Anthea spoke sharply to the dogs and they kept out of kicking distance of her riding boots—but slim, shiny-coated, pleasant-breathed beasts. Edwin certainly was improved by the walks: he'd return flushed and energetic: the presence of Susan in the house had seemed to make him sluggish and moody. But everything was okay, thought Lady Rice. Everything had settled down.

And of course it hadn't. Once sexual betrayal splits a community of apparently like minds, the evil's never over. Households fall, writs fly, children and adults weep alike. Sometimes one could almost believe that if a war, an earthquake or a famine doesn't come along and get in first, people will set out to destroy their own households, their own families, their own communities. As if we build only to break down, as if the human race can't abide the boredom of happiness. As if truly the devil is in them. The fireworks of Bonfire Night are a burnt offering to the Gods of War, to appease them, but no one really wants those gods appeased for long. Peace is boring, war is fun. Non-event is the most terrible thing of all, to people of a certain disposition.

(11)
More

But there was Susan living righteously at Railway Cottage, the snows of winter past, the hollyhocks of summer beginning to burst into purples and mauves and pinks. Susan was beginning to look quite pink and healthy again; she had recovered from the miscarriage, though not yet from what was seen by all around—well, almost—as Humphrey's mistreatment.

Susan herself said very little about the events of the past months, as if by ignoring them they would cease to exist. She lived quietly, though it was known that she had changed her solicitor and her doctor. She was divorcing Humphrey for unreasonable behavior, and Humphrey had decided not to argue about it, for Roland's sake. She would keep Railway Cottage and live there with Roland and he would manage somehow, though his practice had collapsed about his ears. He seemed unable to concentrate or persist in anything. He would visit Roland as often as possible.

"I suppose I should be grateful," was all Susan had to say, "but it's all so typical of poor Humphrey! One day he's violent and furious, the next day he's passive and meek. He has these passions but he can never persist in them. Of course Humphrey's a Gemini. You never know which twin you're kissing. I hope he doesn't visit Roland too often. It isn't good for a child to see too much of a father who's seriously unstable."

It was obvious that Clive, so much and so publicly in love with Susan, could hardly handle the legalities of the divorce; and it was understood that Dr. Rosamund Plaidy no longer suited her as a physician. Susan murmured to one or two friends that Rosamund did rather gossip about her patients. And what sort of doctor was she? Had she not treated her own husband for low spirits with pills, and thus tipped him over into real depression? More, had she not stood between Susan's about-to-be-ex-husband Humphrey and the psychiatrists when it was obvious that Humphrey was raving? Was such behavior ethical? Let alone sensible? No, Dr. Plaidy was not Barley's best doctor. Faith in Rosamund rapidly declined, and an untrusted doctor achieves few cures.

One day Natalie came across Clive weeping into his rose bushes when he should have been at work.
"I suppose you're weeping for love of Susan," said Natalie, helplessly.
"I am," said Clive, just as helpless.
"Not for the grief and trouble you've caused myself and the children, but for yourself? Because you'd rather be with her, not me?"
"Yes," said Clive. "I wish it wasn't true, but it is."
"In that case," said Natalie. "That's the end. I quit trying."

Natalie went upstairs and threw all Clive's clothes and papers out of the windows, out of the house, some into the garden, some into the road. Neighbors gathered. There went his school photographs, his early letters to Natalie, his secret porn videos, his cigarette lighters, his compact discs: his socks, his shirts, armfuls from the wardrobes, old shoes he'd never thrown away. It took her an hour. Clive waited till she was done and then packed what she'd forgotten into cardboard boxes and put the boxes neatly in the back of the car. He scavenged amongst what she'd tossed out for anything he really wanted, which he discovered was very little—the old shoes, his address book—and took those, too. The children watched. Daddy was leaving home. They were too stunned to cry, or too riveted by the drama. Then Natalie opened the bonnet of the car and took out spark plugs and threw them into the brook which ran so prettily through the English country garden.

"I want the car," she said. "It's mine by right. I need it to take the children to school."

Clive called a taxi, and left home in that: taking nothing further but his wallet and a clean shirt. It had begun to rain. Taxi tires drove the mementoes of a happier past further into mud. Later Natalie went out and retrieved his cufflinks, which were gold, and a present to Clive from his mother. Then she took the car and drove it into the stream so the water played and gurgled through anything material which could remind her of her husband, and destroyed it. Later she told her insurers she'd been stung by a wasp, and claimed for the car.

Clive went to Susan and said, "I know you don't love me. But aren't you lonely in Railway Cottage? You and little Roland need looking after. Let me move in with you. Please?"

"No," said Susan.

"But I love you," said Clive. "I've given everything up for you. Home, wife, family. All for you! I'm losing my clients; my business is failing. When you left me, so did others. You're all I have!"

It was true that Clive was losing the confident, well-fed look a successful lawyer needs to have. His little moustache had turned grey. One architect, one lawyer, one doctor down. Who would be next?

"Clive," chided Susan, "don't be absurd! We did have a certain rapprochement for a time, and some good talks. It was wonderful and I don't regret it. But it just wasn't the stuff of which futures-together are made. Can't you get back together with Natalie? I'm sure she loves you. It's all such a great fuss about nothing. You really ought to think about your children." When Clive wouldn't leave, saying he had nowhere to go, no home any more, she put her case more plainly. "Please don't pester me like this, Clive. It's thanks to you and your indiscretions I've lost my husband, and Roland now has to make do without his father. I've been treated so badly. Please don't make it worse. You men are unbelievable."

Clive took a bed-sitting room in town and hung about in the supermarket, hoping to catch sight of Susan. But Susan changed shops, and blamed Clive for that, too. Now her marketing cost more.

"It's really hard to take men with moustaches seriously!" said Susan to Lady Rice, meeting her in the greengrocer's. "Yet Clive seems bent on serious self-destruct. Natalie is being really horrible to me: she cuts me dead in the street: you'd think she'd at least try to stay out of my way, do her marketing mid-afternoon, not mid-morning. It's not my fault her husband's in love with me. She ought to have looked after him better: she's completely frigid sexually. Rosamund Plaidy was treating her. I thought she was on my side but when it comes to it she's as cold as you are, Angelica. You'd all rather have a grievance than a friend. Why doesn't Natalie just ask Clive back and be nice to him? He'd soon get over it. Women make such a fuss about this kind of thing. And so shortsighted of her! If Natalie and I go to the same party and she sees me, she just walks out. It's really stupid: people will stop inviting her if she keeps making scenes."

And Susan was of course right. Susan always got asked out and Natalie didn't. The wronged make depressing companions.

"And Rosamund's another one," said Susan. "She acts strangely towards me, too. It's unprofessional of her."
"But you're no longer her patient, Susan," said Lady Rice.
Susan enthused over the quality and color of local apples, and the greengrocer's wife, with adoring eyes, offered her a bagful free. Susan accepted.

"But Rosamund's such a gossip," said Susan. "All that silly stuff about your having an oestrogen implant, when we all know how much Edwin wants a baby. Remember how he wept when I lost mine? You and Edwin were so good to me, I'll never forget that. You're like sister and brother to me. But Rosamund—why is she the way she is about me?"

"I think she believes Roland is really Lambert's son," said Lady Rice. "Not Humphrey's at all."

Susan turned pale. The color drained from her face. She looked quite gaunt and nearer forty than thirty. She left the shop. Lady Rice followed.

"Angelica, you are to tell everyone that's ridiculous," said Susan. "It's obvious just to look at Roland that he's Humphrey's. Roland has inherited all Humphrey's talents and qualities, thank God. Poor Humphrey; he was emotionally crippled, like so many English men of his generation. But that leaves the genes okay, doesn't it? I never had anything to do with Lambert, though he was always a little bit in love with me, so it wasn't for want of asking! Men get so obsessional, don't they! And so full of fantasies. They'll always claim you've been to bed with them when you haven't; when what's happened is they've tried but you said no. No wonder Rosamund is losing her grip. Of course Lambert's saying the same thing about you, Angelica, do you know that? What a problem village life can be!"

And, apparently quite recovered, Susan went on down the village street, basket over arm, strong stride, fair hair shining, exotic yet domestic; with all the confidence of her own goodness and likeability.

If excited voices clamored within Lady Rice, she did not hear them. She made her deafness her strength.

(12)
Damage

Lady Rice called upon Rosamund. It seemed prudent.

"You and Lambert? I never said any such thing," said Rosamund to Lady Rice. "Susan, or the Great Adulteress of Barley, as some call her, just enjoys stirring up mischief. Roland is indeed in all probability Lambert's child, but fortunately Lambert has gone right off Susan since she had her moments of passion with Edwin. Don't look so stricken: I'm not saying for one moment Susan and Edwin did have an affair, just that Lambert, who tends to be paranoid, believes it, so what's the difference? It suits me that he does believe it."

Lambert was back home again with Rosamund. Susan-damage, as Rosamund observed, had so far been restricted to three households, four children—two of hers, two of Natalie's—and one baby, who never got born. The village had calmed; gossip was stilled. Rosamund was beginning to build up her medical practice again: mostly in the Estate where the humble lived. She had more patients with varicose veins, fewer with emotional problems.

"By the way, Angelica," said Rosamund, "I'm pregnant again. Don't you think it's time you and Edwin thought of starting a family?"

A voice sounded tinnily in her head: "Yes, yes, yes," but she ignored it.

"I don't think so," said Lady Rice quickly. Lady Rice found herself frightened of change, of pain, of swelling up, of sharing her body with another personality. As well grow a monster as a baby. Lady Rice was a little person, with narrow hips. Edwin was big. If the baby inherited Edwin's size, how would it get out? These things hadn't occurred to her before. Maternity, to Lady Rice in her discouraged state, seemed a very bad idea indeed.

How quickly time passed: lava steamed and sizzled in the volcano's crater but didn't quite boil over. Rice Court went on the Heritage brochure as a three-starred family outing. Over the weekends visitors could be counted in thousands. Lady Rice was kept busy. English Heritage took over the day-to-day running of the place, but Edwin liked Lady Rice to keep her hands on the reins, so she did. A small zoo was built: pythons, which the children could hold, were a great attraction. There was a monkey enclosure where if you wore laced shoes you were advised to remove them and put on free canvas pull-ons with the Cowarth crest on them which you could then take home. Lady Rice's idea, and most successful.

"Do come to Roland's birthday party!" said Susan to Sir Edwin and Lady Rice. "He'll be four on Saturday. I've asked Rosamund and Lambert to come. They just have to get over this silly quarrel with me. I asked Humphrey but he says no. He's much too uncivilized. Even if he can't make an effort for me, you'd think he'd do it for his own son, even do a few things about the house. The boiler's leaking again. But no. People round here are so rancorous!"

(13)

The Garden Party

Susan had made the garden pretty for the party. It was her gift to make things pretty. Ropes of colored lights twisted through the flower beds. Little iced cakes were charmingly arranged; there was champagne. Susan had forgotten to provide fruit drinks for the children but they made do perfectly well with water. Lady Rice observed to her husband that it didn't seem so much a children's party as one to celebrate Susan's own continuing childhood.

"You women are so catty about poor Susan," said Edwin. "You must have your scapegoat, I suppose."

Rosamund also declined to come to the party, though all those of note and influence in the neighborhood were attending. It seemed ungenerous of her to stay away, and cutting off her nose to spite her face, as Susan pointed out. Rosamund surely needed to make friends and influence people: to build up her practice. Lambert came though. Lambert wore a shirt unbuttoned to the waist. A piece of string held his trousers up. His shoes were unlaced. But his disorder seemed born of triumph, not tragedy. His eyes sparkled. He was almost manic. He burst into the garden with a hoot and a song, and a beating of fists against his hairy chest.

"Are you okay, Lambert?" asked Lady Rice, startled.
"I'm more than okay," said Lambert. "I left home today. I've left Rosamund. You try living with a doctor!"
And he held Lady Rice by her two shoulders, and stared into her eyes beseechingly.

"Everyone deserves happiness, don't they? I'm a creative person. I can't be put into a mould; I can't live with it."

Well, it was true that everyone had been saying that Rosamund had tried to pressure Lambert into respectability, to make him look and act like a husband and father when actually he was a writer and a genius.

"Rosamund is destroying me," said Lambert. "Susan can't cope here on her own; she gets lonely and frightened. She's asked me to move in with her. I've got a play going on at the National Theatre."

"I'm so pleased for you," murmured Lady Rice, while she tried to collate so much new information all at once. "Fame and fortune are on the way."

"I don't care about any of that," said Lambert. "I only care about Susan."

Susan was laughing and chattering amongst her guests. She held Roland's hand. She had dressed the child in the party attire of a hundred years ago—white *broderie anglaise* flounces, leggings, black patent-leather shoes. He was a quiet, passive child, and just as well.

"What does Rosamund say?" asked Angelica. "Does she mind?"

"Rosamund doesn't know," said Lambert. "I want you to break it to her, Angelica. You're her friend. Rosamund will get over losing me ever so quickly, you'd be surprised. I'm just a handy accessory it's convenient to have around. Rosamund doesn't like me; she just wants to own me, and punish me because I'm an artist. Whatever was ever between us is over. But Susan—Susan knows what love really is."

Susan saw Lambert, waved excitedly, and ran towards him. She was wearing large clumpy sneakers beneath her white floaty dress. Rosamund had told Angelica that Susan suffered from painful corns.

"Wild man," Susan said to Lambert, running her finger over his stubbly chin. "Wild man! Wild animal! I can see I'll have to tame you, groom you a little. Where are your things? Don't say you came with nothing!"

Lambert roared like a lion. People turned and stared. Lambert was certainly livelier in Susan's company than in Rosamund's; or perhaps sudden success had gone to his head. Little Roland was frightened and cried. Susan squeezed the child's hand to allay his fears. Perhaps she squeezed too hard because Roland let out a sharp yell between tears. Lambert picked him up and tossed him in the air and caught him.

"Don't cry!" he said. "Don't cry. Daddy's here!" But the child just howled louder.

"Don't say that!" hissed Susan. "You are not his father!" And such was the force of her protest that Lambert's wildness drained.

"Sorry," he said, quite mildly.

When Lady Rice had recovered a little, she trailed Lambert into the wooded area where once the railway track ran. Susan was attending to her guests.

"Lambert," said Lady Rice, "what about your children? Had you thought? And isn't Rosamund pregnant?"

"When you speak to my wife," said Lambert, "tell her I advise her to get an abortion. That is if she thinks she can't cope. It's her decision. But really Rosamund can cope with anything the world throws her. But I'm the kind of guy who needs a real woman to look after."

"Like Susan?"

"Like Susan. Angelica, I'm going to make up for all the unhappiness of her past. Humphrey, Clive, Edwin: they've all been vile to her. Keep it a secret, Angelica, but Susan's pregnant."

"Well," said Lady Rice, "I'm not going to tell Rosamund a thing, and that's that. Do it yourself."

Lambert stalked off. Lady Rice sat down on a fallen tree trunk, which Susan had not had cleared because it looked so romantic. It had come down in a high wind, six months ago. The next morning Edwin had gone down to look at the fallen tree; he'd called Susan and offered to send a couple of men to winch it up and away, but Susan had declined. Lady Rice wondered why Susan found a stricken tree so romantic. Then she saw what anyone else would see at once: that the ground on the far side of the trunk was green, smooth, soft and mossy. The stream burbled by; very private, very secluded. Yes, it was ever so romantic. It would do very well for an assignation, or two, or three, or hundreds. A changing verdant backdrop: ferns and leaves. And first the blackberry flowers, and then the berries. How pleasantly the seasons would change.

> "Hi, Lady Rice," said Jelly. "Let me introduce myself. My name is Jelly White. What you said to Lambert just now might have sounded rude, but you have my total support. Indeed, you can hold me responsible for saying what had to be said."

Lambert walked towards Lady Rice; helped her to her feet.
"I see your point," said Lambert. "I should tell my wife myself."
They walked together back into the garden. Lambert held Lady Rice's elbow, had to steady her.
"Are you okay?" asked Lambert.
"I thought I heard voices in my head," said Lady Rice. "I expect it's the hot weather." He stopped. She stopped. Lady Rice buried her head in the hairy gap between shirt buttons and shirt buttonholes. The chest smelt pleasantly of scented maleness: he might be dishevelled and distraught but he had washed. No doubt Susan had insisted. No genius of hers could continue to suffer from *nostalgie de la boue*. Rosamund might encourage it: she would not.

Edwin turned up out of nowhere and said, "You two seem to be having an intense conversation."
Lady Rice pulled back from Lambert's chest and said, boldly and angrily, "Don't you 'you two' me, Edwin."
Edwin looked taken aback.

"That's right," said Jelly White. "You stand up to him, Lady Rice!"

"When you forget, and speak naturally, Angelica," said Edwin, "it's with the accent of the streets: common, that is to say."
Lambert said, "For an alleged gentleman you can be very ungentlemanly, Edwin."
Edwin said, "You could make my wife pregnant as well, Plaidy, only fortunately your wife's rendered her sterile."
Lambert said, "I never saw you as a family man, Edwin. Too many drugs. But I understand your problem. You do need an heir to inherit the estate."
Edwin said, "At least I have something to be inherited," wit or repartee not being his forte, but by that time Lady Rice, poor thing, unaccustomed to such open hostility in a social setting, had fainted again.

English country garden flowers are tall: delphiniums, hollyhocks, lilies. Lady Rice simply fell amongst them, breaking blooms and stems. Shorter flowers might have survived better.
"Good God," said Edwin. "Do you have to spoil all Susan's flowers as well?"
"As well as what?" asked Lady Rice, reviving, but he did not reply.

And indeed Susan was to blame Lady Rice for that as well: ruining her flower beds! Lady Rice felt so bad about the damage she'd done that she agreed to tell Rosamund that Lambert had left home, having made Susan pregnant. The shock of the fall seemed to have blotted Jelly White out. There was no help there.

"Jelly?" enquired Lady Rice, acknowledging her alter ego's presence. "Are you there?"
Someone, not Jelly, said, "You are so wet, Lady Rice. No wonder he's fed up with you."
Then there was radio silence.

(14)

Fallout

"Four households and six children destroyed," was what Rosamund said. "Susan is doing well. Natalie and her two, add Humphrey and his one—or so he thought—me and my two, and another on the way. I shan't go through with this pregnancy. Though I daresay Lambert will want to come back to me when he finds she expects him to change a nappy or put up with a tantrum. Susan is very bad with little children. She tends to smack them when no one's look-ing. She's been reported on a couple of occasions but the consensus is always the same: a false accusation, malicious prattle, forget it. In the meantime, Angelica, I have patients to see. I can't waste any more time on this."

The greater the adversity, the brisker she became.

"Is it true that Lambert's got a play on at the National? Is that why he's in favor?" asked Angelica, as the surgery door closed in her face.

"It isn't certain but it looks like it," said Rosamund. "Now he's made it, of course he'll leave me. I'm the sort who see men through the struggling years, then get ditched. Susan's the sort who gets them in their earning prime and destroys them when the money looks like failing."

She spoke without bitterness. Doctors tend to melancholy, not bitterness.

Word got round. A few concerned voices were raised. The man in the Post Office refused to sell Susan a stamp and told her she was a marriage-breaking trollop. But Edwin had a word with Robert Jel-lico and the man in the Post Office, whose name no one could ever remember, lost his job. He was not sufficiently customer-friendly, anyway, to do his job properly. Now so many visitors came to Barley, to admire the church, the old village pump and the quaint country cottages, everyone had to learn to smile and say "Have a nice day." The Rice Estate flourished: Rice Court Heritage Ltd. was in profit. Fungi (Inc.) was back in business. Eight hundred thousand pounds in cash had held the balance of stately funds at a truly critical time.

Susan came up to Rice Court to visit Lady Rice, as she had so often in the old, happy days.

"Thank God the man in the Post Office has gone," she said. "I hate it when people are nasty to me. It's so unfair. The worst I've ever done is love not wisely but too well. Aren't we all meant to look after our own happiness? I can't be held responsible for other people's, can I? We all have to look after ourselves. At least that's what I was taught to do. Where's Edwin?"

"Out," said Lady Rice shortly, but it might have been Jelly. Susan's pregnancy was showing: a swelling beneath autumnal heavy skirt, lichen-dyed, hand-woven. Lady Rice hated the garment, and all such like it.

"It'll be another little boy," said Susan.

"How can you tell?" asked Lady Rice.

"I'm the kind to breed boys," said Susan.

"Lambert's pretty good at girls," said Angelica.

"Personally," said Susan, "I doubt that any of Rosamund's three are Lambert's. Why are you so hostile towards me, Angelica? You English are so un-up-front! What have I done to you?"

"Go on," said the voices, "go on, tell her!"

—and when Lady Rice refused to listen to them and said, "Susan, it's all totally in your head; there's nothing at all the matter!" they muttered darkly amongst themselves.

On that visit Susan asked Angelica about the English laws of inheritance. She seemed disappointed to learn that Edwin's children would inherit nothing. Rice Court was a grace-and-favor house, at Lord Cowarth's discretion. When he died, the older of Edwin's twin brothers would inherit, but there was some confusion as to who was the elder, and everything was tied up in trusts anyway.

"Not even a title?" asked Susan.

"The oldest boy would get a title," said Angelica, vaguely, "I think."

"You *think*?" asked Susan, eyeing Lady Rice with incredulity. "Don't you *know*?"

"No," said Lady Rice. "But I do know, whatever it is, no girl will get it."

Lady Rice and Susan were in the garden. Lady Rice was picking plums: Robert Jellico was trying to persuade Edwin to spray for pests, and Edwin had nearly been convinced, but Susan, whose horror of insecticides was well-known, had dissuaded him. However, Natalie reported Susan using aphid spray, early in the morning when no one was watching. Natalie knew because once she'd been watching the house, sitting in her car, convinced that Clive was inside with Susan.

"Say something," said Jelly.

"No, I can't," said Lady Rice. "I just can't. Everything would break and split and disappear."

"It won't," said Jelly. "Everything round here will split and break and disappear if you don't say something, do something. Or we'll have nothing."

"No," said Lady Rice.

"Did you say something?" said Susan.

"No," said Lady Rice.

She had taken her left foot off the step-ladder: she supported herself
on her right. Now her left foot aimed a deliberate kick at the right.
"Ouch!" cried Lady Rice, and fell off the ladder.
"Are you okay?" asked Susan.
"Just fine," said Lady Rice from the ground. "I thought I'd seen a
wasp, that's all."
"You should never move suddenly if there's a wasp," said Susan.
"They get frightened and sting and then they get blamed for it."
Lady Rice's fingers found themselves going further and further into
the soft purple rotten flesh of a wasp-ridden fallen plum.
She picked it up and threw it out of sight, out of thought. It hit
Susan in the left eye. She screamed. Her hand flew to her eye.
There was plum juice all over her, looking agreeably like blood.
"I'm sorry, I'm so sorry," cried Lady Rice. "I was throwing it on the
compost heap. But I'm just such a bad shot! Will you ever forgive
me? Don't tell Edwin: he certainly won't!"

> "Got her," said Jelly, and all the other voices giggled and chor-
> tled and cheered. "Well aimed, sir! Good shot!"
> "Jesus!" said Lady Rice, with unaccustomed ferocity. "What is
> this? Will you bloody well shut up!" She did display little
> snatches of anger every now and then, but they were for the
> most part directed at herself, not at the outside world.

"Poor Susan," said Lady Rice. "Come to the house and we'll clean
you up." But Susan wouldn't stay. What was the point? Edwin
wasn't there. Enough that her visit would be reported.

Rosamund had an abortion and made no attempt to hide the fact.
The village was censorious. Sympathy returned to Susan and Lambert, who now did their marketing together, and returned to Railway Cottage together, and were seen in the mornings by the
postman nightclothed, bare-footed and cheerful. Poor Lambert, ev-

eryone said. He deserves a little happiness. What a dreadful wife for a man to have. Killing her own baby as an act of revenge! And Susan so charming, so lively, so bright; so much in love. Rosamund had never *loved* Lambert. Career women made bad wives, everyone knew. And mothers bad doctors. They kept having to rush home to their own, instead of tending yours.

Susan gave birth to a little girl, Serena, with the same prominent brown eyes as her brother. Lambert's eyes. People nodded and smiled and wished them well. A family reunited at last! Roland was fortunately a quiet child, so Lambert, once installed in Railway Cottage, was at first able to write in more peace than he had ever enjoyed in the rooms above the Health Center. But after Serena's birth, alas, quiet reflective loving times were out of the question. Serena cried, wept, stormed, shivered: her health demanded constant medical attention: the running of sudden high fevers, the swelling of infant eyelids, the clenching of scarlet baby hands made this unavoidable.

Up at Rice Court Edwin would drift out of the room if anyone referred to Serena's existence, or Susan's difficult labor, but then what man of his kind ever enjoyed gynaecological or paediatric chit-chat?

According to Natalie, who with Susan happened to share a cleaner—Margaret—the wife of the man who had lost his job at the Post Office, now obliged to go out cleaning—Susan would march into the study (once Humphrey's) and thrust Serena into Lambert's paternal arms. "Your baby," she'd say. "You're the father, you look after it; you call the doctor; don't leave everything to me."

Lambert would do his best, but there was a certain problem getting doctors to call: Rosamund's colleagues proved more loyal than expected. Nothing for it but for Lambert to abandon his re-writes mid-sentence and take little Serena to the Emergency hospital twenty miles away. Serena was always well enough when she got there: symptoms of concussion—Roland suffered from sibling rivalry, tending to lash out at his little sister—disappeared, fevers fell and breathing difficulties evaporated at the first smell and sight of a regular medical establishment, a green or white coat, a kindly and enquiring stethoscope. You would almost have thought doctoring ran in the child's blood, she and the medical profession had some special relationship—yet how could that be? Word got round that Rosamund's spirit hovered like an unsatisfied ghost in Railway Cottage, for all that her physical self remained in the Health Center, head high, defying the world's strictures.

One day Natalie called to see Lady Rice, who was often now at home alone in the evenings. Rice Estate business kept Edwin away: he had been to visit his brothers on tropical islands and had not taken his wife with him—"It's for the best, my dear. We are too much in each other's pockets." Lady Rice could see it might be true. And how would the Rice Court visitors get on without her constant attention? The cream in the cream teas—now a favorite line— might sour; the floors stay unpolished; the accounts un-done; the visitors liked to get a glimpse of anyone titled, upstart or not: just the whirl of a headscarf behind a pillar, the flick of a sensible skirt. No, Lady Rice would not evade her responsibilities.
"No such thing," Edwin would laugh, his favorite joke. "No such thing as a free title!"

Natalie said to Lady Rice on another day, "Isn't it odd? I used to be a really nice person. Now I'm not. That's what being betrayed does for you. I hate Susan not because she took Clive from me but because of what she's done to my nature. I hope you never have to learn, Angelica, and can stay nice for ever. You're right to be blind; it's the best way."
"What do you mean?" asked Lady Rice. She found it remarkable

the way her friends would project their own predicament, whatever it was, on to her. "How do you mean, I'm blind?"

"Never mind," said Natalie. "I'm quite happy, these days. I have a new hobby; a game called Persecuting Clive. I'm asking for more and more alimony, so I get to see his accounts. I allow him no privacy. He doesn't deserve any; he's paying Susan's mortgage."

"He's what?" Lady Rice was startled.

"Humphrey can't keep her: he's gone bankrupt; so Clive's taken over, with money which is ours by rights."

"But doesn't Lambert contribute?"

"Lambert?" derided Natalie. "Lambert's on his way out."

"I don't believe it."

"According to Margaret, the minute Lambert leaves the house in the morning to take Roland to school, Susan's on the phone to Clive. Lambert gets back at a quarter to nine and at a quarter to nine minus thirty seconds Susan and Clive stop talking."

"Margaret isn't a reliable witness. She hates Susan."

"Why you go on supporting Susan I can't imagine, Angelica," said Natalie.

"But Susan and Lambert really love each other," said Lady Rice, piteously.

"Susan needed a babysitter once Humphrey was gone," said Natalie, "and Clive was fine as a live-out lover, but as a live-in partner he'd be hopeless. So she went for Lambert instead, because of the play at the National. She thought she'd get to meet interesting people. But according to Margaret the National keeps calling and asking for the re-writes but Lambert never delivers, and never will. I think you should keep away from Lambert, Angelica: the urge to self-destruct is catching. The village says you're hopelessly in love with him."

"The village what?"

"You were seen kissing him down by the old railway track at Susan's party."

"I don't believe it!"

"Don't then," said Natalie. "They'll soon think of something else, anyway. Shall I tell Lambert Susan's carrying on with Clive again?"

"Yes," said Jelly White, back again. "Yes, yes, yes: encourage Natalie to tell Lambert. At least it will stir things up."
"You are such a trouble-maker," said Lady Rice to Jelly. "And, anyway, I don't want Susan on the loose again."
"How you let yourself be trampled on," said Jelly. "All you ever do is throw yourself flat on your face in the mud, and say to people, 'oh, please walk all over me, please.' "
"You mean me falling off the ladder into the rotten plums?" asked Lady Rice. "*You* did that to me."
"No, you did!" said Jelly. "You kicked your own ankle," and the now familiar cacophony of hoots and whistles and jeers began.

"I think you should tell Lambert," said Lady Rice to Natalie, who was waiting for an answer. "It seems only fair."
"I'm not interested in fairness," said Natalie. "I'm interested in causing trouble. Mind you, I can see anyone might need Clive as an antidote to Lambert. Lambert's got big feet, damp and smelly: he's fleshy: you'd have this great white belly bumping up and down on you every night. He's not one, they say, to let an opportunity go by. He quite exhausted Rosamund. Whereas Clive—he's so neat and contained, and he never smells, and he hardly breathes, and he has this little piston thing, deadly accurate. I loved him: now there's no one."

Natalie started to cry. Doing without familiar sex, when you've been married for years and never thought you'd lose it, can be hard.

Lady Rice obligingly told Edwin, who naturally told Lambert, who then left Susan and went back to Rosamund, leaving a vacancy in

Railway Cottage. This vacancy was filled by Clive, which Natalie had not anticipated.

"If only I had a re-run button for my life," she mourned to Lady Rice, "I'd wind it back to when I came across Clive weeping in the rose garden. I'd have made him a cup of tea and resisted the drama of throwing him out. Now I'll have to put up with the kids spending Sundays at Railway Cottage, while Susan bitches at them. I think I'll die."

"See what you did?" said Lady Rice to Jelly White.

"Sorry," said Jelly. "Poor Natalie!"

"Better poor Natalie than *pauvres nous, ma cherie*," said another voice in a cutesy French accent. "One must rejoice. If it hadn't been Clive, it might have been Edwin. And not at Railway Cottage, up at Rice Court. Her in, you out!"

"That is just absurd," said Lady Rice. "You're insane. And who are you, anyway? How dare you even think things like that!"

"Just call me Angelique," said the new entity. "I'm what you might have been. I like things just so. Very neat. I can't abide a mess. Do you remember when we were sent to that educational psychologist, and he diagnosed us as anal obsessive?"

"Everyone agreed that was a mistake," said Lady Rice, "(a) he hated us and (b) he'd got the wrong file."

"*Ce n'est pas vrai*," said Angelique. "He was talking about me, that's all. *Moi*. I was the only one he noticed, understandably."

"Go away, go away, go away," called out the others. "You're an offshoot, an upstart. We have a crisis brewing here. You aren't necessary. Eat shit and die!"

"Yes, you just get the hell out of here," said Lady Rice, with unusual vigor. "You'll only depress me."

Angelique said, "*Ça va, ça va*, but don't say I didn't warn you," and went, and fortunately was never heard of again.

"It wasn't working out between Lambert and me," Susan explained to Lady Rice at the chemist's. "It was becoming a destructive relationship. It's difficult for two creative artists to live under the same roof; and now his play's been turned down by the National, Lambert's been impossible. Jealous, possessive: he even tried to strangle me, just like Humphrey did. Caught me by the throat and squeezed and squeezed. It seems to be my fate to hang out with crazies. If Rosamund can cope with Lambert, she's welcome; she is his wife; she deserves him. Rosamund really ought to take more responsibility for things. Clive's moved in, by the way. He's using Lambert's study as an office. He's only the lodger, of course. Nothing else, before the accusations fly. I'm glad to have someone sharing Railway Cottage, especially at night. Sometimes I get the feeling the place is haunted. But I guess I'm just being the over-imaginative artist!"

"I guess," said Lady Rice.

"Is that Natalie over there?" asked Susan, her bony arm on Lady Rice's, and Lady Rice looked and said, "No. Just someone who looks rather like her."

"I keep thinking I see Natalie," said Susan. "Not that I want to. She hasn't been much of a friend. What a dance she led poor Clive. People see sex in everything. Clive moving into Railway Cottage isn't a sex thing. I really hope people realize that. You will tell them?"

"Of course," said Lady Rice.

Clive, she thought, in and out, in and out, like a piston through the night, blotting out ghosts, blotting out poor Natalie, his wife.

(15)

Dinner Party

Lady Rice was so busy! She was glad of it. The busier she was, the fainter the voices. Trauma and leisure both seemed to stir them up. Ventura Lady Cowarth had a bad back—she'd had a fall from her horse and, though to be blind drunk is meant to relax and protect a rider from injury, she had nevertheless disabled herself badly. She could barely wash, though she got herself hoisted on to horseback to follow the Hunt and managed that. "I can't fuck," Ventura told Lady Rice, "but at least I can still chase a fox. Always preferred it, anyway, when it came to your father-in-law."

Lord Cowarth was upset and knocking away again at his teeth, such few as were left, and they were mostly at the back so he had to open his mouth wide to do it. Horrible.

Lady Rice was needed up at Cowarth Castle four or five times a week, nursing, shopping, answering the phone, parrying Milord's insults and oddities, preparing for the visit of the twins, back from the Caribbean for business reasons but unaccountably laggardly in visiting their ancestral home. Or perhaps they were just exhausted: some fathers just exhaust their children, sapping their strength. If only I had a baby, thought Lady Rice, it would be a proper baby on a proper scale, ordinary and wonderful! I'd be allowed to focus my family responsibilities in my own home. I wouldn't be so tired. But too late for that now.

These days Edwin said he didn't want children. He said he didn't want the family insanity passed on, and he was serious.

"Isn't there some bill going through the House of Commons," asked Lady Rice, "which will give women equal rights of land inheritance, and overrule the old charters? So the oldest child inherits, whether boy or girl? Title as well?"

"It'll never get through," said Edwin, shortly. "It's absurd."

Lady Rice asked Rosamund Plaidy if insanity was inherited, but she was no help. She just said what did she know, she was giving up medicine altogether, the better to look after her children. Bad enough coping with Lambert. He was living at home again.

Rosamund, Lambert told anyone who would listen, was on a masochistic binge; she was doing it on purpose to mortify him, but he declined to be mortified. Apparently Rosamund refused to speak to Lambert, other than when she felt it to be entirely necessary. She encouraged the children, Matty and Sonia, in the same behavior. Rosamund told them Lambert was only a temporary kind of husband and father, there today, gone tomorrow, best not to get too close to him, if only because closeness was what drove him away. He was emotionally immature, Rosamund told Matty and Sonia, as if definition somehow improved matters. The children nodded, trying to understand, being ever-willing, ever-hopeful, ever-forgiving. They loved both parents but obeyed their mother. Lambert claimed to like the surrounding silence: it allowed him to get on with his work. Oddly, the family seemed to enjoy their lives together and when a social researcher, enquiring into the domestic lives of doctors, asked them one by one to rate their "happiness," all replied "good." "Let's ask Susan and Clive to dinner one night," said Edwin. "We never get to see them these days. We need to get the social scene round here going again. If we don't, who will? *Noblesse oblige.*"

He'd felt reclusive lately, and had put on weight, which depressed him further. He'd stay in bed till late in the morning, as he'd used to

at the beginning of the marriage, only now unaccompanied by Angelica. He snapped at her and found fault. But now suddenly, at the
prospect of a party, he had his arms round her; he seemed full of
resolution and Lady Rice was happy. She remembered what times
past had been, and saw they could be good again. Skies could cloud
so gradually you hardly noticed when bright turned to overcast; and
then suddenly there'd be the sun again, and you realized what you'd
been missing.

"But perhaps we shouldn't ask them," said Angelica. "It will upset a
lot of people if we do."

And Edwin and she counted them up: those to whom the social
acceptance or otherwise of disturbed and disturbing, shifting and
changing couples mattered. They listed —

> Humphrey.
> Rosamund, Lambert, and their two children Matty and Sonia.
> Natalie, and little Jane and little Jonathan.
> Roland, who missed Humphrey, and little Serena, into whom
> the spirit of Rosamund's aborted baby had entered, or so it was
> said.
> X, the name given by Angelica to Susan's miscarried baby.

"But you can't lay all the responsibility at Susan's door," said
Edwin.

"I do," said Lady Rice, but nevertheless she invited Clive and Susan
to dinner, because they were better company than any of those
listed. They were accepted back into society, recognized as a couple, as a new nation is recognized, allowed to fly its own flag, its
sovereignty acknowledged. But it is a mistake to believe that a social
circle, once lapsed, can ever be revived, any more than can a former
empire. Once the myth has gone, whether of lasting friendship or of
power, that's it. But people try, ever hopeful. Send out invitations,
set warships prowling; gestures only.

Another mistake: Edwin wanted to invite Tully Toffener and his wife, Sara, in the hope, he said, of diluting the social mix.

Tully Toffener and Sara were weekenders. That is to say, they lived in London but, by virtue of their capacity to pull strings and influence others—namely, Robert Jellico—were one of the few families permitted to rent but not live full-time in Barley. They came down at weekends to sun themselves and restore their spirits in the countryside; during the week their cottage, which faced directly on to the village green, remained curtained and blank. The Rice Estate discouraged such parasitical occupancy of Barley: it did not want its award-winning village to be one of those communities which came to life only at weekends. But Tully Toffener was a Junior Minister of the Crown and might be able to pull a financial or political string or two to make the life of the Rice Estate easier. He had unfortunately been moved out of Heritage into the Department of Social Security, almost as soon as the leasehold of Roly Cottage was granted him by special dispensation of Lord Cowarth, but he might one day move back again—it was his ambition—and in the meantime could put in a good word here and there. His age was indeterminate. He had the clear skin of the undersexed and overweight; he was the cartoonist's dream: his whiny voice made him sound both earnest and honest; his clamping jaw intimidated; he had a full soft lower lip, very bright and pink.

Lady Rice, who disliked so few people, disliked Tully Toffener. She said to Edwin, "I suppose it is wise to ask the Toffeners?"
"Why shouldn't it be?" he asked. "What's wrong with them?"

Angelica would have put it to Edwin that Tully's work didn't make him exactly likeable, that as spokesperson for, and power behind, the Ministry of Welfare, it was he who recommended, if only by proxy, that little old ladies should pay more for their heating, that the lame should be obliged to limp to the dole office, that the poor should drink the rain from heaven, not water from the taps. Yet at the same time Tully professed to love the old, the lame, the poor. Tully was politically ambitious: he would not want his hypocrisies made public; he did not want his desire to obliterate the lot of them made known publicly, though he was always happy to have it said over the dinner table.

But Angelica had been subsumed into Lady Rice; she had forgotten the idealism of her youth; she had, if only she could come to think of it, almost forgotten her youth altogether, and though she visited Ventura Lady Cowarth often, hardly ever gave her mother a thought, let alone called upon her. It was as if, in her own regard, she had sprung into life on the day she married Edwin, and was presented with her new name, Lady Rice: she had taken over at the first available trauma. These days she vaguely assumed that the rich deserved to be rich and happy, and that the poor deserved to be miserable. If she cut old school friends dead in the street it was not, as they supposed, that she felt herself too good for them, but that she really could not remember them.

"The Toffeners can only talk about politics and inheritance," Lady Rice said, vaguely.
"It's better than gossip," said Edwin, and said, "They'll lighten the mix."

Sara and Tully had no children, but they had each other. They would hold hands as they strolled by the duck pond, and it should have been charming but it wasn't. Sara was pale and puffy, school-girlish. He and she lived, apparently, in a pleasant enough apart-ment near Westminster, but it was their on-going ambition to obtain legal possession of a large property in Chelsea, which Sara felt to be hers by right; the place was named, agreeably enough, Lodestar House, and belonged to her grandmother, Lady Wendy Musgrave. The shortcomings of Lady Wendy, the folly of her re-marriage to a penniless adventurer at an advanced age, the neglect of Lodestar House, formed the basis of Sara's conversation; the pro-pensities of one-parent families and the elderly to rob the State that of Tully's. At least when he had been with the Ministry of Heritage he had talked of the tendency of rooks to drop twigs down ancient chimneys and set castles ablaze, and the disgusting personal habits of gypsies and hippie vagrants, and been diverting: now he was ran-corous and noisy.

But, as Edwin said, the Toffeners would lighten the mix.

"Okay," said Lady Rice.

"Darling Angelica," said Susan. 'I thought you'd never ask. Every-one's been so unsociable lately. Shall we just all start over? Ask Rosamund, Natalie, Lambert, everyone? Shall I bring a chocolate mousse? Pity about the Toffeners, but one can't exclude them for-ever. She's such a bore, but I do find him quite attractive, in spite of his looks. Why don't you ask that new man at the church, the Rev. Hossle? We could have a civilized dinner and a service of recon-ciliation over coffee. People do it all the time back home. Every-one's got so horrid to everyone, and we all used to be such friends!"

Lady Rice called round and did indeed invite other guests; neutrals, semi-strangers—the Letchworths, the Stephenses, Eric Naggard the TV director—but not Rosamund, Lambert or Natalie. Not yet. It might take a couple of years but she would do it.

Pre-dinner champagne was by the log fire. The dogs looked con-tented, as if all was well with the world: golden heads between golden paws, huffing and snuffing. Mrs. MacArthur insisted on tak-ing round drinks. Lady Rice felt she would be better employed in the kitchen, but Mrs. MacArthur still did as she wanted. Susan wore a new black shift dress which disguised her boniness. Lady Rice wore pretty much the same, and was outshone. Edwin said, "Lovely dress, Susan!" but made no mention of his wife's. Clive had on a white shirt and a bright yellow waistcoat—Susan was cleaning him up; she had never quite managed it with Lambert. He had shaved off his moustache. Sara Toffener wore a too-tight bright green dress in a stiff, shiny fabric. Tully Toffener wore a striped pink and white shirt which matched his complexion. Sara Toffener entertained everyone with the difficulties she was having with her Filipina servant, who was so frightened of the English countryside and ran away at the sight of cows. Everyone smiled politely, and Lady Rice suddenly said, "Wouldn't it be more merciful to leave her in London, then?" and Sara replied, "Oh no! She might steal everything and run off."

"Knew she'd say that," said Jelly. "That's why I asked."
"For God's sake," said Lady Rice. "Go away. Not now! Not in the middle of a dinner party."
"Okay, okay," said Jelly.

Tully Toffener said fortunately he had the best lawyer in the business to handle the matter of Lodestar House and the challenging of Sara's grandmother's will; a legal eagle who looked promising. Brian Moss was his name, at a firm called Catterwall & Moss, and everyone was able to agree that legal firms could have very strange names indeed. Waite & Waite, or Burgle, Havem & Lost, or Gotobed & Snort were mentioned. Edwin revealed that Catterwall & Moss had handled much of the personal side of the Rice Estate for nearly half a century, in a sleepy kind of way, but that young Brian Moss, grandson of the original Moss, was a whizz on matters of divorce, and now, it seemed, inheritance.

"So how come Edwin knows that this Brian Moss handles a good divorce?" asked Jelly.
"Shut up," said Angelica. "It must be the Boffy Dee connec-

tion." Boffy forever threatened her current husband with divorce, and sometimes went through with it.

"Yeah, yeah," said Jelly.

"Go away," said Lady Rice.

Tully Toffener said, well, since it was Robert Jellico who had recommended Brian Moss in the first place, it was not surprising that he and Edwin shared the same solicitor. It was possible, if the lawsuit succeeded, that the Rice Estate would help Tully out with the development of Lodestar into a block of high-rental apartments.

"Told you so," said Lady Rice.

"Tully's like Edwin," said Jelly. "He may move slowly, but he thinks quickly. He saw your eyebrows rise."

"It's ridiculous," said Tully. "Two old people living for nothing, and in squalid conditions, in a space you could fit two hundred!"

"Planning permission won't be too much of a problem," said Sara. "It's a Grade II listed building but Tully has such good friends in the Ministry of Heritage."

Lady Rice was sorry she'd invited the Toffeners: teeth were being gritted and even the dogs were looking wearily out of their sleep-hooded eyes. But it was like being back in the old days, when the ire of the group was projected towards outsiders, not turned inward.

The guests had moved into the dining hall—the occasion being too formal for kitchen eating. Lady Rice was serving the lobster bisque when there came a ring at the great front door. The bell echoed harshly to the vaulted timber ceiling, which was these days lyrically described in the *Guide to the Cowarth Estates Handbook*. Family friends and guests normally used one of the humbler and lighter side doors.

"Trouble," said Jelly.

"I can't hear you," said Lady Rice.

"Blind, deaf and dumb," said Jelly. "I don't know how you get through your day."

"What was I to do?" asked Mrs. MacArthur later, deprived of her normal composure and gentility. "That bell rings, you answer it. No mistake! I thought it would be Anthea, had a riding accident or run out of whisky. Or I wouldn't have answered it."

Mrs. MacArthur had to unplug and unlink various security devices to open the great carved door. Once, in more innocent days, the door had stood half-open day and night, all summer long. Only an inrush of winter cold ever led to its closing. But now thieves were everywhere, who knew who came and went amongst the visitors? The Handbook referred to the value of everything: tarnished silver had been polished and dull gold made known for what it was; what looked like Woolworth's fake Chinese turned out to be fourth century B.C. Korean, so now the guards stood at the door by day, and at dusk the visitors would be shooed away and it would be closed and the alarm system activated. Robert Jellico even wanted the gentle Labradors replaced by German shepherds but Edwin would have none of it, and Anthea had told Lady Rice that Robert Jellico was a bear of very little brains let alone breeding or he wouldn't have said such a thing. One did not trade in one's dogs as if they were cars or wives.

"She's dangerous—careful," said Jelly.

"For God's sake," said Lady Rice. "She's old, and a family friend. In fact, she *is* family."

Anthea lived in the Dower House next to Cowarth Castle and was a distant cousin of Edwin's, and ten years older than he. She had a splendid-booted, narrow-waisted figure and a raddled, out-of-doors, wind-toughened face and a voice made husky and attractive by drink and exercise. She did not involve herself in what she referred to as Angelica's bohemerie, being more at home with the Castle's hunting and braying set, as she dismissively but affectionately called them. She would sweep into Rice Court by day or night, regardless of inconvenience to the keepers at the gate, calling, "Bingo! . . . Solo!"—the dogs—and as often or not "Stupid!" as well, by whom she meant Edwin, who would appear dutifully like a third dumb beast for his long, healthy walk.

But when Mrs. MacArthur opened the door on that evening, it was not Anthea who stood there, but Natalie. Natalie pushed her to one side and walked into the dining room. Soup spoons froze—only Tully Toffener continued eating, fishing the yellowy soup for morsels of lobster flesh.

Natalie was also dressed in black; but black as in shroud, not elegance. Hollow eyes stared from a gaunt face. Once she'd been plump, lively and smiling. Susan maintained that Natalie liked to make the most of her misfortunes, and the consensus had come to be that she did: that her hollow eyes were as much the result of smudged kohl as distress. Barley society, these days, taking their lead from Susan, maintained that times were changing, that it was folly to believe that wives owned husbands, or husbands wives. If one or the other lost interest in the arrangement, fell out of love or into it, that was that. Everyone must try to behave well, not let bitterness spoil social engagements or interfere with the children's education.

And here Natalie now was, bent apparently on justifying the suspicions of her critics, self-pitying and worse, out of touch, advancing upon Edwin and Angelica's dinner table. Now she swept the very spoon out of Susan's hand. A splodge of hot lobster soup landed on Susan's brow. Edwin was on his feet at once, restraining a struggling Natalie, who was trying to strangle Susan.

"Bitch, bitch!" yelled Natalie, as well as she could for Edwin's vast hand around her throat.

"Get this cow off me!" Susan shrieked, or tried to shriek.

Now Clive tried to rescue Natalie from Edwin's clasp. Everyone was on their feet except the Toffeners, who tried to pretend that nothing untoward was happening, and the Stephenses: she kept her eyes closed and he held her hand.

Naggard said, over and over, "Look here, look here!" Hannah Letchworth made little moaning noises.

"Leave my wife alone, you bastard fornicator," shouted Clive at Edwin. Edwin, surprised, let go of Natalie. Natalie let Susan go. Susan's hand went to her throat, to her face, where a blob of yellow soup still remained.

"If you've bruised me, if you've scarred me, I shall sue," said Susan. Edwin dipped his napkin in sparkling water and gently removed the mess from Susan's brow.

Natalie looked disgusted and turned on Lady Rice.

"Why don't you do something about him and her, you idiot!" she said.

"What's she talking about?" Lady Rice asked Jelly, frightened, but Jelly seemed to have gone off duty. Lady Rice was alone.

"None of you English women have the least idea how to look after your husbands," said Susan. "If you lost him, you deserved to, Natalie, you self-pitying, frigid bitch."

Natalie sat down in the spare chair. Mrs. MacArthur laid her a place

and gave her some soup and some bread. She left the soup but ate the bread. Edwin suddenly laughed and said to Susan, "Jesus, Susan, you're a troublesome child."
Everyone laughed in relief. Mrs. Stephens opened her eyes.
Clive remarked, "Hell hath no fury like a woman scorned. I apologize for Natalie."
Sara Toffener said, "That was a good entrance, Natalie!"
Tully Toffener said, as if he were a child, "Any seconds of soup?"
Natalie said, "Itemized telephone bills are a boon to domestic understanding."
Susan said, "What do you mean, Natalie?"
Natalie said, "I have yours, Susan, for the last three months. Margaret gave them to me."
Susan said, "She's fired."
Natalie said, "She's left already. She's tired of you sleeping around and slapping your children about, and then complaining she hasn't dusted the tops of the doors. As for you, Clive, when you're busy taking Lambert's children to school, Susan's on the phone to guess who? Her first husband, the artist, Alan Adliss. And she meets him once a week, on Tuesday evenings, at Royston Car Park."
Clive said to Susan, "But that's when you go to Philosophy class."
Lady Rice said, "I hear Alan Adliss is having a major retrospective at the Tate."
Tully Toffener said, "Of course, my ambition is to be Minister of the Arts, but don't tell Robert Jellico."
Susan said, "Natalie has flipped her lid. She suffers from vaginismus, poor thing. Most uncomfortable for any sexual partner. Abstinence has driven her mad."
Lady Rice said, "Tell you what, shall we call this dinner party off? Just all of us go home, everyone?"
Natalie said, "The point is, Clive, Susan just keeps you as a babysitter while she waits for Mr. Next. I'm sorry for the current Mrs. Adliss: she doesn't stand a chance."

Sara Toffener, who, as it transpired, had drunk more champagne than anyone, said, "There's no need to rely on one's vagina. One can simply by-pass it. Apparently men go to prostitutes because then they can do it, you know, the other way. And then men get sort of addicted."

Tully Toffener said, "You've drunk more than enough, Sara," and huffed and puffed, and explained that his wife did charity work in the East End.

Sara Toffener asked, as if she really wanted to know, "Is that the secret of your success with men, Susan? One longs to know."

"I'm going home," said Susan. "Clive, take me home."

"I have something to show you, Clive," said Natalie. And she put photos down on the table. There, in a car-park setting, a car. There on the front seat Susan's head of blonde hair, buried in the famous artist's lap: he with an expression of mesmerized distraction on his face.

"I suppose in a public car-park that's about all you can do," said Sara Toffener, "until after dark at any rate."

"Clive," said Natalie to her ex-husband, "now will you please take me home and stop leaping about like Susan's pet poodle?"

Without a further look at Susan, Clive took Natalie away. Susan sat stunned. Then tears came to Susan's eyes, but whether of grief, shock or outrage, genuine or contrived, who was to say? Mrs. MacArthur cleared the soup and brought in chicken, salad, and *pommes dauphin*. Edwin put his arm round Susan; he at any rate assumed she needed comforting. Lady Rice caught just a glimpse of a look from Susan before Susan tearfully buried her head in Edwin's shoulder, as Susan made sure that Lady Rice understood that she, Lady Rice, was finally defeated.

"Take me home now," said Susan to Edwin, and Edwin excused himself to his wife, and guests, and did so.

"But I need you to carve," said Lady Rice, woefully. Her husband didn't hear.

"This is a divorcing matter," said Jelly.

"He's just being a good host," said Lady Rice.

"Pull the other one," said Jelly.

Lady Rice carved the chicken herself, though Tully Toffener offered. Then she passed food round. Still Edwin did not return.
Mory and Hannah Letchworth, who both designed fabrics, came to
life and made everyone move up their chairs so the two blank spaces
weren't so obvious, and started prattling about craft fairs; and Harry
and Cynthia Stephens, who ran the Barley bookshop, chattered
about publishing, and Eric Naggard, the TV director, the extra man
who makes a dinner party go, talked about take-over bids in the
industry.

All left in due course with cries of "lovely evening, darling: nothing
like a little real life drama! Give our love to Edwin when" (by inference "if") "he gets back," and so on, and Lady Rice became aware
almost for the first time that envy and resentment interwove others'
liking for her. Lady Rice was too pretty, too young, too favored by
fortune, too (once upon a time) successful and rich, too happy with
Edwin—or was that in the past, she could hardly remember; how
did the present become the past: at what juncture?—to enjoy the
unadulterated support of others. They were happy when she was
cast down.

Lady Rice wept and Mrs. MacArthur helped her to bed. For once,
Lady Rice was grateful for her presence.

"I told you she was trouble," said Mrs. MacArthur. "You young
women are such fools. Some women are born marriage-breakers.
They ought to be stoned to death."

"But everyone likes Susan," moaned Lady Rice. "Everyone likes to
be in Susan's company. Why is Edwin taking so long?"

"Because I expect he likes to be in her company, too," said Mrs.

MacArthur tartly. "She comes round here too often for my liking. Especially when you're out. Lady Anthea's a different matter. She's family. And she's too old for him anyway."

Edwin returned home just after three.
"I had to calm Susan down," he said. "But she's very angry with you, Angelica."
"Angry with me?" Angelica was astonished.
"You set the whole thing up, one presumes. Told your friend Natalie you'd invited Susan."
"I did no such thing," said Angelica. "Have you gone mad? I didn't set anything up. I was doing what you wanted."
"Don't hide behind me," said Edwin. "Someone has to have told Natalie. You've had it in for Susan for a long time. You've even suspected me of sleeping with her, which hurts her very much and it certainly insults me. You've done untold damage to Susan and her children. What are we going to do with you, Angelica?"

Edwin undressed and slipped into bed beside his wife. His body, which should have been cold from the journey home, was warm. He lay still for a moment and then pulled her out of bed roughly, propelled her across the room and stood her against a wall, and possessed her, careless of her pleasure or composure, as if she was some girl he'd met in a pub and the master bedroom of Rice Court was an alleyway.
"You're easy enough with other men," he said, "to all accounts. You're only ever reluctant with me. Why?"
·She was too surprised to say anything; too hurt, too proud, and— discovering she had enjoyed this assault on her dignity almost to the point of orgasm—too alarmed to protest. She got back into bed; he lay at the far side of it without touching.
"God, you're a bitch," he said, and then he fell asleep. To her own surprise, so did she.

(16)
Friends

Lady Rice, craven, called Susan the next day. "Susan, what's the matter?" she said. "I thought we were friends. It's ridiculous to suggest to Edwin that I set you up. I trust you; why can't you trust me? I don't even object if Edwin takes you home mid—dinner party and doesn't come home till three. Much. What have I ever done to you, except be supportive, speak up for you, take your side—surely, after everything—"

"I don't know what 'everything' you're talking about," Susan said. "I've never needed your support. Why should I need speaking up for? But we all have to pick and choose in life, don't we? And some friends suit for a time, and then don't. So we have to discard them. I hope you don't think I'm being brutal. But that was no favor you did me last night. I no longer count you as a friend."

"So long as you discard Edwin as well," said Angelica, "not just me."

"There you go again, Angelica," said Susan. "This is exactly what I mean. You've changed. You used to be good fun but you've become a jealous and closety sort of person. As for me and Edwin, men and women can be very close friends indeed without sex entering into it at all. But you don't seem to understand that. And these days surely people aren't expected to have to have friends in couples. Edwin's my friend; you aren't. Shall we leave it at that? We'll smile and talk if we meet in a social situation, naturally, but that's the limit of it. Don't call me again." And Susan put down the phone.

Lady Rice wondered if she could get a posse together to go round and burn Susan alive in Railway Cottage as a witch. Or perhaps they could stone her to death as an adulteress. She said as much to

Edwin, who looked at his wife askance and asked her not to cause more trouble than she had already.

And the day after that, when Lady Rice was doing the filing in the Rice Court office, still trembling with shock, confusion and upset, and Edwin was off for the day somewhere with Robert Jellico, Anthea came in without knocking. She was looking, she said, for Edwin. "He said he'd be up at Wellesley Hall at ten," said Anthea. She seemed annoyed. She brought in a flurry of wind and weather with her: outdoors had suddenly taken over from indoors. Anthea was wearing green wellies, a blackish anorak, and a horsy headscarf damp with rain. Her hair fell over her eyes. She carried a riding crop, from a force of habit. "Edwin's too bad. He was meant to be looking over Henry Cabot, with a view to purchase."
"Henry Cabot?" Angelica was bewildered.
"A horse, darling, for the new stables."
"The new stables?"
"Darling," said Anthea kindly, "he says you don't notice very much, and you don't seem to. What is all this secretarial stuff?"

She drew Angelica away from the files, the computer, the fax; she led her, protesting, into the drawing room, flinging aside the ropes that kept the visitors confined to the established pathways through the house, snatching up labels and throwing them to the ground as she went. She called for Mrs. MacArthur and told her to light the fire—always laid but never lit—which Mrs. MacArthur meekly did.

"You're meant to be Lady Rice, not some office factotum," Anthea said. "And it's pissing Edwin off. I thought I should warn you. And what are these village creeps you keep mixing with? Very sordid things are happening, to all accounts. You and Edwin should stick to your own kind. Well, Edwin's kind. You started off fine, exotic and eccentric; we can do with wild cards to liven up the bloodstock, but you've turned into some kind of dozy housewife and what's more you haven't even bred. So what's the point of you? That's what Edwin's beginning to wonder."

Anthea had her boots and her anorak off; she lay back in a leather armchair, unbooted feet stuck towards the fire. Her sweater was ancient and thin.

"And, darling," said Anthea, "infidelity runs in the Rice blood. A capacity to chew women up and spit them out. Women of all classes, including their own. You served your other purpose: you were basically respectable, lower-middle class; got Edwin off drugs and back on the straight and narrow okay. But that's done and here you are, demoting yourself to domestic/secretarial, and he's taken the Great Barley Adulteress for his mistress while he works out who to marry next. I'm telling you this because I like you. You're hopelessly out of your depth, but it's not your fault. You're the choirmaster's daughter, and an amateur choir at that."

"You've been drinking," said Angelica. "God, how you lot drink."
And indeed Anthea was helping herself to whisky even as she spoke, delivered her bombshell.

"You haven't even decanted this stuff, Angelica," complained Anthea, and winced at a smeary glass. Since her hands were covered with mud and some kind of rural slime, Angelica did not take this seriously.

Lady Rice pointed out politely that since Edwin was married to her, he could hardly marry Anthea; that she, Lady Rice, knew well enough how to run her own life, and that the matter of the artist-mistress—if Anthea was referring to Susan—was nothing but mischievous rumor; that she, Lady Rice, trusted Edwin with her life; that she had to get back to her work, and re-print all the labels Anthea had destroyed, and would Anthea please leave and come back when she was sober.

Anthea said, "My God, Edwin's right. You simply do not know how to behave. This is the end."

Anthea left, but not before saying at least Edwin didn't intend to father children outside the family. He had taken the Adulteress to be aborted at the time she'd had domestic trouble and was staying up at Rice Court. Just as well because stray babies could lead to nasty wars of succession.

> "I tried to tell you," said Jelly, wearily. "Now don't you go to pieces on me."
> "Just as well there was an abortion," said another voice, consolingly. "Think of it like that."

Lady Rice went back to the office and wept into her computer. Still Edwin did not return.
"I hope you weren't rude to her," said Mrs. MacArthur. "It isn't wise to queer your pitch with people like that. They're the ones with the real power."

Lady Rice got in her little car—a runabout fit for country roads; Edwin kept the Mercedes and the Range Rover for himself—and went down to Railway Cottage. It seemed empty. The door, usually wide open and inviting, was locked. Angelica looked in the windows and saw that everything was neat, tidy and, as usual, prettily arranged. But there were no flowers in the vases. They stood drained, polished and upside down on the sill.

Lady Rice stood indecisively in the pretty English country garden. Andrew Nellor, the retired evangelist who lived in the cottage next door to Susan, in neurotic twitchiness and rumbling disapproval of everything and everyone, came up Susan's path. He was weeping. His trousers were old, and, as were Lambert's from time to time, held up with string. His little wife looked anxiously out from the top window. She was well-kept and pretty, like Susan's garden.

"She's gone," said Andrew Nellor. "Susan's gone. She kissed me and said she loved me, she wouldn't forget me, and she left. I always loved her. God forgive me, I lusted after her. It was her body I wanted. She had no soul. I prayed, my wife prayed, but the lust wouldn't go away. Such a strong, vibrant person. She had no shame: she was proud of her body. She didn't mind what I saw, what my wife saw. She'd undress with the light on, she'd lie sunbathing naked in the garden. She saw nothing wrong with nudity. She wanted to give me pleasure. I think in her heart she loved me, wanted me. I painted her, secretly. My wife didn't understand. She'd cut her dead in the street. I'm sure that's what drove Susan away. I try to forgive my wife, but I can't. I shall hang the painting in my study, I don't care what she says."

"Who exactly did Susan leave with?" asked Lady Rice. "I'm sure she didn't leave alone."

"With the painter Alan Adliss," said Andrew Nellor. "Susan loved me but I had nothing to offer her. I'm not rich and famous as he is. All the same, nobody will ever understand Susan as I did. She would have been happy with me."

"Fine about the love," said Angelica. "Pity about the wife. Did she take the kids with her or did she ditch them?"

"She told me she was taking Roland to his father. He needed discipline."

Lady Rice went down to the surgery, which Rosamund Plaidy now opened only twice a week for four hours only. It was out-of-hours: the surgery was closed: when was it ever not? Lambert and little Roland sat upon the stone wall opposite. Little Roland was snivelling. "I want my mummy," he sing-sang. He was not an appealing child. The wail betokened petulance, not major grief, but what did Lady Rice know? She had no children of her own.

"Just be glad," said Jelly White, who was in a bad, bad mood, "that the bitch has left town. And with someone else's husband, not yours. Time you woke up, Lady Rice. You're beginning to be a bore."

"Go fuck yourself," said a voice.

"Chance would be a fine thing," said Jelly White, and there was a burble of hoots and jeers behind the voice which made Lady Rice's hair stand on end. Whose were they?

"Rosamund's thrown me out," Lambert said to Lady Rice. "She went away with the kids. She locked me out when Susan dumped Roland on me. I haven't got a key. And Roland's wet his pants and is smelling."

"Then break the door down," said Lady Rice.

"I don't feel like doing that," said Lambert, as if what a man felt like doing and what he did were one and the same thing. He was in no fit state to be left with a child. He, like Andrew Nellor, was unwashed and unshaven. "I haven't been feeling too good lately," Lambert said. "I've kept to my bed a lot. I don't blame Rosamund, I blame myself. You just don't know, do you," he said, "when first you fuck your neighbor's wife, the kind of thing that can happen. She took Serena round to Clive and Natalie's, and left her there. She says Clive's Serena's father. I expect Natalie's hysterical again."

Lady Rice took Lambert and Roland home, since there seemed nowhere else for them to go. Edwin was still out. That was something.

Lady Rice put both Lambert and Roland to bed in the spare room at the top of the house and then slipped in beside them. She did this to keep them warm, no more, and provide them, and indeed herself, with some human comfort. And she was so tired. Little Roland dived down to the bottom of the bed, to be further from these suddenly and unaccountably close adults. Lady Rice was fully clothed. So was Lambert. The night was cold; the spare room, the one the chimney had fallen through in better days, was at the top of the house, where the heating, even though newly replaced, never quite reached.

"Where's Edwin?" asked Lambert, shivering beneath the bed-clothes, only vaguely aware of his surroundings, but trying to be polite. His face was flushed and unhealthy against white linen: yellow beard springing amongst pimples. Upset made him spotty, as if he were an adolescent.

"I don't know," said Lady Rice, "but at least Susan is with Alan Adliss. I used to worry about Edwin and Susan."

"No need," said Lambert. "Susan never could get Edwin. She tried, but she failed. She got all the men in the neighborhood except Edwin; and he was the one she really wanted, because of the title, because of this house, because he stood out against her. She never liked you, Angelica, but she admired you. She didn't understand the power you had over Edwin."

"I love him," said Lady Rice, as if this explained everything. Then she heard Edwin clanking and calling about the house. She was too proud to get out of bed, and too tired and cold besides, and when Edwin burst in, kicking and shouting—behaving as if the door was locked when of course it wasn't: it was just the ancient cross latch which worked the way you wouldn't expect, as he ought to very well know—and there she was in bed with Lambert, albeit with so many clothes on she could not reasonably be supposed to be sexually motivated. She was just, like Lambert, tired, cold and emotionally strung-out. But if Edwin assumed she was there with erotic intent, Lady Rice was not going to produce little Roland from under the bedclothes as chaperon: why should she, why would she?

"Whore, bitch, slut," shouted Edwin, yanking Lady Rice out of bed, hitting her, but leaving Lambert alone, as is often the habit of men who discover their wives with other men. They beat the woman but respect their rival, who after all has defeated them.

Edwin dragged Lady Rice down the stairs, sometimes by her hair, sometimes by an arm or a leg. She lost some clothing on the way. She hit her hand frequently on step and stone. Mrs. MacArthur stood at the bottom of the stairs and watched, aghast.

"Help me," cried Lady Rice, but Mrs. MacArthur did not. She had been at Rice Court when Angelica came and she sure as hell would be there when Angelica left.

"But I'm Angelica," Angelica cried to her husband. "Don't do this to me," but he wasn't listening.

Edwin pushed his wife out of the side door and locked it. She saw the little red security lights shining in the ancient stone walls.

"Told you so!" said Jelly. "But you wouldn't listen."

"Why didn't someone tell me what was going on?" wailed Angelica.

"I did my best," moaned Lady Rice.

"I've lost fucking handfuls of hair," complained someone else unidentifiable.

Edwin's wife lay on the ground outside Rice Court and moaned and groaned, but no help came. She thought she might die of cold and exhaustion.

"Get up," said Jelly.

"What's the difference if I'm up or down?" said Lady Rice. "I'd rather be dead, anyway."

"Well, I wouldn't," said Angelica. "So get up and start walking."

"Where do I go?" asked Lady Rice.

"To Mum's," said Jelly. "Where else?"

Edwin's wife walked for an hour and reached her mother's house. Lavender Hatherley opened the door, wearing an apron she'd been wearing as long as Angelica could remember. Behind was a glimpse of familiar shapes and colors, but a new, strange man in her father's armchair.

"Quite the stranger!" said Lavender Hatherley, with a touch of anger in the voice, but she took her errant daughter in, washed her, warmed her, fed her and put her to bed as if she were six.

News got round Barley that Lady Rice had left her husband and gone to her mother. She'd been discovered in bed with Lambert Plaidy, and Rosamund had walked out on Lambert as a result, taking the children. Lady Rice's name was mud, but what could be expected from a rock-star? Angelica White should have accepted the position God had given her in the world: stayed a girl from the estate, daughter of the school choirmaster, and married a local boy. But like mother like daughter—think how Lavender White had behaved!

Barley mourned the loss of Susan, and saw merit in the fact that she'd gone back to her first husband, her one true love. They blamed Lady Rice for Susan's departure: news of the dinner party had got round, and it was thought that Lady Rice and Natalie had conspired to bring about Susan's humiliation and hurl lobster soup in her face. It was as if blame and Susan were of the same magnetic pole: you could bring them together, think you had closed the gap, then at the last moment they'd veer suddenly away. By all the laws of nature they were unable to meet.

And that was the end of that.

(17)
Angelica Barred from Home

Angelica simply doesn't know what to do.

The doors of Rice Court are locked against her. She has not been allowed in to collect even her personal belongings. Any security guard who might recognize the former lady of the house and pity her has been replaced. Those who now man the gates have been shown photographs and been told she is a madwoman, and when she appears weeping and distraught, to beat upon the doors or batter her hands upon the uniforms of their strong breasts, they can see that she is indeed mad. They catch her small wrists in their big hands and call for police and ambulance to restrain and help her, but by the time the authorities turn up she has always gone.

A suitcase of her clothes, her toothbrush, and so forth, turns up at her mother's house, dropped off by Robert Jellico, to demonstrate that she has no ally in him.
"Where's her eight hundred thousand pounds?" Lavender Hatherley calls after him, and she could swear he replied, "What eight thousand pounds?" but he was revving his Range Rover at the time to get away as fast as he could, and Lavender cannot be sure.

Sir Edwin will not receive his wife's telephone calls. Lambert Plaidy has gone to Australia with Roland. Rosamund has given up her medical practice altogether. Even Natalie shuts the door in Angelica's face; she has Serena to look after now. Natalie is bringing her up as part of her own family. She wants to put the past behind her and Lady Rice is part of that past. The greengrocer gives Angelica the smallest, meanest apples. Ventura Lady Cowarth receives her, but in the kitchen. Lord Cowarth is ill in bed with suppurating mouth ulcers, but that is probably just a story. Lady Rice is out, out, out. Ventura tells Lady Rice she will be happier out of Barley altogether, and recommends a London divorce solicitor, one Barney Evans.

"But I don't want to be divorced," cries Lady Rice. "I want to be back home with Edwin and happy again. I can't bear him thinking badly of me."

"Then you shouldn't have been such a silly girl," says Ventura.

> "Her back's still bad," says Jelly. "You can see when she moves."
> "Good," says Angelica.

Angelica is not sure whether or not she wants a divorce: she knows she needs money. She has none. She goes to the bank and finds the joint-account closed. One of her credit cards still works, however. Her friends from the old days are out of sympathy with her. Music is all rap and funk and acid house, and the drugs have changed. She is alone. She can't stay home with her mother; Mary Hatherley, once her friend, now her step-sister, sleeps in her bed and Angelica is left with the sofa.

She takes her story and her plight to Barney Evans. He is a large, fleshy man with a double chin and a benign and bumbling air. He wears a dusty suit, a pink shirt and a pinky-yellow tie.

> "What does that remind you of?" asks Angelica.
> "The lobster soup the night of the dinner party," says Lady Rice.

"So it does," says Angelica. "When your memories are strong enough, I have them too."

"We'd better pay attention," says Jelly. "This is important."

In real adversity they are quite companionable.

"Are you sure you're telling me the truth?" Barney Evans is asking her. "It may be hard for a court to take your story at face-value. Fully clothed, you say?"

"Yes," says Angelica.

"You have witnesses?"

"No," says Angelica. "By the time Mrs. MacArthur saw me I had hardly any clothes on at all. He'd ripped them from me."

"And you walked to your mother's in that state?"

"Yes. There was a child in the bed, too."

Barney Evans raises his eyebrows.

"The quieter we are about that one the better," he says. "You know how people's minds work these days."

"We were all just keeping warm," she says.

Barney Evans stares at her.

"You make my life difficult if you don't tell me the truth," he says. "However, we will work with what we have. If you do decide to divorce, it seems unlikely that you have any claim on the matrimonial home or contents," says Barney Evans, "since both are owned by the Rice Estate. As for alimony, the Court may well take the view that you are young and healthy and have earned very well in the past, and can earn again; and will award you very little."

"What about my £832,000? The money I brought to the marriage?"

"But you seem to have no receipts, no documents."

"I handed the cash over to Robert Jellico. He was very grateful. He'll tell you. He's a trustworthy man, everyone knows that. It will be in his books somewhere."

"The Rice Estate has creative accountants: sometimes things show

up in their books, sometimes they don't. Depends what they want to happen. And it is Robert Jellico's job to appear trustworthy."
Barney Evans smiled at Lady Angelica Rice.

"Things don't look too good, do they?" remarks Jelly.
"No," reply Angelica and Lady Rice together.
"I'm sorry," says Lady Rice. "I haven't managed any of this very well."
"You didn't even get any good fucks either," says the so far unidentified voice, querulously.

"Never mind," says Barney Evans. "Cheer up! I'll look after you. I'll take my chances with your fees. I daresay you'll end up with a penny or two. I'm not pressuring you, but it might be a good idea to start proceedings before your husband does. The one who initiates the divorce normally has the Court's sympathy."
"Edwin would never divorce me," says Lady Rice. "All this is just a temporary upset."

Barney Evans raised his bushy grey eyebrows.

And here ends Jelly's formal and official account of how Angelica Lamb split, and took her life into her own hands.

Part Three

A Perforated House

(1)
Sir Edwin Begins Divorce Proceedings

Angered by receiving a divorce petition from Sir Edwin stuffed full of malicious and lying allegations, from lesbianism to bestiality, bad cooking to adultery, Angelica booked into The Claremont, using the credit card Sir Edwin's advisors had forgotten to cancel.

On her way to the hotel Angelica stopped at Fenwicks, the Bond Street department store, and there bought suede leather thigh boots, open mesh stockings, a small silver skirt, a white singlet and a leather jacket. She charged these to her card. She changed out of her depressed and dowdy country clothes in the powder room, and would have surely dumped the full, long floral skirt, chunky sweater and sensible laced and muddy shoes behind, but Lady Rice said that would be a wicked waste of money and insisted on stuffing the discarded garments into bags and carrying them about with her.

Lady Rice was made nervous by Angelica's general desire to stride free, shove what she needed in a pocket and leave her purse at home. On the way out of the store, Jelly stopped Angelica in her confident lope and made her buy knee-length skirts, white blouses, cashmere sweaters and plain little-heeled shoes, and a collection of wigs. Angelica explained to the salesgirl, who regarded the kind of clothes she was required to sell with obvious distaste, that these were for her sister, who was acting the part of an office worker in a TV commercial. "No-one," said Angelica, "would be seen dead in these—in real life."
"Bitch!" hissed Jelly White.

The salesgirl pretended she had not heard: it was that or take on as an antagonist this lanky, limby, foul-mouthed, forceful, un-smiling, unpretty but attractive person, who would doubtless win any engagement.

"Enjoy," was all the salesgirl said.

As Jelly White, Angelica took a three-day refresher course in computer technology, and brushed up her shorthand skills. She called Catterwall & Moss and determined that the firm who provided their secretarial staff was called the Acme Agency. She contacted them and produced references on Rice Estate headed paper signed by Robert Jellico, and from Rice Court signed by herself. Within weeks she organized herself a temporary post at Catterwall & Moss, and within days of arriving was working exclusively for Brian Moss, and had proper access to all *Rice v. Rice* files. With her new computer skills she deleted all references to the credit card she retained, other than those which automatically made payments as and when required. It was all perfectly simple.

As Lady Rice said, "At least it keeps me in touch with Edwin. I don't feel so alone." Jelly said, "I'm a prudent person. Forget the divorce, a gal needs something to fall back upon, and indeed into. Secretarial skills and Brian Moss's arms are not to be sneezed at. What a pity he's a married man!" Angelica said, "Jesus, you are both so wet!"

(2)
Lady Rice's Petition

In her petition, Lady Angelica Rice alleged adultery between Anthea Box and her husband over a six-month period previous to the date on which she, Lady Rice, had left the matrimonial home.

Lady Rice claimed physical assault; over-frequent and perverted sexual activity which led to her humiliation; drunkenness, drug-taking and financial irresponsibility on the part of her husband; she asserted that her husband's relationship with his dogs was of a sexual nature. She claimed she had been eased out of her home, Rice Court, to make way for Sir Edwin's paramour, Lady Anthea Box. Lady Rice, on the other hand, had throughout the marriage been a good and faithful wife. Sir Edwin had behaved intolerably and she wanted this reflected in any property settlement. And she wanted her £832,000 back.

"An out-of-London court!" exclaimed Brian Moss, this seeming to be the part of Barney Evans' letter-plus-enclosures which most affected him. "What a nightmare! I have no influence whatsoever in the provinces. A nod in London is simply not as good as a wink anywhere else. How ever are we to get this case settled? And how strange: the wife has claimed almost the same unreasonable behavior as has the husband."
"I expect it's because they were married so long," said Jelly. "They can read each other's minds."
"Eleven years isn't a long marriage," said Brian Moss. "There was a couple in here the other day in their nineties wanting a divorce by

consent. I asked them why they'd left it so long and they said they'd
been waiting for the children to die."

He laughed; a deep, hoarse, unexpected laugh at a pitch which
made the many racing prints on the wall rattle, and Jelly laughed
too, at his joke. Her tinkly little laugh made nothing rattle, but he
pinched the swell of her bosom where it disappeared under her
blouse. Just a little pinch; friendly.

"What do you think about the money?" asked Jelly.
"She hasn't a hope," said Brian Moss. "It'll be so far buried in the
Rice accounts it would cost her a fortune to get it out. And we'll get
Sir Edwin's allowance reduced to zero for the nonce, so she can't
claim that either. The woman's clearly a trollop and a bitch."

Outside the elegant Regency windows, central London's traffic
flowed, or tried to flow. Only emergency vehicles seemed able to
make progress—police, fire, ambulance. Their sirens approached,
passed, faded, with enviable speed.

"I make a good living," observed Brian Moss, "out of other people's
need to be in the right; they like to claim the privilege of being the
victim. It helps to call her a trollop and a bitch if I'm doing her
down, but who's at fault in the Rice debacle is of no importance.
The property is all that matters, and we'll make sure she doesn't get
her greedy little fingers on too much of that. Clients assume that
conduct during marriage will have an effect on a property settlement and steer it in the direction of natural justice, but it's rash to
make any such assumption. Or only in the most extreme cases."

"You don't see the Rice divorce as extreme, then? Merely run of the
mill?" enquired Jelly.
"Very much run of the mill," said Brian Moss, "other than that both

parties do have to go to considerable lengths to hide their income."
It was fortunate, he said, for Sir Edwin that the Rice Estate had
books of magical complexity.

"I imagine it is," said Jelly White placidly.

He loved her calmness, her interest in his work. If only his wife Oriole had the same. Oriole's sweaters were covered in baby milk and
vomit: she had new twins; she could think of nothing but babies.

"Otherwise," said Brian Moss, "it's just a normal divorce. Both parties vie for the moral high ground, never noticing that a major land-
slip has already carried the whole mountain away. And both parties
enrich me, thank God."

"You are a very poetic kind of man," said Jelly White, and Brian
Moss caught up a little of her fair hair between his fingers and
tugged, and she smiled obligingly, and Lady Rice sighed.

Thus Lady Angelica Rice had once smiled at Sir Edwin, her husband. Now Jelly smiled with measured guile, not an overflow of innocence. Trust and amiability had done Angelica Rice no good at
all.

Lady Rice had a problem with lies and cunning. It was as well that
Jelly White did not. Self-interest was intrinsic to her persona, and
just as well, or they would all be alone, humiliated and penniless in
the world. Someone had to earn the money.

(3)

The Velcro That Is Marriage

In the long sad hours of her sleepless nights, Lady Rice, still love-sick for Edwin, still distracted by the end of her marriage, came into her own. The others left her. They slept and partly slept. They had to get up and go to work in the morning. Grief and remorse were luxuries. Dimly, they listened to her explanations, the account of herself she gave them.

"I was married to Edwin for eleven years, and the Velcro that's marriage got well and truly stuck. The stuff is the devil to wrest apart; it can rip and tear if your efforts are too strenuous. The cheap little sticky fibers do their work well. 'Overuse,' they say, weakens Velcro. If 'overused'—a strange concept: should you fasten only so often?—is there some moral implication here?—you can hardly get Velcro to stick at all. But I was not overused in the beginning. On the contrary. When Edwin and I married, when I stopped being Angelica White and became Lady Rice, I was seventeen and a virgin, though no one would have known it. Chastity is not usually associated with leathers, studs, boots, crops, whips and the more extreme edges of the pop scene which I then frequented. But my velcroing capacity to be at one with the man I loved, in spite of appearances, was pristine, firm, ready for service. Velcro hot off the loom. I 'waited' for marriage, as my father told me to. Extraordinary, in retrospect. So many opportunities lost! I blame you, Angelica: you were in charge in those days. When you abandoned me you left me with the habit of over-discrimination in sexual matters: as Lady Rice I had neither your appeal nor any sexual appetite. I was indeed a different woman to the one Edwin married, but didn't realize it.

"On a good night, tucked up in my high, soft bed at The Claremont with its pure white, real cotton sheets, I see myself as an avenging angel. Then I laugh aloud at my own audacity and admire myself. Fancy getting a job with your husband's lawyer's firm! I have to thank you for that, Jelly. On a bad night, like this one, when the fine fabric of the pillows is so wet with my tears that the down within gets dark, matted and uncomfortable, when I feel tossed about in a sea of dejection, bafflement, loss—a sea that keeps me buoyant, mind you, made extra salty by my own grief—why, then I know I am just any other abandoned and rejected woman, half mad, worthy of nothing. Then I see that taking a job at Catterwall & Moss, in the heart of the enemy camp, is mere folly, presumption and insanity, and not in the least dashing, or clever or funny. And I worry dreadfully in case I'm found out: I don't totally trust you, Angelica, or even you, Jelly, to see me through it."

In the early mornings, while Lady Rice slept from sheer emotional exhaustion, Angelica would in her turn confide in Jelly.
"What a poor, passive creature Lady Rice is! This is what marriage has made of her. She'd lie about in The Claremont suffering all day if I let her. She wouldn't even bother to answer Barney Evans' letters. I, Angelica, am the one who has to get her to work each day, dress her up as Jelly White, take her to the gym, keep her on a diet, stop her smoking. I am, I like to think, the original, pre-married persona. Why she maintains she's the dominant personality round here I can't imagine. Perhaps it's because she has a title: perhaps it's because she can't face the small-town girl that's me, which is part of her and always will be. What do you think, Jelly?"
But Jelly, wisely, was asleep. She actually had to go to work. She couldn't afford to waste her energy arguing.

(4)

Lady Rice's Sea of Sorrow

On a bad night Lady Rice rocks in a sea of sorrow, half-sleeping, half-dreaming. The sea is so salt with tears she can never sink: see how she is buoyed up by her own grief. Sometimes the sea grows wild and stormy, whipped by winds of anger, hate, violent resentments: how she turns and tosses then. She's afraid: she will be sucked down into whirlpools; she will drown, she will drown, in a tempest of her own making. All she can do then is pray; much good it does her. Dear Father, dear God, save me from my enemies. Help me. I will be good, I will be. Let the storm cease. She takes a sleeping pill.

Ghostly barques glide by, in fog; pirates' swords, the swords of wrath, glinting, slashing, disembowelling, castrating. Steady the mind, steady the hand, in case the sword turns against the one who wields it. Lady Rice is pirate and victim both. She knows it. The sea of sorrow, nevertheless, sustains and nourishes her. In her head it is called the Sea of Alimony. It might be on the moon, for all she knows, like the Sea of Tranquillity; she might be in her mother's womb. She might be in some drowned church, knocking up against stone walls, as the current pulls her here and there; her father's church. Certainly she is bruised, body and soul. Dear Father, dear God, forgive me my sins. Let the weight of Thy wrath depart from me.

Sometimes the Sea of Alimony is calm; the rocking sensuous, almost sweet. She is sorry then to surface. She is a mermaid, stunned, beached up upon the white sands of The Claremont's delicate sheets, rolled back by waves into the sea, tossed up again, to surface with the dawn, to wake to the World of Alimony, Brian Moss, work, and the chafing parts of the self: but also to alimony, healing, sustenance. Grief nourishes; it is a drug; she is dependent upon it now: all three of her; or is it four? She sleeps as one, she wakes as many. The sea of sorrow sucks her in as one, whirls her down, washes her up fragmented—or is it the telephone which thus shatters her? A man's voice.

"Good morning, Lady Rice. It's seven thirty. This is your wake-up call."

Lady Rice looks in her morning mirror at a face puffy with restless sleep: last night she did not take off her make-up. She collects cold water in cupped hands; it gushes plentifully from large-mouthed taps, antique or mock antique, who cares? The antique leak lead into the water, the new do not. Lead is good for the complexion, bad for the brain. She splashes her face; she does not use the white face flannels provided in some number. She despises them. They are too small. This morning she will despise anything. The handle comes away in her hand. Nothing is dependable, nothing is solid. She does not bother to call Housekeeping.

Lady Rice goes back to bed. But the voices in her head are loud again; clear enough to distinguish easily one from another; not pleasing this morning in what they say. She would rather just be in bed and weep: they won't let her. They are full of reproaches, complaints, eggings on to action, all unwelcome. She is beached, beached. She has tried to incorporate these bickering women, these alter egos, back into herself; now she tries to regain her sense of self, but she can't. She must listen to them, and answer them.

"It's too bad," moans Jelly. "Can't you even clean our face off at night? This is the quickest way to a bad complexion, and you don't even care."

"I was tired," explains Lady Rice feebly. "I've been so distressed by the divorce, surely I'm allowed to be tired."

"You can't afford to be tired," says Angelica. "We've got to get out of this mess somehow. How are we going to live? You and your take-over bids. You can't survive without us. Look what happened at Rice Court! We can't stay in this hotel for ever. Sooner or later they'll throw us out."

"They'd never do that," says Lady Rice. "I'm a member of the Rice family. Edwin would never let it happen."

"Of course he would," says Angelica. "You have a replacement. You're old news. What does he care about you? Nothing as ex as an almost ex wife! The most hated object."

Lady Rice dissolves in further tears; the grief is harsh, not languorous.

"Get her up, for God's sake," says Jelly. "You have more influence than me. I hate being late for work. You just deliver me and go away. You don't have to stand around to receive the flack."

"I think if I had a fuck," says the other voice, out of nowhere, "I'd feel better. Brian Moss will do very well. The only cure for one man is another man."

"Who *is* that?" asks Jelly.

"She shouldn't use that language, whoever she is," says Angelica, shocked. "And surely we can do without a man for a month or so? Men are the source of the problem, not the cure."

"I think it was I who said that," says Lady Rice, remorseful. "I just came out with it. But now it's said, it might be true."

"Perhaps Brian Moss is our karma," says Jelly cunningly. "So shall we just get up and go and meet our destiny?"

And Lady Rice finally drags herself from her bed, just to shut them up, since they won't leave her alone. She can see they might make good company. She need never be lonely: and loneliness, for all that others speak of aloneness, is what she most fears. Once her feet are on the floor she resigns and Angelica cuts in.

(5)
Initial Transformations

Angelica rose and dressed. She left for work in black leather jacket, black wig and dark glasses, looking not at all like Lady Rice—that wronged, tearful, virtuous, needy creature—but like the rather ferocious and determined mistress of some important guest at The Claremont. She carried a holdall in which, neatly folded (by Jelly: Jelly was good at folding, Angelica was not), were Jelly's working clothes.

Angelica it was who would step into her chauffeur-driven, hired Volvo at exactly 7.48. Nearly every morning the car was there, parked in Davis Street. Nearly every morning she stepped in as Angelica, stepped out as Jelly. Once in the car, she would take off Angelica's wig to reveal Jelly's short, shiny, straight blonde hair: she would take off her leather jacket and put on a pale blue blazer with brass buttons, made in a cheap, uncrushable fabric. She would drag her hair back behind a pale pink satin headband, and hang a long string of artificial pearls round her neck, to fall over her tight, white woollen jumper. She wore a bra which under-played her breasts: the tightness of the sweater was more to do with fashion than sexuality. She would wipe off her more extravagant make-up and put on owl glasses. She would become Jelly White, with Angelica's knowledge and consent.

But occasionally the Volvo was not there, not waiting in Davis Street when she left the hotel. The car service was stretched that time of the morning, they would explain. Or they were short of drivers; there was a flu epidemic. Could she wait? Half an hour, perhaps? And she could not, and would have to travel to work by public transport. Then she would make the ego change in a Ladies' room at the Inns of Court, so boldly entering the passages marked "Private," passing without shame through doors marked "Staff Only," to find this safe, high, private, empty, well-disinfected, still slightly odorous place, leaving with so prim and self-righteous a mien that in neither personality was she ever challenged.

But she preferred the back of the Volvo: the darkened windows, the stiff back of the driver the other side of the glass, leather upholstery made sticky by the contact of flesh, albeit her own.

And there she would be as Jelly White, she of the highly developed super-ego, the eye for detail, the capacity to distinguish between right and wrong, and the self-righteousness, the priggishness, that goes with it; a clean, tidy, cologne-scented, apparently unambitious young woman with a self image not high, not low, but realistic, well aware of her own virtues, her own faults; Daddy's girl, the one who stays safe for his sake, who never ventures far, who marries someone reliable and nice on the right day at the right time, the one in whom incestuous desires are decently repressed, the one in whom deceit runs rampant, the one to whom lies come naturally, and are always justified, the one to whom rank and order of authority matter; Jelly, for this reason, fit to be underpaid and overworked, the one who stays late to get the mail done, who just occasionally pursues the flirtation with the boss, to sue for sexual harassment later. Office bait: a sweet smile, a gentle look, but an eye for the main chance. Daddy never frowned on that. "You get what you can out of it, my girl!" "Never *be* the boss; no, *use* the boss."

While you're at the office, incognito, Jelly is the girl to be. No use being Angelica, anyway: life would be one long error, coffee spill and misfiling: one long chafing under instruction: a yearning for freedom, a throwing open of windows to let the air in, and letting wind and rain in instead, to everyone's dismay.

Angelica would threaten Brian Moss's marriage to Oriole as Jelly never would. He would never employ Angelica. The Jellys of the world, sealed off from real emotion, seldom create it in others. Lust; yes: yearning; no. They sit at the office desk and one might be another. Angelicas come singly, and because they suffer, also inflict suffering.

Angelica tried out Jelly's role for size, and found that not only did it fit, but could be discarded easily. Jelly put up no resistance: she was wonderfully practical: good at emergencies; never dithered: or threw her hands in the air or acted like a startled child.

Sir Edwin arranged a meeting with Lady Rice and her solicitor, Barney Evans, at Brian Moss's office. They would try to settle things swiftly and amicably. Sir Edwin would offer a final settlement of a small apartment at the end of a suburban line somewhere. He had no property of his own, and no income, and documents to prove it. He was the younger son in the fairytale, who by tradition had nothing, so you had to marry him for love. Brian Moss rubbed his hands. Barney Evans would not accept the deal, but it was a start.

It was easy enough for Jelly to slip into the powder room and turn into Lady Rice: take off the owl glasses, pull a little black velvet hat down over her hair, change the city high-heels for a steadier, more country kind, put on blue eyeshadow and bright red lipstick, adjust the expression on her face and there she was, an unhappy version of a once happy Lady Rice, and all Sir Edwin's fault.

The powder room where Jelly achieved this transformation was one of the original back bedrooms of the pleasant Georgian house in which Catterwall & Moss was housed, haphazardly converted. The room was high and large; plaster flaked from the ceiling. Thick cream paint covered the walls and ancient plumbing alike. Draughts whistled under the doors. Go into the loo as typist, adopt the body language of those who command, rather than those commanded, and come out the client.

As it happened, Sir Edwin had not turned up. Lady Rice flounced out, sidled back into the powder room and changed back into Jelly, by-passing Angelica. Jelly realized she could exist without Angelica. She had her own existence. Perforation was approaching split.

"Just as well he didn't turn up," said Jelly. "There'd only have been a scene."

"Chickened out," said Angelica, and retired for a time, defeated, disappointed in spite of herself.

"I love him," moaned Lady Rice. "If only I could just see him, meet him, talk things over, he'd realize that he really loved me; he couldn't possibly prefer Anthea to me. She's ten years older than he is."

"Face it," said the other voice, "you were a dull fuck. You deserve what happened."

(6)
Office Business

Both lawyers were now trying to persuade Lady Rice to accept an out-of-court, once-and-for-all, clean-break settlement, which Lady Rice was not prepared to do. Prompted and nudged by Angelica, she was prepared to fight.

"Such settlements may suit the Courts and the lawyers," said Angelica, in the form of Lady Rice, boldly to Barney Evans. "They save the Court time and trouble, but they don't suit me. Why should I let Edwin get away with his crimes against my life, my spirit? Let my husband be answerable to me for the rest of his life: let him support me for ever. He can disguise his assets temporarily, but in the end truth emerges. Doesn't it?"

Barney Evans, a fine dray horse compared to Brian Moss's swift and elegant steed, sniffed and trumpeted and avoiding saying, "No. In my opinion and experience truth rarely emerges." Clients had to be protected from the world, allowed to keep their illusions. Yes, justice exists: yes, heaven exists. This was the task of the lawyer, as it was that of the priest. "Lo, there shall be no corruption, no mortality! The law protects you; Jesus saves you."

"I demand justice," Lady Rice persisted in crying, as did so many who came up against the legal system in any land under the sun. "I will never rest till I have it, and nor should you!"

Oh, Lady Rice was a nuisance: the virtuous one. Barney Evans and Brian Moss agreed, by a look exchanged, a soft sigh of common understanding. It is never easy to be reminded of what one has come to.

"I'm sure I've seen Lady Rice somewhere before," said Brian Moss to Jelly White after Barney Evans had shared another sherry with him and departed, and the *Rice v. Rice* files were once again put away.

"She was almost a celebrity once upon a time," said Jelly White, head turned towards the computer, stretching and bending her fingers so as to save herself from Repetitive Strain Injury *(Wisdom v. BT)*, which can so wretchedly affect the computer worker. "That was before she married Sir Edwin, back when she was a pop star. She was No. 1 for eight whole weeks with 'Kinky Virgin,' and on TV a lot. After that she was lead singer in a group of the same name; they toured quite successfully. But that was all. Marriage put paid to her showbiz ambitions."

"I don't look at TV," said Brian Moss. "I don't have the time. When I get home I have to bath the babies. We have twins, you know. Fifteen months old. I'm a New Man. Why did Edwin Rice marry a pop star in the first place? Didn't he need someone he could take to hunt balls? It's so much easier to marry a woman other men ignore. That's what I did when I married Oriole. I knew I would be safe; Oriole would always be faithful: I make a real effort to be the same. Anthea Box will suit Sir Edwin much better than his first wife ever did, so long as she can stay off the drink. Those are hard-drinking circles, I believe. She's out of the same stable as he is, that's the main thing when it comes to marriage. Isn't she some kind of cousin? I hope there's nothing unfortunate in the genes. I find Barney Evans a very pleasant and helpful chap. I was at school with his brother. Salt of the earth."

"Aren't you lawyers meant to be somehow antagonistic," asked Jelly, "if only on behalf of your client? I was surprised you were so friendly."

"We go through the motions," said Brian Moss, "but, like anyone else, all we really want is as much profit and as little fuss as possible. We professionals are all on one side, the punters on the other."

The pace of the divorce and the property settlement was labored and slow. Lady Rice withdrew her petition and let Sir Edwin's stand, since a nod and a wink from Brian Moss suggested to Barney Evans that Sir Edwin would be generous if she did. Sir Edwin's refusal to communicate directly with his wife continued. Lady Rice complained of undue influence from Anthea Box. And indeed, a letter from Brian Moss's office suggesting that Sir Edwin make another attempt to meet Lady Rice and sort things out in a friendly fashion was fielded by a phone call from Anthea, saying it was out of the question. Jelly, who took the call, said she'd let Brian Moss know. She did nothing of the kind, of course, since Brian Moss was unaware of the initial letter: she had written it herself.

Lady Rice received a letter from Barney Evans saying it was in his client's interests to move the hearings from the provincial Courts to London, since they would get a better hearing there with a more sympathetic judge. Lady Rice wrote back to say no, the provinces would do her very well. She would rather trust an impartial judge than a sympathetic one. Sympathy could sway like a tree in a high wind; first here, then there. Lady Rice did not know whence this wisdom sprang; sometimes she felt she was older than her years.

Lady Rice remained vague as to her whereabouts. She gave Barney Evans her mother's address for correspondence. Let Edwin have a sense of her as Lilith, whom Adam discarded, the original, wronged wife, who wanders the outskirts of the universe, bringing trouble to mankind, never resting, for ever spiteful, for ever grieving, making others feel bad.

The best place to hide, she knew, is beneath the nose of the searcher. It was obvious to Jelly White that such staff at Catterwall & Moss whose job it was to look after Sir Edwin's private finances would have neither time nor inclination to look through the files when the hotel account arrived. Who would be bothered to check that Rice, Sir E., didn't have "and Lady A." tucked in next to it? No one. Nor would The Claremont think it prudent to point out to anyone that Lady A., according to the newspapers recovering from bulimia and anorexia in a nursing home somewhere in the Midlands, was to their knowledge living in their Bridal Suite. It suited them well enough to have a titled lady in residence, although that lady went incognito.

(7)
Angel Is Born

One Tuesday morning Lady Rice woke from her sea of sorrow and went to work as usual, climbing into the Volvo as Angelica, preparing to leave it as Jelly. The driver was obliged to make an emergency stop as a police car chased a young car thief down the wrong side of the road.

"Okay?" he turned to ask his passenger.

"Just fine," she said, but her heart had been in her mouth, and her head had banged against the glass partition. She thought she had recovered, and no harm had been done, but she found herself howling aloud. She howled as in films the man who turns into a werewolf howls, body and mind stretching and deforming: all had gone into overload. She was giving birth to yet another self. Her name was Angel, and no angel, she.

Ram the chauffeur, seated behind the glass partition which cut off employer from servant, stopped the car, turned his head and fixed Angelica/Jelly with startled eyes. His eyes were dark, well-fringed, kind, albeit male. Angelica's dress was up to her knees. She was changing her slimming black stockings to Jelly's ankle-thickening beige. But her leg from ankle to knee, whatever she wore, remained long, slim and fetching. She moved her knees quickly together, but too late.

"Is that my exhaust holed?" the driver asked. "Or is it you?"

Lady Rice, Angelica, Jelly, Angel howled again. They howled because it was a Tuesday morning, and on Monday nights Anthea often stayed over at Rice Court. So much Mrs. MacArthur had told Lady Rice, whilst explaining that whatever evidence Edwin Rice required her to give in Court, she would. If Edwin said Lady Rice and Lambert were in the big fourposter bed, not the spare room, so be it. Her loyalty was to him, not the newcomer Lady Rice. It was Sir Edwin who paid her wages, and Lady Anthea knew how to treat staff: not as if they were friends, but keeping a courteous distance.

Since this conversation it had been the habit of the female combo that was Angelica to drug herself to sleep on Monday nights, so heavily that it would be nearly Tuesday lunchtime before the three awoke. But the exigencies of employment had made that impossible, and here they were, caught halfway between Angelica and Jelly, at eight thirty on a Tuesday, knowing that this was when her husband's enjoyment and capacity for sex was at its highest—many's the time she had slipped out of bed early so as not to encounter it, as she remembered to her pain—and, worse, the chance thereby increased of his saying something intimate, loving, kind to her rival. And at that very moment, if she thought about it, that rival, like as not, would be in the marital bed. Of course the entity howled.

They made no further effort to move their legs together. They were in any case wearing French knickers which hardly hid a thing. In fact they found themselves moving their legs further apart.

> "For God's sake, what are you doing?" pleaded Angelica, suddenly alarmed. "This is no answer to anything."
> "You don't know this man from Adam," warned Jelly. "Remember AIDS."
> "I do as I like," said Angel, for it was she, moving her legs further apart. "And I have what I want, and what I want, as ever, is sex."
> "What is going on in here?" demanded Lady Rice, who had

been dozing, but was startled sufficiently to be back at least notionally in charge. "I know I said I wanted a fuck, but I was speaking theoretically."

"Oh no you weren't," said Angel. "And that was me speaking, anyway. Hi, everyone, I'm Angel."

"I don't want someone like you in my head," said Lady Rice, panicky. "I just know you'll be trouble."

"We don't want you interfering," said the other three. They were already ganging up on her. "You had your chance and a fine mess you made of it."

"Oh, thanks," said Lady Rice bitterly. "Thanks, everyone. Edwin, Anthea, Mrs. MacArthur, and all my Barley friends: thanks to the inside of my head now too, it seems, for trying to destroy me. I'm getting out of here."

And Lady Rice retired, part hurt, part glad to have been given permission, to some brooding part of her being, to rock in her sea of sorrow and absorb its mournful nutrients. She was finally glad she'd been an only child, had never had sisters.

"Please don't make that noise," Ram pleaded. "It makes it difficult to drive." He was, Angel supposed, for she was looking at him closely, as Jelly never did and Angelica never would, in his late twenties. He was fair-complexioned and had well-manicured nails which rested with confidence on the well-padded wheel; he was blessed with the strong jaw and sharp eyes of a business executive. Only the chauffeur's cap suggested that the car was the tool of his trade, not the badge of his status. But the emergent halfway woman didn't really care who he was or what he said, or indeed what he saw—one stocking half rolled off, the other un-suspended, and the suspender straps with their plastic button device falling loose— tights are tricky to change in confined surroundings; stockings less of a problem, but still provide some difficulty—that person half way between a couple of I's and a she uttered another howl, and tears ran down her face.

Ram turned the Volvo without so much as a comment, let alone asking for permission from his multi-faceted employer, into an underground car park. "Spaces" flashed out in red lights in the narrow street outside. As the car turned in, the barrier to the entrance rose, apparently of its own accord. (The electronic world is so much in tune, these days, with the living one, it is not surprising we get confused, see ourselves programmed, incapable of political or social protest, as we go about the routine of our lives.) The car approached, access was willed, the barrier rose: the horror of the scene thus revealed—the dark mouths of concrete stalls, the puddled floor, the scrawled tormented walls, the stench of urine—seems an inevitable consequence of that very willing. Forget it, don't argue, don't fight, don't attempt to reform; technology doesn't, why should you? You are less than the machinery which serves you, and by serving you controls you; more prone to error, the ramshackle entropy, than when you were poorer but more in control. The human spirit splits and fractures, it has to, to make an amoeboid movement round technology, to engulf it, as flesh forms round a splinter, the better to protect itself. The four-fold entity of Lady Rice is not yet commonplace, but may well yet be.

Ram took his vehicle deeper and deeper underground. Angel swayed, first this way, then that, as it traversed the descending levels, the bare stretch of thigh above her stocking tops sticking, first this side, then that, on hot leather, until there was nowhere else for the car to go but the furthest, deepest, blackest stall, after which the entrance signs turned to exit signs. Ram McDonald reversed the Volvo into this small space, with considerable skill. The vehicle's windows were of darkened glass. The occupants could see out; no one could see in. The rich like to travel thus, and the journeys, after all, were

on Sir Edwin's charge account. Ram left the front seat and joined
Angel in the back. She did not protest. Anthea clasped Edwin,
Edwin clasped Anthea; the sun did not go out, nor society disap-
prove. What matter then who clasped whom, in lust or love, since
decency and justice had foundered anyway?

The core of the amoeba is fluid; its outer parts jelly-like. When the
amoeba wishes to move, fluid is converted to jelly at the leading end
of the body, and jelly is converted to fluid at the other end, and so
the whole animal moves along. The concept of "wish" is vague, and
there seems no point within this single-cell creature which could
generate an emotion, or drive, yet "wish" it does. It wishes to move,
or chooses to move, or fails to remain still. However you put it, the
amoeba demonstrates intent: just so Lady Rice's body, flowing, in-
corporating, changing from fluid to jelly, jelly to fluid, announced
to her and demonstrated to her parts its joint intent to experience a
unified and unifying orgasm, as Ram strove and stroked.

> "That's better," said Angel to the others, shuddering and jud-
> dering. Ram pulled her close to him. "That's what you lot
> needed. A good fuck."
> "Speak for yourself," said Angelica. "It was the last thing I ever
> wanted," and she turned her mouth away from Ram's. "Edwin
> and I always got on well enough without. I liked being wooed
> and I liked being kissed, but I hate being out of control." Angel
> made Angelica turn her mouth back to Ram's. His lips were
> heavy on hers and Jelly could feel the bristles of his chin
> roughening the delicate skin of her cheek, but had to let the
> matter rest.
> "He's not even wearing a condom," agitated Jelly into Lady
> Rice's ear; surely that would make an impact. "For God's sake,
> put a stop to all this—"
> "It's beyond me," murmured Lady Rice, consenting to make a

final comment, but quite without affect. "My mother used to tell me there was no stopping a man once he's begun, or you get yourself raped. So why begin it? Just get it over. But aren't you going to be late for the office? All right for you to be as late as you like; just not all right for me to stay in bed in the mornings."

Jelly and Angelica wept, Lady Rice sulked, Angel responded to Ram in energetic fashion, though her own gratification had been long since gained.

"We must do this again," said Ram. "Tomorrow?"
They wondered what to reply. They talked amongst themselves.

"Get involved with a chauffeur?" demanded Angelica. "You must be joking."
"Impossible. I must keep my mind on my work," said Jelly. "I can't afford diversion."
"Never, never, never," cried Lady Rice, panicked back into existence. She was having trouble staying away, for all her hurt feelings. "Edwin might find out." But they discounted her. She was the one who loved Edwin. The others had long given up. Love, they could see, was a luxury they could ill afford. The humiliation of love spurned was what made women on the edge of a divorce give up their rights so easily. "Take it all," they cry. "I don't want a thing." Later, when love's over, they can see their mistake. The man seldom has any such qualms. Winner takes all.

"Of course we'll do it again tomorrow," said Angel, and, as she had use of the mouth and the whole body felt good and at ease, it was Angel Ram heard. "Unless you're free this evening. But shall we concentrate on now?"

"Slut, whore, bitch! Anybody's! Stone her to death," came Angelica's response. She *was* in a temper. Angel bit her own lip
and let out a yelp. Ram licked the sore place better.
"And what time of the month is it?" Jelly asked. "Forget AIDS,
what about pregnancy? Christ, you're irresponsible."

Lady Rice just gave up and thought about other things. Let Angelica, Jelly and Angel emote; it left her free to reflect in tranquillity. She had wanted a fuck and got one but, when it came to it, this
was no kind of answer. She supposed she was in the power of the
statistic, yet again. She was one of the 34 percent of women who
engage in untoward sexual activity when first apart from their husbands and suffering, as a consequence, from low self-esteem. Her
own behavior, she could see, was nothing to do with her, not her
responsibility at all.

Interesting, she noted, that Angel's stretched arms fell apart from
around Ram's neck at the moment of orgasm. Jelly would have
clasped hers the tighter, in surprise. Angel, on orgasm, felt gratification, not surprise. Angel's body fell automatically loose and languid
at such a moment. Angelica would have tautly stretched and sidestepped: first the stretch to better experience, but then the last-
minute sidestep to avoid the fluid to jelly, jelly to fluid of orgasmic
takeover. Fidgeting, defensive Angelica; self-interested, manipula-
tive Jelly; serve them both right to be overwhelmed by the desires of
lustful, conscienceless Angel!

What pleasure then, as out of the sepulchral gloom which sur-
rounds the death of marriage, this brilliance dawned, this Angel,
sweeping away humiliation, self-interest, discrimination, with such
powerful wings. Or this at least was how Angel would have liked her
compatriots to view her birth. If only the others could have seen it

so. This new source of lustful energy streamed out waves of stormy, light-dappled dark; and in the flickering blackness of the car-park Ram McDonald also gained his power; hairy male arms and legs entwined with her angelic smooth white limbs.

"King Crab Ram," Angel called him, and when he asked her why, said he's clearly crawled out from under a rock, perfectly at home in his watery parking lot; monstrous yet everyday; the handsome, healthiest crab you ever saw; king of the rock pool, all-important till you got a glimpse of the ocean. A chauffeur today, but who tomorrow?

If Angel fluttered through clouds of sexual glory, it was to rejoice in their turbulence. Good Bad Angel, thought Lady Rice; her little sister Angel, who loved to feel the stickiness of hot leather on naked thighs, who rejoiced in the rush of non-identity to the head, the feel of long skinny legs opened, the satisfaction of the thrust of strange hard flesh felt between; and the familiar flurry and panting begin, the search for the soul of the other, buried so obtusely in flesh. Leave it all to Angel.

> Angel cried out, in urgent anticipation of her coming to birth.
> "Be quiet," begged Jelly. "Don't make that dreadful noise."
> "Don't overdo it," warned Angelica. "He'll think you're faking."

Good Bad Angel, little sister! Lady Rice denied maternal status. She would be Angel's sister; that much she could allow, but she could never see herself as mother in charge. She had had enough of all that, in marriage. In charge of Rice Court, in charge of her husband's happiness, in charge of everyone's morals, as good wives are: inexorably, little by little, simply by virtue of knowing best, being turned into mother, albeit one without children. What even halfway decent man could allow himself to stay married to his mother, once that status had become unequivocal? Her spirit began to wander.

"By the way," said Angel, humping and pumping away. "My full name's Angel Lamb." Lamb was Angelica's mother's maiden name. "I am the Angel and the Id together," she introduced herself. "I am the internalized sibling of Lady Rice, Angelica Barley (a passing stage name) and Jelly White, our father's daughter. Now just shut up and let me get on with this. There's no stopping me now I'm here. The time you've wasted; the journeys you've taken with this gorgeous hunk of manhood and done nothing about it! Too bad!"

Angelica winced at the phraseology, and Jelly lamented the folly of what had been done, and Lady Rice drowsed and sniffed her unhappiness and got out of the mind altogether.

(8)

Anthea in the Linen Room

In her drowsiness, Lady Rice became telepathic, saw visions, moved about her own house like a ghost. Since they would not let her through the door, she had no choice but to move through walls. Rice Court was her home. And if the inside of a body, a head, gets too crowded, one or other of the inhabitants is likely to go for a walk. The spirit of Lady Rice went wandering, and shot unbidden to Rice Court.

As Ram leaned over Angel, shuffling off his blue serge trousers in the back of the Volvo, and Angel inclined further backwards on the real leather seats—with their added helpful spray of leather aroma—pulling her narrow skirt further up around her hips to demonstrate her assent, to quieten her howling, Edwin entered Anthea, not in the marital bed but in the second floor linen room of Rice Court and Lady Rice witnessed it. Here the shelves were neatly stacked with bedding of the old and tasteful kind, linens and cottons well-washed to a delicate flimsiness, folded neatly and flatly by Mrs. MacArthur or her staff: woollen blankets likewise: not an acrylic duvet or a man-made fiber in sight.

Lady Rice thought she saw a fanged monster slouch by outside the linen room: a bulky thing straight out of hell, with a leathery hide and red eyes, but it was waiting for Edwin, not for her. It moved by, almost touching her, and she did not mind. Perhaps it was her beast? Perhaps she owned it?

Edwin, massively built, broad-shouldered, a softness of flesh cover-
ing muscle and nerve, smooth-chested, warm-skinned in spite of his
blue blood, a chin naturally commanding but with a nature per-
petually retreating, these days appeared to the outside world as a
man extremely fortunate in his heredity, both physical and financial. He was supremely rational, calmly confident, pleasant and co-
operative, and intelligent enough, with untold shares invested in
mysterious companies abroad. This man, this paragon, this foolish
Prince now grown into Kingship, leaned back against the slatted
laundry shelves, parted Anthea's knees with his, pushed up between
her thighs and with no ceremony entered her. Anthea barely
blenched, though Lady Rice did. Anthea wore a familiar headscarf
of heavy cream silk, with a splatter of anchor chains and horses
upon it. Edwin, Lady Rice perceived, liked Anthea to wear the
headscarf in the house and out of it, and Anthea, conscious always
that her hair was probably in need of washing, made no objection to
doing so. The headscarf, at this moment, was all she wore. She was
narrow-hipped to the point of skinniness. Lady Rice, watching,
found the woman wholly eclipsed by the man, by so many inches
did his width surpass hers. They had to use the linen cupboard,
clearly, because Mrs. MacArthur too often surprised them: bringing
their breakfast on a tray, or saying the cleaners wanted to get in, or
the plumber, or Robert Jellico needed Edwin's presence. Here they
were safe, for at least an hour or so.

So much for the spirit of Lady Rice.

It was understood, but seldom said, that Edwin had succumbed to a
passing infatuation when he married Angelica; he had married
someone hopelessly unsuitable; a young woman with no background, who not only wouldn't ride to hounds but spoke up for the
hunt saboteurs; who would unfairly refuse her husband his marital
rights on one pretext or another, while still claiming his title. Of
course he had looked elsewhere. Anthea understood that the way to

keep a man happy was to give him as much sex as possible but no intellectual challenges. Men liked to rest, once adolescence was over.

See Anthea now, as did the spirit of Lady Rice, leaning back into pieces of soap-scented linen, arms outstretched as if crucified against the shelves, hands clenching and un-clenching; eyes rolling, gasping: more, more! Oh darling! They seldom kiss—it seems too personal. That's how Edwin likes sex; so does Anthea. Lots of sex, and all of it impersonal.

My problem, thought Lady Rice, or one of them, was that the original Angelica, ex–Kinky Virgin, turned out to be over-fussy. Angelica required wooing; she had a notion of romance; she liked kissing, endearment, sweet words, tired easily, and in the end would rather plainly not fuck at all if she could help it. A man can grow weary of that kind of thing. Seduction and persuasion, foreplaying and tantalizing, are all very well for a year or two, but ten years into a childless marriage can begin to seem onerous.

The spirit of Lady Rice was called back to the Volvo, urgently. The snarl of the monster had for a time drowned her alter egos' cries for help.

> "Jesus!" cried Angelica. "I can't keep Angel in her place. She's taking over. Where are you, Lady Rice?"
> "She won't listen to us," moaned Jelly. "There'll be no holding her. She simply will not abide by a consensus. She isn't safe."
> "I'm just trying to get a few things straight in my head," said Lady Rice vaguely. "Trying to be a nicer person."
> "That is a luxury we can't afford," screeched Angelica. "This slut is budding off from you. Do something! She's your unconscious, not ours."
> "Oh dear," said Lady Rice, and returned to her body, relieved

of the attempt to be reasonable, to overcome jealousy, and see things from Edwin's point of view. But she was too late.

For even as in the second floor linen cupboard of the ancestral home her rightful husband shuddered within her rival, in the back of Ram's car Angel let out the bellow which was her birth-cry. The umbilical cord that tied Angel to Lady Rice was cut. Angel understood, as Angelica had not, or Jelly either, that life could be good. You just had to accept what it offered, and if the offering was male, you'd take it.

Angel adjusted her dress and Ram took up his place in the front seat and took her to the very door of the office, not just the corner of the square. Could someone so precious be expected to walk even a few yards when the chauffeur was at hand?

(9)
Jelly at Work

"I'm sorry to be so late," said Jelly to Brian Moss of the velvety smooth voice, cunning eye and beautifully cut suit. "I had to go to the doctor. I hope you haven't opened the post," she added. "You always get everything in such a muddle."

"I leave detail to you, my dear," he said. "I look after the major issues, the wider sweep, as befits the male. Shall we have coffee now?"

"You mean will I make it?" she asked, and did.

These days a good legal secretary is hard to find and, if they are found, are usually elderly women—the young ones decline to take work both so responsible and so poorly paid. Legal secretaries often start out with crabby natures—those with an eye to detail often have these—and impatience with human folly gets the better of them, and feeds into the original disposition. It is not easy or pleasant to get correct, day after day, the detail by which human beings try to wrest justice from a world determined not to deliver it. People, it soon becomes clear to the legal secretary, veer either to the delinquent or to the boring. At the delinquent end of the scale, in criminal or family law, there is too much distress; at the tedious end—contractual or constitutional law—there is just yawning boredom. And even that boredom exists as a fragile, if opaque, lid on a bubbling cauldron of iniquity and roguery; scams so great, from the stealing of pension funds to the selling of junk bonds to the hijacking of nations, it is hard to believe it is happening. The detail of fraud is not so much interesting as incomprehensible to the noncriminal mind. Spelling mistakes creep in. Negatives where negatives should not be. The computer operator, the legal secretary, to whom the shameless effrontery of others so often is initially apparent, tends to shut up and stay silent. A bad dream induced by boredom, they tell themselves. It can't be happening. Shut up, stay quiet, don't stir things up, look after yourself, keep the job. The world can't be as bad as this, nor the people in it so villainous, so confident in their grey-suited villainy: the stories unfolding before my eyes upon the screen, she moans, must surely be fiction. But no.

And, after all, the legal secretary, the computer operator, has by virtue of training and inclination no need for desperate action, seldom any personal craving for wealth or power, and finding so little villainy in herself, even on close self-inspection, is not looking out for it in others. This may be a pleasant characteristic, but it is also dangerous. "I didn't believe it; I didn't want to rock the boat" are the initial pleas. "I thought they must know what they were doing" comes next; "I was only obeying orders" comes last and hellishly.

Good legal secretaries come too expensive to have their time wasted on coffee-making, but Brian Moss, a New Man in the home, was a Former Man in the office and liked Jelly to prepare his sustenance. Nor, when it came to it, did Jelly much mind. Brian Moss was too impatient to let the water boil and the coffee he made was lackluster.

"Excuse me," said Jelly later in the morning, when she was taking dictation.
"Well, what is it? Grammar? Correct it as you go along. We have a lot of post to get through." Brian Moss was impatient. She liked the way his fingers tapped upon the table: imperative and irritable. It seemed to her the proper way for a man to be. He had just concluded a letter to a would-be father suing a Health Authority for

causing his wife's infertility. "My best regards to your wife. I hope
the poodles are keeping bright and bushy-tailed."

"Poodles get their tails docked at birth," said Jelly. "Perhaps 'bushy-
tailed' is inappropriate."

"Replace it with some similar jocularity," said Brian Moss. "I leave
it all to you."

He stood behind Jelly's chair and his hands slid round beneath her
breasts, feeling the weight of each one. She felt her identity scatter
as her pearls had scattered earlier in the day in the back of the
Volvo. Sexual desire was inimical, it seemed, to single-mindedness.
"You're not wearing your pearls today," he said. "I like your pearls."

"They broke on the way to work this morning," said Angel, speaking
through Jelly's lips.

"Please," begged Angelica, "not this too! Don't mess this job
up, as you did my marriage."

"Who, me?" enquired Angel, all innocence. "That was Lady
Rice. I wasn't even born when you were married."

Angelica managed to maneuver the wavering Jelly out of the room
and back to her desk. Brian Moss followed them both, believing
them to be one person.

The secretarial quarters at Catterwall & Moss were small, high-
ceilinged squares of rooms looking out on to a soot-blackened wall,
requiring always artificial light. Jelly's was the partitioned end of the
former Georgian library which served as Brian Moss's office, which
was grand, formal, old-fashioned, panelled in oak, but dispropor-
tioned as a result of that very partitioning. Brian Moss seldom entered the small room. He found it gloomy, not surprisingly. He
spoke through the intercom and summoned whoever it was sat
there; they changed with the years. Now he followed Jelly.

"We've nowhere near finished the post," Brian Moss complained.

"Some of these letters really have to go off today. You will just have to excuse the inexcusable, Miss White, if so it was, come back into my office and get on."

Brian Moss looked at his secretary pleadingly, little-boy-like. He had blue eyes and a face reckoned handsome, in the English manner: clean cut and under apparent control; his expression imbued with a gentle melancholy. At first Jelly did not reply: she was busy collecting personal belongings from her desk drawer, saving what was on the computer, evidently preparing the place for her successor.

"Please," said Brian Moss. "I really am sorry. I shan't lay hands on you again. Promise."

It was in Brian Moss's favor, Jelly told Angelica, that he was prepared to talk about his infringement of her body space. Many a man would maul you and then say nothing; would prefer to pretend, if the advances were rejected, that the advance had never occurred. Many a man, come to that, put in Angel, would spend a night with you and never refer to that event again either, and the woman, feeling rejected and diminished, would all too often collude and fall silent too. As if the very past were male, defined by the man's memory of it, forget the female's.

"Do stop looking at me like that," he said. "Say something. Or, if you won't, couldn't we just get back to work?"

"I doubt it," said Jelly. "According to the small print of my agency contract with you, I am free, in the event of sexual harassment, to terminate my employment without penalty."

"You'd have to prove sexual harassment," said Brian Moss, "and that would be difficult, even impossible. Your word against mine. Why do you think we agreed to that clause being there in the first place? Because it is meaningless, and because women like to see it there. It makes them believe they're being taken seriously. But all that is by the by. I am actually a perfectly decent guy and don't want to take advantage of you. You had your blouse unbuttoned so far down that I could see your nipples. And you're not wearing a bra. So I didn't think you'd mind. I'm sorry. It won't happen again."

Jelly quickly buttoned her blouse, which was indeed undone, but not to the extent Brian Moss suggested. Angel had no doubt managed to slip a button or so through a hole or so when she, Jelly, was thinking of something else. And how did she come to be bra-less? What Angel did was only vaguely recalled by Jelly, Angelica or Lady Rice, but the marks left upon the body—their nipples were sore and there were bite marks on their neck—stood between them and total forgetfulness.

Jelly conceded that she might, albeit unknowingly, have provoked him, and consented to go back to work.

Brian Moss told Jelly a little about his wife, Oriole, whom he loved but who was so forgetful she would never even remember to comb her hair in the mornings, and would collect his older children by a previous marriage from school in a car into which she'd forgotten to put petrol. She was a danger to them. Once she'd left the iron on so it burned right through a ceiling; it was a regular occurrence for Oriole to let the bath overflow.
"Would that count as unreasonable behavior in a divorce court?" Jelly asked, and Brian Moss looked quite disconcerted at the thought, and said he and Oriole were Catholics so there was no question of that anyway. But she now understood why he watched her own smooth, quick, certain movements with a kind of longing, a subdued passion for what was effective, efficient and reliable. She was pleased to see it. It was part of herself which had never in the past been properly appreciated.

Jelly worked late; so did Brian Moss: both of them in their separate rooms. The building was darkened. Computer screens gave off a luminous sheen; pot plants seemed to breathe, and to swell and diminish minutely with each breath.

Jelly could feel Angel whispering and nudging her: saying, "Look, here's your chance. Do something! Strip off: just leave on your suspender belt and stockings. Very nice too. And then just walk like that into Brian Moss's office."

"But why?" Jelly asked. "What would be the point of that?"

"You'd end up with a rise," said Angel. "No pun intended. And you could make him do what you want."

"You are just disgusting, Angel," said Angelica.

"You're not really here to earn a salary, anyway," murmured Lady Rice. "Our original plan was to interfere with the natural course of justice, so I get some kind of decent alimony from Edwin."

"And you'll as likely find yourself fired by morning," said Angelica.

"What about revenge?" asked Angel. "Edwin's having a good time with Anthea. Anthea's living in our house, sleeping in our bed—aren't women meant to get their own back?"

"Don't make me think about it," said Lady Rice, bile rising in her throat.

"Brian Moss could stop you thinking about it," said Angel. "He could stop you thinking about it for at least twenty minutes. Think how well Ram did only this morning. If one man fancies you, another man will. Make the most of it."

"Brian Moss has a wife at home," said Jelly. "I don't do things like that. I don't go with married men. Because Lady Rice is unhappy, why should Oriole Moss be unhappy, too?"

"For that very reason," gritted Angel, bad Angel, avenging angel, in Jelly's ear. "If you spread the misery wide, you make it thinner for yourself," and Angel bit into the base of Jelly's thumb so hard there was a mark for days, almost as sore as her breasts where Ram had pecked and nibbled at them.

"I won't do any such thing," said Jelly. "Angelica is right. I'd only get fired. That's what happens in office romances."

"This is not an office romance," gritted Angel. "It is you fucking your boss in your own best interests."

"No," said Jelly.

"But I want to. I mean to," yelled Angel in her head, drowning out reason. "I want Brian Moss *now*, you mean old bitch, and I'll have him."

"Shut up," said Jelly, biting the other thumb. Lady Rice was humming to herself somewhere else; some sad, melancholy, typical tune. "Don't put this pressure on me. I'm tied to the mast, understand? And I'm not listening to you. I can cope with Lady Rice, I can cope with Angelica, but you, Angel, I can tell you're a menace! Get out of my life!"

"That's right, blame me!" shrieked Angel. "Hang me up by my thumbs. After all I did for you! You'd never have had the nerve and you know you loved it, all of you."

"I'm going home now," called out Brian Moss to Jelly White. "Must be home to bathe the babies."

"That's fine," called his secretary in reply. "I'll turn the lights off and set the alarm."

Brian went home by train. Jelly took the subway, squashed with a thousand others into a space fit for a hundred, the smell of despair adding humidity to the air she breathed. How do I escape, how do I not do this? How not to be herded, squashed, insulted, abused? See, there's the hem of my coat caught in the door: it will brush through the soot of ancient tunnels; that woman's high heel driving between my toes, removing skin; that man's crotch, that woman's arse, rubbing against mine. We share the same torment, rebreathe each other's air, use the strategies of the traumatized to escape all remembrance of the journey: the slaves were whipped to the pyramids, simply for the fun of it, the pain of it, for a whipped slave works half as well, but a man must know when he's beaten. So have his masters from the beginning of time insisted on the humiliation of their workforce. These days, through their Lodges and Confederations, they have got together over champagne and devised the public transport they never travel in to whip the workers to work: and are not jobs short and is not the living hard and precarious, and who can argue any more?

Do we not suffer?—the multi-voiced air of the subway rose to heaven, spoke to heaven—Who will save us? But there came no reply. Suffering does not necessarily suggest its own relief: because things start does not mean they must end: oppression does not necessitate the rise of the hero, nor sin its savior. And besides, everyone disliked each other too much to do anything about any of it. White hated black, black hated white, and all stations in between: parent hated child, child hated parent; police hated citizen, citizen hated police, man hated woman, woman hated man, the old hated the young, the young hated the old, and everyone hated the uniformed staff who cried aloud, "Mind the doors, please," and sometimes with a strong hand in the middle of some wretch's back—serve them right!—shoved yet another human unit to judder up against the sighing, sodden, juddering mass inside. In London, in Tokyo, in Moscow, or New York, Johannesburg or Toronto, in Seoul and Samarkand in the rush hour it is the same.

Brotherly love comes in off-peak hours.

Thus Jelly traveled to Bond Street Station, where she alighted. By the time she arrived at The Claremont she imagined she would, as usual, be Lady Angelica Rice again, albeit incognito, albeit with bruised and painful breasts and a sore chin and a bitten thumb. It had been a long day, starting with Ram, ending with jam. Angel laughed at the thought. She loved a pun. She skittered into The

Claremont and the doorman looked after her, not recognizing her as Lady Rice, and wondering what agency she was from and why he had no commission for her. His normal introduction fee was 10 percent.

"We can't live at The Claremont for ever, paying our bill by false pretences," said Angelica to Lady Rice.

"A girl needs her own house and home, if only to put a red light above the door," said Angel, "and write 'model' by the bell. You can't do that in a hotel."

"I want a nice little apartment somewhere," said Jelly, "which I can make my own, where I can get my life going again. Why don't we just accept Edwin's offer; it would be so much easier than all this? Just give up and start over. I hate living off men anyway."

But Lady Rice wasn't listening. She was home and weeping again.

(10)
Postcoital

Lady Rice continues to brood on the subject of alimony. Lady Rice will not let herself be deflected by Angel, who is really only a source of entertainment, though Lady Rice at least now appreciates the usages of sex. Lady Rice still wants her pound of flesh, but is grateful to Angel for trying. Nor will she listen to Jelly, who is beginning to say if this divorce drags on and on in uncertainty, her health will begin to suffer. She sees the temptation to cry "enough, enough" and just give in, but she won't. She is stubborn, and angry.

To do without anger, Lady Rice explains to her sub-sisters, would be to do without the nourishment she has come to depend upon. These days she relies on the bread of outrage, well spiced by bitter gall rising to the throat. It is bread well-buttered and well-slavered with hatred of Anthea. Unholy, unhealthy emotions all, but satisfactory, better than misery: anger is the knife between the teeth of the embattled warrior; an unchancy weapon, metal against ivory, sharp edge turned outward, but, of course, if you fall, that's what disembowels you—your own enmity, forget the enemy. Hate, like sex, is an addiction, explains Lady Rice: you feel you can live on it for ever; that you're born one fix of hatred under par; but of course all the time it's enticing you, luring you, killing you. And it can kill you quick, if you overdose, as heroin does: you can choke pretty fast on your own bile. It's the opposite of a quiet death—it's death by intemperance, spite, righteous anger, the nausea of revulsion. Or else it can kill you slowly; you can retreat howling, as Jelly did in the Volvo, parking in a concrete stall, leaving the field to others, licking obviously fatal wounds, a savage beast holed up in a rancid cave, pitiful, dying but dangerous.

If anyone demonstrates kindness, Lady Rice sneers, she who once gave such nice dinner parties; if anyone goes near, the creature will repay that kindness, that approach, by tearing the innocent to bits in its death throes. Beware the howling of the injured. Angel, don't feel too safe in the body you think you control. You may be out of your depth. Jelly does nothing to annoy; Angelica is almost a friend; but Angel has left Lady Rice with her knicker elastic snapped and Lady Rice may not like it; let Angel not rely too much on the gratitude of Lady Rice, divorcee-in-waiting. Lady Rice speaks nicely but let even her own sisters beware. Not push her too far.

(11)
Alimony as Justice

Lady Rice, now she has the knack of it, sends her spirit out to her lawyer, so that he will believe her and represent her interests better. He sleeps and snores beside his grey-haired wife, who dreams of lovers she has never known. Lady Rice speaks for all of her.

"We need alimony! We want nourishment: we are cracking and splitting. We are thin and brittle for lack of love: we have lost two stone in six months. If our husband won't recognize our rights, then society must come to our aid: law courts and lawyers must stand in for a corrupted individual conscience. Your duty is great, Barney Evans.

"We are not motivated by vengeance or greed. On the contrary. No. Our plea is that if the scales of justice are to remain in balance there must be brought into existence, recreating itself moment by moment, the proper, decent, material reflection of 'spiritual good.' Lost goods—in this case love, illusion, hope (worse than lost, this latter: stolen!) have an equivalent in money; this equivalent needs to be paid monthly to the end of time. That is to say, 'in her lifetime,' which for the individual, of course, is the same thing. Alimony!

"The great and complex construct which is marriage—a construct made up of a hundred little kindnesses, a thousand little bitings back of spite, tens of thousands of minor actions of good intent—be they the saving of a face, the interception of an ant, the plucking of a hair, the laughing at a bad joke, the overlooking of errors, the forgiveness of sins—this cannot, must not, as an institution, all be brought down in ruins. Let the props be financial; if this is all that remains, they have to be so.

"If we—by whom I mean myself (Lady Rice), Angelica, Jelly and yes, I fear, Angel—don't get alimony from Edwin, the whole caboodle will crumble: I can feel it. A lot rests on this. The stars themselves will implode. The scales which balance real against unreal will be shoved so far out of kilter they will tip and topple and the point of our existence, and therefore existence itself, will be gone. We will all vanish like a puff of smoke. Or implode like a collapsing marshmallow man. In the end it is money which keeps us in being, inasmuch as money is the only recognized good we have: being both abstract and real. You cannot live off justice, but you can live off money."

Barney Evans slept. The beast slouched by outside the windows, its moon-shadow clear. It was real though Lady Rice was not: it had at this moment more corporeal existence than she. Mrs. Evans moaned in her sleep: the good dreams were turning bad.

"I know we can fail," said the spirit of Lady Rice to the sleeping lawyer. "A Court might decide, as Edwin hopes it will and as you tell me often enough, that we're perfectly well equipped to look after ourself, and since the doctrine of No Fault prevails in our divorce courts, and the great injustices one human being can render to another are now apparently neither here nor there, the Court may say what the hell, who is this hopeless wife, this ex–pop star who never rode to hounds at her husband's side, who was found in bed with her best friend's husband?—who can possibly believe her account of how she got to be there, or how little happened in it?— give the woman nothing! Yes, they are capable, I hear, of awarding the four of us nothing at all. Should all my hopes for justice fail, how will any of us live? Why, as the birds do, do I hear you say?—picking at nothing. We could always take to blackmail. We may yet have to. A word or two in a media ear would have the whole flock of them down like starlings. Do you want that?"

Barney Evans snuffled. Mrs. Evans' eyes flew open. She woke Barney. "There's someone in the room," she said. But of course there was no one. "I have to be in Court tomorrow," he grumbled and went back to sleep, but before he did they embraced cosily.

"Blackmail's out of fashion," Jelly's employer Brian Moss happened to say to her the next day, "because no one's ashamed of anything any more," and she nodded and smiled politely but thought, "what do you know?" Other people's imaginations clearly didn't run the way hers did. These days she had a pocket full of floppy discs, stolen from the files, the way others had pockets full of rainbows, or claimed to. She'd take home to The Claremont in her shopping bag files containing letters and transcripts of bugged conversations, depositions and affidavits from many sources, and not just those relating to *Rice v. Rice*, matrimonial. People do chatter on to their solicitors, and Jelly was beginning to take an interest in someone other than herself, or selves. The great thing about employment, as Lavender White always used to say, is that it takes a girl away from the personal.

As for Lady Rice, she doesn't react much, can't react: she is too eaten up with anger to marvel at anything, even her alter ego Jelly's delinquency, or Angelica's pickiness, let alone Angel's whorishness. Lady Rice likes to rant on about justice, and finds some relief in it, but is still not relieved of the burden of sexual jealousy. She makes herself contemplate the reality of her husband in the arms of another, but familiarity with the source of distress, looking it in the eye, unflinching, does not weaken it as it is meant to. It makes it worse. Still jealousy rages: it gives her a pain in her midriff: it exhausts her.

But what Lady Rice can now see, at least, thanks to Angel, is that when it comes to it she's no lady.

(12)

An Unbelievable Narrator

The stress of living at The Claremont on stolen credit cards is telling on Angelica. When the phone goes, she jumps. Supposing it's the management, telling them they must move on? They will be found out, thrown out, punished, disgraced!

Angelica has always lived in fear of being found out. Never mind how much money she has in the bank, if the telephone behind the grille buzzes while she's at the counter she thinks the call must relate to her—she's been discovered as an imposter.

Angel loves to order champagne and endless club sandwiches from room service. Angelica, for no good reason, feels she will be safer if she orders Coke and Danish pastries. Lady Rice can only pick at a steamed lobster. Angel offers to seduce the bellboy who brings these goodies so he forgets to charge them if that makes Angelica feel safer, but Angelica shudders and declines. A great deal of food is ordered, but very little eaten.

Lady Rice signs the account the Hotel Manager proffers weekly, and Jelly waves him away. So far, it seems, the account is accepted and paid without question, however unwillingly, by the Rice Estate. Angelica moans and groans about theft and cheating.

But Angelica has been hearing other voices in her head. The one most predominant is male, she's sure of it. It happens when the others are sleeping. The voice is preoccupied with Robert Jellico's sins and self. It drones on, creating a rumbling background of aggressive discontent.

"I'd like to ram a red-hot poker up Jellico's arse," grumbles the voice. "I'll do it. I will. I'll get him. He'll rue the day he was ever born. The man's a thief, as well as a criminal; ought to be strung up, crucified. I'm on your side, baby. If anyone gives you a hard time, let me know . . . I'll tear his eyes out for you . . ." and so on. Sometimes the voice becomes brisker and more intelligent, the threats and imprecations more subtle. It is as if the new self—which Angelica fears it is—is looking for some definite, suitable, and lasting identity before making itself properly known.

She does not tell the others. She is ashamed to have a male inside her, part of herself, as Angel turned out to be part of Lady Rice. What will they think? She feels unnatural and debased.

Angelica finds herself trying to mend the gold taps in the marble bathroom, fixing the shower, instead of waiting for Housekeeping to come along and do it. She has wrenched the fitments unnecessarily hard and broken them. She has kicked the television because by so doing she can make it change stations without need of the remote control.

"What are you *doing?*" begs Jelly. "You are breaking the place up. Are you losing your wits?"
Angelica laughs hollowly.
"Cheap muck!" complains the voice. "God, this place is a rip-off. You know all this marble is plastic veneer?"
"Who's that?" asks Lady Rice suspiciously.
"Just me in a bad mood," says Angelica, but she knows it isn't true. A man is taking shape inside her, as Angel took shape in

Lady Rice. Angelica feels polluted and disgraced, but can see that if she could accept the male part of herself she would be a fuller, rounder, more effective person. The man has a good appetite: Angelica finds herself devouring hamburgers and chips, sausages and mashed potato. He orders beer. Angelica has bought some weights on the way home from work. She stands in front of the mirror and body-builds. Swing, lift, lower; swing, lift, lower.

"Stop it!" shrieks Angel. "I don't want muscles. That's the last thing a girl needs."

"I'm too tired," moans Lady Rice, "for all this."

"Keep us healthy," Jelly concedes. "We don't get enough exercise."

"Sex is the best exercise there is!" says Angel. "We get plenty. What, do you want more? I'm easy!"

Three times a week they go with Ram to the car-park. He picks them up three-quarters of an hour early so they're not late for Brian Moss. On the other mornings he's booked for other regulars—though none, he assures them, that involve his sexual services. They all begin to like him really quite a lot.

Swing, lift, lower; swing, lift, lower: there's no stopping Angelica. She waits till the others are asleep. Listens.

"Hi," she says. "Who are you?"

"An A, a J, an A, add X, the unknown factor."

"Ajax," she says.

"Ah-ha!" he says. "So what's your problem?" and is gone.

Angelica thinks about her problem and comes up with an answer. It's this: "Call my problem X and solve it. Too many Xs for a simple equation: quadruple equation either. X = ex.

"Ex-virgin, ex–pop star, ex-wife, ex-socialite, ex–convent girl, ex-everything, ex-everyone, that's me: primarily ex-daughter of a radio ham. When Daddy wasn't running the Barley school choir he was up in the small back study, where Lavender never went, surrounded by banks of electronic equipment, tangled in wires, deafened by headphones, in touch with others everywhere just like him, who'd rather say 'hi' to a perfect stranger, and 'well, have a nice day' to a ship's telegrapher, than kiss his wife or cuddle his child. Daddy, Daddy, speak to me! I can't my darling, my angel, I'm saving ships at sea. What ships, Daddy, what sea? I don't know, my darling, my angel, but sooner or later, if I search the airwaves long enough, I'll rescue someone, somewhere, and you'll be proud of me. In the meantime, sweetheart, just leave Daddy in peace.

"Are you Daddy's darling or Mother's little helper? God knows.

"My problem is I feel as Zeus must have before Athena burst out of the top of his head. The pressure on me is tremendous: the others sleep, I cannot; I am an insomniac; guilt and anxiety stop me sleeping: velociraptors, velcro-raptors prowl within my head, as well as my sisters'. A black band as if the head itself were a hat, begins to confine and tighten. The whole bulging swarm of identities is getting a terrible headache and I'm the one who feels it. Something has to give.

"I repeat: I can't live for ever in an hotel room, no matter how grand and marble-lined, so pinkly frilled, so golden brown its furniture and exquisite its fitments, so profoundly desired its address, so lordly my fellow guests. I can't just live here under a false name, growing alternative personalities as if they were pot plants, feeding them, nurturing them for lack of anything else to do, while I wait and wait for my life to resolve itself, for the legal profession to catch up with itself; all because it suits Edwin to claim I committed adultery with my erstwhile best friend Susan's lover Lambert. Lies, all lies! What really happened is that Edwin wanted to marry Anthea, and organized my exit from his life. Edwin was tired of me, that was all. What I thought was marriage, would endure for all our life because apart we were nothing but together we were something, oh yes, something, was just Edwin's way of growing up. I hate Edwin now for what he did to me, for the loss of my faith in the goodness of people; he has stolen my capacity for love, and doesn't care enough for me, doesn't remember me clearly enough, even to discuss the matter with me. Used and abused, that's me, but, worse still, forgotten.

"Or look at it another way: I am the twisted cord of a telephone wire: dangle it and watch the rapidity with which it untwists itself; so rapidly indeed that it then twists the other way, almost as badly, and who then has the patience to wait for it to settle? Not me, whoever I may be. I'd rather wrench the whole thing from the wall and go cordless. But how can I shake off these others, who travel with me wherever I go?

"Too much unravelling, that is my problem. Too many exes, and too much unravelling. Of course I have a headache."

Still there was no response from Ajax.

Angelica thinks that perhaps a bath may soothe her. The baths at The Claremont are deep, wide and made of marble. They are also, she notices, difficult to clean. She takes the scouring powder from the cupboard beneath the basin, and with the help of a damp face-cloth, stretches to reach the section the maid has failed to clean and, when she straightens up, catches her head on the shower fitment.

She staggers to the bed. She lies down. Her headache is much, much, much worse.

(13)
The Perforated Personality

"I've been observing the phenomena," said Ajax, in cultured tones over Angelica's breakfast. "And I have some observations to make. Angelica, Jelly and Angel are not three split-off parts of Lady Rice, as she supposes. No. All are equals. Each can and should be held responsible legally, fiscally and spiritually for the others. There is no question here of the one hand not knowing what the other is doing; one personality dominant, controlling lesser ones, capable of taking the others by surprise. In classic cases of split personality, respectable A will wake in the morning and discover herself, say, bruised and smeared with honey, or in strange clothes and with sums of money in her pocket, be puzzled and distressed, and have no notion at all of what her other persona B was up to during the night, or where B went, or what she did—indeed have no idea that B even exists. But B does exist and, what is more, exists alongside, quite probably, C, D and occasionally emerging others, E, F and G; who will either know all about the others, or know nothing about the others, or have some degree of knowledge, depending on whether they are, as it were, on A or B's team, and to what degree trusted by their controllers. The main split, the A/B split, lies between the steady, the good, the nice and the cautious, and the licentious, delinquent, spiteful and spontaneous.

"In the case of Lady Rice, the split is better described as a perforation: not yet complete: a rather extreme case of voices in the head. Only if torn will the actual split occur, as when you tear your round Road Tax disc from its embracing square. As it is, if Angelica murders someone, Jelly and Angel cannot be excused: they ought to have controlled her, and had the capacity so to do. If Jelly develops repetitive strain injury at Catterwall & Moss, Angelica and Angel can hardly complain: it was their own fingers they overworked, in excessive zeal. If Angel gets herpes, or AIDS, Angelica and Jelly can hardly be surprised: they should not have colluded: the truth is that they, too, were sexually tempted. The three must, and should, take their place together, as one, in the eyes of the world even if, among themselves, they continue to hold endless speculative conversations. A phenomenon not yet clinical, and with any luck never to be clinical. Each knows everything about the other and individual parts continue to make up a recognizable whole. The square still contains the circle. So far.

"Now the conglomerate persona that consists of Angelica, Jelly and Angel, which on marriage formed itself into Lady Rice, received nothing but affection and kindness—so far as any parent is capable of wholly admirable and pure behavior—from her parents Lavender and Stephen White. Evil, psychosis, trauma, do not necessarily fit the equation; they are not necessary to the creation of a perforated personality. Split is clinical and distressing, morbid: perforation is a far more common occurrence. Many of us suffer from mild perforation, a vague feeling of disassociation, the gentle murmuring of voices in the head. Poor me, poor me, with variations: for example, I don't know what came over me! It happens to the most sensitive, not those most oppressed by worldly misfortune.

"To be thus divided into three is what many women report. When they stare at themselves in mirrors, twirl on delicate toes, they are Angelica: when they go to work, industriously, impersonally, they are Jelly: when they go to the bad, take another drink, smoke an illicit joint, leave the child un-babysat, leap at the genitals of another sex, why then they are Angel. They sign their letters 'Lady Rice' with a kind of conjoined formality.

"When a woman says, 'If only I could find myself,' all three personae speak at once: they feel over–Jellyfied, Angelicized, or Angelated, and don't like it: they search for a balance.

"When she says, 'I must fulfil myself,' it is the Jelly in her speaking (looking up from her work, wondering what the matter is, deciding it's lack of babies), trying to leave Angelica behind and get Angel out of her system somehow.

"When women keep husbands as pets to fetch their handbags, won't have sex with them and affect a general air of moral superiority, then Angelica predominates. It is Angelica who says all men are rapists at heart and are nasty, messy, aggressive creatures in general. Animals!

"When a woman runs off with her best friend's husband and says this thing is bigger than me, or all I have to do is snap my fingers and I'll have your boyfriend, why that's Angel, and she probably will have him. Beware. Her heart is kind, but her passions are great and her morals few.

"Lady Rice has 'trouble coming to terms with her situation,' as the newspaper therapists calmly put it; that is to say giant stars in her psyche implode and black holes yawn: reeling, she takes refuge in Angelica, Jelly, Angel.

"You will notice," says Ajax, "that I leave myself out of the equation. The three of you make one. But I am male, separate and indivisible. And I am in charge round here."

There is a stunned silence from the women.

"Angelica," says Jelly, "put that man away at once."

"I'll try," says Angelica.

"It isn't decent having a man in here anyway," says Lady Rice. "It makes me feel very peculiar."

"I like it," says Angel. "He makes me feel ever so sexy. You don't have to listen to what he says. He's only a man."

But Ajax has gone anyway. Angelica tries to locate him. Somewhere she hears shouts and bellows, and the creak of ships' timbers, and the call of sea birds, and the sound of sword upon shield comes to her ears, and the crashing of wave upon rock, as if Ajax the Hero, Ulysses' friend and compatriot, was taking over from Ajax the expert on Multiple Personality. More fun, perhaps: a more active and satisfactory life for a brawny, full-blooded man than trying to share a head with three women, and lecturing them on their condition.

Jelly does not go to work that day. Angelica is too fretful to get Lady Rice out of bed. Ram waits fruitlessly at the hotel entrance. Even Angel can't be bothered with thrills. The whole personality shudders and shakes; it has been more upset than it knew by the sudden eruption of Ajax out of Angelica, and by his clinical definition of their state. Everything was easier when it was undefined.

"Trust a man," weeps Lady Rice. "I need Edwin to look after me and he isn't here to do it any more. I'm on my own!"

The others don't even have the energy to explain yet again that she is not.

But it is true that times are worsening. Trauma approaches. And from whence and how will rescue come? The union soul is under attack; the confederation falters; the flag is torn—poor Lady Rice can't tell good from bad, nothing seems real, nothing can be trusted, her past has become meaningless, her future is obscured; even friends are no longer friends. The very plates from which she was accustomed to eat are apparently not hers at all, but Rice family heirlooms, or so Sir Edwin writes to Brian Moss. Lady Rice has no

access to her satin sheets, neatly folded in the master bedroom press;
worse, her rival Anthea leans up against piles of healthy, folded, natural fabric in the second floor linen room to be pleasured by her
husband. If the linen room is now reckoned to be haunted, and
Mrs. MacArthur will not now go into it unaccompanied, because of
a chilly feeling in the air and prickles up her spine, it is not surprising. Anthea and Edwin notice nothing: the warmth of their passion
overwhelms everything.

Poor Lady Rice. See how now she goes through her life stunned,
flickering out of one persona, into another, as men and women do
when they discover that concepts of love, of home, of permanence,
are not placed on rock, but on shifting sand. When the Velcro splits
and tears and the trousers and the knickers fall down and everyone
laughs, even those who live in luxurious hotels can be pitied.

No wonder people put their trust in Jesus. Jesus never fails. Upon
this rock this Church is built, if only you can overlook a little histori-
cal evidence, a South Sea scroll or two. South Sea Scroll, that
phrase being the melding of South Sea Bubble, that great financial
scandal, and the Dead Sea—that arid waste, that bitter pond. South
Sea Scroll, article of lost faith.

Alimony is the rock, in Lady Rice's eyes, on which such future as
she can have will be founded; Angelica planning, Jelly working,
Angel fucking, Ajax irritating.

(14)
Breaking Out

Lady Rice, that perforated, split personality, that collection of identities loosely bound in the one body, sat in The Claremont in her
silk wrap, bought from the hotel boutique, paid for on Sir Edwin's
credit card, looked in her mirror, felt lonely, wept and could no longer contain herself. "I can't stand it!" she cried, and indeed she
could not. Most people say they can't stand it, and lie: they do stand
it, having no choice. But the spasms of emotional pain that overwhelmed Lady Rice were so intense that she was driven not out of
herself but into more of her selves.
Perforations deepened.

"Pull yourself together, for God's sake," Jelly said to Lady Rice,
out of the mirror. But she added, more kindly, "It's been a
long, hard day."
"In future," said Angelica, "we'll go home by bus, not Underground. It's easier on the nerves. And do stop crying, before
our eyes get red and puffy. Jesus! What a sight!"
"Let's go downstairs to the bar," said Angel, "and make out
with some rich businessman. Have a fun night out, some sex—
good or bad; I grant you that's a risk. We'll score if we can and
make ourselves some money."
"Score?" asked Lady Rice.
"Drugs," said Angel.
Lady Rice uttered a little scream.
Lady Rice found herself looking out her best lingerie and trying it on, while Jelly agitated.

"You'll do no such thing," said Jelly. "You need a good night's sleep. You have to go to work in the morning," at which Angel pinched Jelly's arm and left a nasty little bruise, so Jelly shut up, while Angelica just looked on in horror, and Lady Rice screamed again and collapsed altogether into her separate parts and there seemed nothing left of her at all.

She lay down on the bed and left it to the others to get on with the night.

(15)
Angel's Outing

The bartender smiled at Angel. He was young and Greek; he had soft brown eyes, a snowy white shirt and tight trousers; he leapt about from one end of the bar to the other at the behest of his slow-moving customers. Angel, considering his small, muscular buttocks, actually licked her lips. She allowed the edge of her small pink tongue to show, running around her carmined mouth.

Angelica seldom wore make-up; Jelly went in for soft shadings and a discreetly artificial look; Angel just liked lots and lots of everything. Her skirt was up at her thighs, her silver shoes high-heeled; her midriff showed: black leather jacket fastened with an enamelled rose, the kind of thing a sheik might buy at Aspreys for a very lucky girl.

The barman nodded to an empty table in the panelled corner, softly lit. The bar was done out in tasteful pinks and greys. Angelica loathed it, Jelly loved it, Angel didn't notice, excited even by the feel of her own tongue on her own lips. Who cared now about Edwin, marriage, injustice, alimony, law: all that was another world.

"I'm supposed to discourage single ladies," said the barman, "but business is so bad you could only do it some good."

Jelly began to say that this was outrageous—an affront to her principles, if not single women then why single men?—but Angelica and Angel made her hold her tongue. Angel sat down with her drink, and casually slid her skirt even further up her legs, stretching them to show them to advantage. The elderly, well-coupled rich who this evening, more's the pity, frequented the bar, looked, and looked away, and the wives looked at the barman for help, but he had his back to them, and a couple of the husbands sneaked a speculative after-glance or so.

"Oh God," said Jelly, "this is so crude and shameful."

"What do you expect?" asked Angelica, bitterly. "Angel's a very crude person."

"She'll be sorry in the morning," said Jelly. "That's all I can say. We all will."

"Just shut up, the pair of you," said Angel, hitching open her leather jacket so that more swelling bosom was revealed. "I certainly won't be sorry."

"I don't believe this," said Jelly. "Angelica, this is intolerable. Shall we go?" and Angelica made an effort and stood up, but the stiff drink had weakened her legs—Lady Rice rarely drank anything stronger than tonic water—so she had to sit down again quickly.

At last two possible prospects, two on-the-face-of-it heterosexual men without women, came into the bar: they were in, she supposed, their late forties, solid, red-faced, probably American; not the suave, moneyed, boardroom types on better days to be found in the bar, nor the eloquent, quick-moving, dangerous Arabs who moved in groups, liked a big-breasted girl and possessed her in order of precedence, status: no, these were, say, engineers: they'd have started out as practical men, good with their hands, and ended up on the executive floor; steak-and-chips men, not the caviare kind; prone to simple human affections, to weeping not beating; they'd have solid, plain wives whom they loved; they shuffled and grinned foolishly, more at home in the bar than the nightclub. Angel sighed.

"Two little lambs who've gone astray," murmured Angelica, reviving, "in unknown pastures, and God knows when they last washed. Angel, how can you?"

"Shut up," said Angel, so fiercely that Angelica did. "If I want to be the reward, their good night out on the town, that's my privilege. If I make them happy, I'm glad. You're so mean, the lot of you."

A murmur in the barman's ear: he nodded towards Angel. The two turned to stare at her, speculatively.

"Hang on a moment, Angel," reasoned Jelly. "Jesus! I know that kind of barman. He just wants you out of here. You're bringing down the tone of his bar. He could have fixed you up with anyone. It's an insult, an outrage. At least settle for a millionaire. For God's sake, Angel, don't just throw us away!"

"Fucking shut up," said Angel, and pinched Jelly's arm again, and had to smile through her own grimace as the two approached, carrying two whiskies for themselves and a double gin for her. "At least I give good value for money."

The punters would, after all, get three of her for the price of one, though no doubt Angelica would be reluctant, and Jelly a wet-blanket; but sex is sex: the moment the body was engaged in its instinctive business the other two shouldn't prove too much of a problem; might even add a frisson or so to Angel's own entertainment.

Lady Rice slept. Where did she get her worldly wisdom? She had led an emotionally-trying but narrow and sheltered life—it was enough to make you believe in the group unconscious. If you delved too deep into it you'd find the accumulated wisdom and experience of not just three but all the women in the world, and all the false assumptions and conditioned responses too. And no sense yet made of any of it. Lady Rice is no angel: that she's sure of, or she wouldn't be in this company.

Michael, with thick silver hair and the single gold tooth, sat at Angel's left. David, with thinning red hair and crinkly blue eyes, sat on her right. Glad to make her acquaintance, they said. They were strangers in town. She smiled and said nothing in particular. They were staying, they said, in a hotel down the road. That figured: their suits did not have quite the flat smoothness of the ones usually seen at The Claremont. They had been first packed, then unpacked, and not seen the services of a first class valet.

Michael and David pressed more gin upon Angel, intently watching her drink. She told them her name was Angel; that she was a private nurse. That she was employed to look after a stroke victim, an elderly lady currently a guest at The Claremont. It did not do to present herself as either too up-market, or too obvious in her profession. Amateurs did better in this game than professionals.

"Angel by name," they said, "Angel by nature." They expected she needed something to cheer her up, and she agreed that she did.

Michael laid a well-manicured hand on one arm, David on the other.

"Ask them if they're married," said Jelly in Angel's ear.
"What, to each other?" snapped Angel, aloud. "For God's sake, leave me alone."
"Did you say that to me?" asked Michael, surprised.
"I'm sorry," said Angel. "Sometimes I do talk to myself. You'll get used to it."

David leant over and squeezed her lips gently together with thumb
and forefinger. "That's to stop you," he said. "Women shouldn't talk
too much. It gets them into trouble." She could see the gold wedding band on his third finger: there was no avoiding it. He had a
wife.

Angelica said, "Don't you have any respect for anything?"
Jelly said, "Oh, give up, Angelica. There's no stopping her.
Let's just go with the flow," and for a time they did.

Michael said to David, concerned, "If you hold her lips together,
she won't be able to drink," and David took his hand away and
Angel beamed happily from one to the other. The barman held the
door open for them, and they helped Angel across the room.
"I'm so drunk I can hardly stand," she confessed to the barman, giving him a little kiss for good measure.
"Wrong man!" said David, pulling her away.
"Isn't that Lady Angelica Rice?" asked the doorman of the barman,
in the marble foyer, as the three went off down the road, in search of
their lesser hotel.
"Of course that's not Lady Rice," said the barman. "That's some
pick-up, using and abusing my bar. I just get them drunk and out as
fast as possible."
"Lady Rice is here incognito," said the doorman, "so in theory it's
not our concern. She'll just have to look after herself."

On the way down Davis Street, towards Oxford Street, Angelica
kept looking over her shoulder.

"Why are you doing that?" asked Jelly, annoyed. "I need to
concentrate. I'm trying to keep her steady on her feet."
"It's all too easy," said Angelica. "I'm nervous. We've been set
up. Supposing we've been recognized? Supposing Edwin gets

to know? Supposing we're being spied on? Supposing it affects our alimony?"

"You're being paranoid," said Jelly. "Personally, I'm glad of the opportunity to widen the field of my experience."

"You're a hopeless little slut at heart," said Angelica, bitterly. "No better than Angel."

Angel tripped and nearly fell, and was buoyed up on either side by Michael and David. Michael had his hand inside her jacket, she noticed, fingering her bosom. She liked that.

"This goes too far," said Angelica, and shut her eyes. "I've changed my mind. I'm going to join Lady Rice."

"So am I," said Jelly. "Angel, you're on your own."

Before she retired, Jelly managed to extract one of her high heels from a grating, instead of merely leaving the whole shoe behind as Angel was happy enough to do. Angel was neither prudent nor scrupulous. She enjoyed waste. The shoes were silvery net—an expensive pair Lady Rice had seldom had opportunity to wear: in Rice circles shoes were usually plain and serviceable. Presently Jelly became aware that Lady Rice was lying semi-clothed on a bed, not in The Claremont but in some strange hotel: the less she knew about any of it the better. She just hoped to live. Casual sex was insane. Serial killers, HIV rapists were at the outer edges of the sex-with-strangers experience: further in, nearer home, sadists, bullies, men on power trips, men anxious to humiliate. If Jelly knew this, how come Angel so readily took Lady Rice into danger? Or perhaps Angel thought horror a small price to pay for sex. What did two men want with one woman? Or did one woman merely save the cost of two?

When it came to it, David and Michael seemed more interested in one another's orifices than in Angel's. Angel served, as Angelica acidly observed in the morning, safely back in The Claremont, as witness to passion, even love, and as a kind of soft, sweet, fleshly jam spread on harder, crusty, rather stale bread, in the hope that the latter would be made appealing. To which Jelly replied, "You are such a mass of euphemisms, Angelica. It was disgusting. Men are beasts. They just wanted somewhere extra for a ramrod to ram, should it run out of places. There was no love in it, none." To which Angel murmured but they seemed to love each other: who cared about love, anyway? She, Angel, had a good time and earned herself a hundred pounds cash; and then, as Angelica filled and scented the bath and Jelly folded the clothes and tut-tutted over the scuffed heel, Angel lapsed into exhausted silence and went into hiding.

When she was gone, Jelly said to Angelica, "What are we going to *do* about her? She'll get us into terrible trouble," and Angelica, anointing her sore parts with healing jellies, said, "I don't know. I don't know."
Over breakfast, Angelica said, "I thought I saw that nice barman when Angel came in. I had the feeling he'd been waiting up. It was obvious what we'd been up to. Drunk, unescorted, skirt torn, four in the morning. Supposing he took a photograph?"
Jelly said brusquely, "Nonsense. We'd have seen the flash."
Angelica said, "We were in no condition to notice anything."
Jelly said, brightly, "At least we're 'we' again. A good night out can work wonders."
Angelica said, "Speak for yourself. I'm ashamed and humiliated. But I expect it's no more than I deserve."

They enjoyed their coffee. It was black and strong. The croissants were fresh, and there was a Danish pastry, well filled with apple and quite delectable. Sun shone in.
"Only four hours' sleep," said Lady Rice, herself again, "and a full day's work ahead! God knows what comes over me, sometimes."

As a day, of course, it was a dead loss. Lady Rice stumbled through it as Jelly, hungover and sleepless, but the speculative pain was muted, the outrage and blind fury that Edwin preferred another woman to her, that that other woman had so easily taken her husband, her property, her home, her very life from under her nose, had somewhat abated. Lady Rice used her alter egos as strategies for survival. What else was she to do?

Jelly forgot to save a file on her computer and lost a whole day's work, including a letter to Barney Evans, which she omitted to mention to Brian Moss. If a letter came in complaining of undue delay, she could lose that one too, when it arrived. She had stopped being in a hurry. Now she was playing for time. She could see that some kind of healing process had begun. The others agreed.

Not too much damage had been done, as it so happened, by Angel's delinquency.

"Sex, money and alcohol make a dangerous mixture," said Jelly primly. Since Angel could not do without the first, and all of them needed the second, they decided never to get drunk again. There were too many divorcees around who relied upon alcohol to get them through the night, and so seldom got through the days.

(16)

The Wicked and the Good

Tully Toffener called Brian Moss. Jelly received the call. She said Brian Moss was at a meeting, though he wasn't. She said she would ask Brian to return the call, but she didn't.

"Why don't we like him?" Angelica asked.

"He was unsympathetic," said Lady Rice vaguely. "Not quite our sort."

Memories of the marriage were fading, had only properly been Lady Rice's anyway, at any rate in the latter days of the marriage. A few vivid incidents stood out: watching the chimney fall through the roof, handing over money to Robert Jellico, nursing Lady Ventura, the dinner when Natalie burned Susan's cheek with lobster soup. Yes, Tully Toffener had been there that night, but what had he said, what had he done? She remembered Sara Toffener complaining about the servants. But these incidents now floated like star-ships in a kind of space, without beginning, without end. They had nothing much to do with Lady Rice any more. She had not seen or spoken to Edwin for six months, though he had called Brian Moss on a few occasions, and she had put the call through. Edwin had not even recognized her voice. She had seen his scrawled signature on the bottom of letters, and had pressed the writing to her lips for comfort, for all Jelly tried to stop her, crying out in disgust, "My God, talk about women who love too much! The man's a monster." Lady Rice had used ruse after ruse to get through to Sir Edwin on the phone, but he had changed his private number. Anthea would

answer, or Mrs. MacArthur, and Lady Rice would put the phone
down, heart beating and leaping all over the place.

That Anthea now moved about her, Lady Rice's, kitchen, used her
pots and pans, lay in her bed with her husband, seemed to Lady
Rice the stuff of nightmare, though to the rest of the world, and
indeed to Jelly, Angelica and Angel, it seemed ordinary enough.
These days, of course, men and women had serial spouses; who
could forever be changing houses, buying new when partners
changed? Children, if there were any, required continuity. No sympathetic magic would be allowed to lie in the cutlery or china, the
pillows and sideboards, that had accompanied a marriage: it was
simply not practical. Did not a new man now sit in Angelica's father's armchair, without apparent fear of a haunting? Let the new
partner water the old partner's pot plants, it was all that was required. Lady Rice thanked God now she had no children, to tear
her apart, loving and hating them, needing and rejecting them, as
she saw the father appear in them. Nor did she believe any longer
that if she had had a child it would have made much difference to
the marriage. He would have seen his wife in his child, and dismissed the child as well, that was all.

Angelica yawned.
Jelly yawned.
Angel yawned.
"Forget the past," they said. "What a bore it is."
Lady Rice tried to explain that it was no longer the past which
upset her so, but her increasing and intensifying lack of one.
Edwin looked through her and by her: he was trying to make
her feel she did not exist, and had never existed, and he was
succeeding. He was vanishing her.
"We'll sustain you," said the others. "We live in the here and
now; we don't need a past."

She was grateful, but felt they did not understand quite how she suffered. Even in her dreams now, sometimes, Edwin's face would be checkered over by changing squares, as if he were someone on TV who did not wish to be recognized. It hurt her more than anything. He had stolen her home from her, and now he robbed her even of memories of him. He had stolen twelve years. She had no choice, if she were to live at all, but to go back to being the person she was when she married him: like a child too long and too often away from school, how would she ever catch up? She would have to limp along behind everyone else for ever.

Alimony, hate, resentment, these three. Oh, she was having trouble with herself.

(17)
Jelly Takes Over

Tully Toffener finally managed to get through to Brian. He called from the House of Commons.

"What's the matter with that secretary of yours?" he asked. "You stuffing her, or what? She hasn't got her mind on her job."

Brian made excuses on Jelly's behalf. Tully Toffener wanted to know what his chances were of getting his wife's grandmother and her husband put in a lunatic asylum and getting himself made executor of their estate. Brian Moss said he thought Tully's chances were slim, since there was an inheritance involved, and Tully lost his temper. Brian handed the phone to Jelly, to save himself. Jelly listened and remembered why she didn't like Tully Toffener.

"Don't give me any of that shit," yelled Tully, "about old people not being paper parcels, and having a will and rights of their own. I get that all the time in this lousy job they've sidestepped me into. If I had my way, everyone in this country over eighty would be tied up with string like the parcels they are, and put into a furnace. There's the division bell. There's a three-line whip and I have to go and vote with the ayes in the free-fuel-for-pensioners bill. You're no fucking use to me at all, Moss. And you're not doing much for my friend Edwin Rice, by all accounts, to save him from that horrid little wife of his. She was a dreadful cook."

And the phone clicked down.

"Being an ex-wife," said Jelly to her boss, "is like being dead, but no one speaking good of you."

"How very strange," said Brian Moss. "That's exactly what my wife said to me."

Next time Jelly stood up, he slid his arms around her waist and hugged her and said, "I'd like to save you from all the horrors of the world."

"You're meant to do that for your wife," said Jelly.

"I can do that for her as well," he said. "There's plenty to go round."

But still Jelly refuses him. Angelica insists. Brian Moss has told Jelly that a woman trying to extract alimony from a man should be very careful not to be seen to be having sexual relations with another man. A nod and a wink between judges and lawyers can happen. Less money if she's still attractive and likely to catch a man; more money if she's old, plain and likely to be alone for ever.

> "That is a disgraceful state of affairs," says Lady Rice.
>
> "Not particularly," says Angel. "It makes sense to me."
>
> "It would," says Angelica, scornfully.
>
> They're all exhausted.
>
> "We have to work out some system," says Jelly, "of sharing this lady out. Supposing you three just go away for a time and leave me to run things?"
>
> "That's a fine system," jeers Angel. "Everything for you, nothing for us."
>
> "Do you want to take over?" asks Jelly, crossly.
>
> Angel backs off at once: she likes a night on the town, but doesn't want any responsibility. She says she's too young.

The others compromise. Angel will stay with Jelly, who'll keep an eye on her. Lady Rice and Angelica will back off for a time. Something has to happen. Nights have been disturbed. Angel is in the middle of an AIDS panic. Lady Rice longs as ever for temporary obliteration (and even admits to the others that, if it were not for them, she might well have sought permanent peace by means of pills and plastic bag). Angelica's nerves are worn to a frazzle by anxiety, lest she be exposed by The Claremont's management as a cheat and a thief. And Ram has to be out of the country for a month. That's the clincher. Angelica and Lady Rice wave good-bye to Jelly and Angel and depart for a holiday from the intellect and the senses. Jelly frees her mind—the full content of which she has learned to conceal from the others—and hugs to herself the knowledge that if Brian Moss wants to fuck Jelly, he can. He just has to stop hinting and ask. All moral scruple, especially her own, has evaporated. And Angel won't be interested in stopping her.

But that is Jelly's idea of the matter, not Brian's: let no woman if not a wife, and not even then, think she is ever unconditionally wanted.

(18)
The Relief of Tension

Tully was on the phone again to Brian Moss. Sara's grandmother, Lady Wendy Musgrave, aged ninety-six, and her husband Congo, seventy-five, had both been found dead of natural causes—failure of the heart. The bodies had lain undiscovered for a week. The one had died of shock, it was assumed, on finding the other dead. But which one first?

"They must have loved each other very much," said Brian Moss sentimentally, trying to keep his breath even. Jelly knelt in front of him, her mouth round his member, sucking upon it as if it were a nipple. She enquired with her eyebrows whether she should stop, but he shook his head vigorously.

"Jesus!" said Tully Toffener. "What's that got to do with anything?"

"Sorry," said Brian Moss.

"I've had a word with the coroner," said Tully, "but the man's a fool. He says in lack of any other evidence it's supposed that the older dies first. That affects the inheritance. No one can find the will: she may even have died intestate. That means everything goes not to Sara but to the husband and he's left the lot to his niece."

"That's nice for the niece."

"Christ, Moss, I'll get you for negligence if it's the last thing I do!"

And Tully slammed the phone down. Jelly and Brian brought their joint activity to its natural end and Jelly said, "Brian, we can't do this so often. It's beginning to take up too much of your time and energy. It's addictive."

"I know," said Brian.

"And frankly," said Jelly, "it isn't altogether satisfactory for me."

"But I can't be unfaithful to my wife," moaned Brian Moss.

"You really think this doesn't count?" enquired Jelly.

"Of course it doesn't," said Brian Moss. "Oh God, what am I going to do?"

Jelly thought she heard a faint titter from the other three, but hoped she had not. She was sent by Brian to search amongst Sara Toffener's papers—old Gerald Catterwall, who founded the firm, had at one time had Wendy Musgrave as a client—to see if by any chance the missing will was amongst them, and indeed it was, yellowed and tied with red ribbon. Wendy had left Lodestar House to her daughter Una, Sara's mother, who had disappeared sometime in the 1950s; or in the event of her prior decease, to a cats' home. Brian remembered old Catterwall telling him Una had been involved in the white slave trade—on the management side, not the victims'—and he had declined to keep her as a client, while continuing to look after little Sara's interests.

"Those were the days," said Brian Moss, "when we could afford to pick and choose our clients on moral grounds. I suppose I could try and find Una Musgrave, but I don't think I will. Let Tully Toffener's inheritance go by default."

(19)
Jelly Alone

Jelly has other reasons for wanting to be alone, free of criticism and comment from her sisters. Nightly, Jelly now fills her notebooks: scraps of fact, fiction, essay; written descriptions of what goes on in the world, what things look like, feel like; recording the numerous assessments the writer can make on paper about the nature of people, things and fate, as if only in the recording does anything ever become real. Yes, she believes, this defines her: she is a writer. Angelica, Lady Rice and Angel are content just to emote, and judge, and act; enough for them just to *be*, without any particular aspiration, other than to be happy and free of plaintive or passionate emotion. Jelly wants to recreate the world in her own image, and needs space in her head to do it: she wants to be able to reflect at leisure, and not have her spare time taken up with endless triangles and discussions. Just for a time, she tells herself; she will start missing them soon.

•

She keeps her stolen floppy discs and files in the back of the shoe cupboard and, staring at her shoes, is astonished. Their number has increased, yet she has no memory of buying them. Jelly herself favors little neat low-heeled court shoes, comfortable but smart. Angelica likes great clomping things, large heavy objects weighing down ethereal spirit, rooting her being. Lady Rice likes sensible brogues. Angel runs to black suede thigh boots jangling with gold chains. Six-inch platforms—how can anyone walk in those? Yet they've been worn, walked-in, but when?

At night Jelly ties a cotton thread to her wrist and to the bedpost, in case one of the others cheats and the body is used overnight without her knowledge, but what's that going to prove? She gives up and hopes for the best, which is also in her nature. Perhaps, when she allows them back in, they could all have some kind of therapy: but then, what are their conversations but co-counselling? It is pleasant in the meanwhile to be relieved of the running anxiety that blights Angelica's existence: and the undercurrent of sorrow that Lady Rice provides; but Jelly does miss Angel—the half-delinquent, always exciting sense that adventure is just around the corner, and that if it doesn't come running to meet you, you'll stretch out a bangled arm and yank it back and by God confront it.

Jelly had a clear-out. She picked a mound of useless clothes out of the wardrobe and shelves: see-through blouses, metal belts, leather trews, purple velvet leggings, cloche hats with flowers, absurd knickers, crotchless tights, lacey suspender belts—unused, unworn mostly, with the price labels still on them—masses of cheap jewellery, expensive face creams gone sour and caked because they'd been inspected, not used, and the lid left off; cheap and cheerful cosmetics, hair curlers, wigs. She gave them all to the corridor maid, who did not seem particularly grateful.

With these out of the way, and nothing but the sensible skirts, pastel jumpers and warm coats left, she felt more herself, and that if the others didn't have clothes and accessories they would not be so likely to try take-over bids. She and Angel got along just fine: Angelica and Lady Rice, she realized, were just too moral for their own good.

(20)
Edwin's Offer

Edwin writes to Brian Moss to see if there is any legal way he can strip his wife of her title upon divorce. She betrayed him, insulted him, humiliated him in front of his friends, turned out to be a different person than the one he married—couldn't he seek an annulment rather than a divorce, on this account? And then strip her of her apparent right to keep a title she had obtained by deception? Her use of the title shows her contempt for all things decent. Shouldn't she be compelled to disclose her whereabouts? Jelly is late one morning and Brian gets the letter.

Brian Moss writes back to say that the Courts are not likely to allow Angelica to go completely unmaintained. If Sir Edwin offers his wife a small suburban apartment and £1,000 a month, as a starting offer, it is likely that Lady Rice will withdraw her counter-petition, and his divorce can go quietly ahead and he can anticipate being married to Anthea before the year is out.

Jelly puts an extra zero on the £1,000, changes "small apartment" to "substantial house in a good central area," prints out the letter, wipes out the changes on the computer and re-enters the original. When Edwin writes back saying that he will offer her half that sum and that he does not want his ex-wife living anywhere near him, she destroys the letter and substitutes for it one requesting Brian Moss offer his wife £5,000 a month, signs it, and gives it to Brian Moss to read. She changes Brian's reply, omitting his expressions of surprise at the generosity of Sir Edwin's offer.

At this point, Jelly allows the natural correspondence to flow untampered with. Any inconsistencies she can iron out as she goes along. She is good at Edwin's signature; she keeps in her desk drawer sheets hand-signed by Brian Moss a-plenty. The important thing is that she is not late for work, or ill, so that Brian Moss doesn't get to open his own mail. It seems to her that she can manage her life well enough without her sisters' advice and intimate co-operation.

Jelly as Lady Rice speaks by telephone to Barney Evans, refraining from saying that if she had taken his advice and declined to counter-petition, she would not now be in so strong a position; she asks Barney to write to Brian Moss saying the financial offer made is ludicrously small, considering the length of the marriage, and Sir Edwin's conduct; how about £7,500 a month. Brian Moss passes the message back to Sir Edwin.

Jelly kisses the back of the envelope before dropping it into the letter box. She is not sure why she does it. Perhaps Lady Rice surfaced again, stirred up by this almost-contact with Edwin? Jelly fears it might be so; Lady Rice's enduring love for Edwin may infect the others by some kind of osmosis; more positively, it just is that the several personae have the need for money and comfort in common. But at least the letter gets posted. Jelly can make quick decisions — hardly ever seeing the need for decision, come to that: the right step is always so obvious — so it was as well it was she, not Angelica, Angel or Lady Rice, who did the posting. Or the letter would have stayed in the back of a drawer while she made up her mind. Or thus she persuades herself. She is quite a Pollyanna.

All is looking well for Jelly, until a letter arrives from Edwin asking Brian Moss to hurry the whole thing up, get everything settled, he wants to marry Anthea, they want to have babies.

Babies! Jelly, opening this bombshell first thing in the morning, has
no immediate reaction. Oh yes, babies. Why not? But she begins to
feel sick, has to go to the powder room, almost faints, recovers, begins to cry. No, she can't cope. She calls her sisters back. They arrive, but can't quell the tears.

> "Bet Anthea wrote it," says Angel, comfortingly. "If you can
> write Brian's letters she can write Edwin's. She may just be
> making it up."
> "Or it could be Edwin just twisting knives," says Lady Rice.
> But Jelly won't be comforted.

Jelly, now composite again, continues to cry and has to tell Brian
Moss when he comes in that she's allergic to the poppies on her
desk. He flings open the window and tosses poppies, vase and all
out, in a gesture which reminds her of Edwin, so she cries some
more. Brian Moss clasps her and tells her tears in a woman always
affect him: he'd like to make love to her properly there and then.

Jelly pushes him away, and says certainly not, this is appalling sexual harassment. He says that weeping is its own form of harassment,
but goes into his office and sulks for the rest of the day. Lady Rice is
back in control: much weeping always revives her. It's Jelly now
who has to go into hiding, keep the company of Angelica and
Angel. With Jelly there to control her, at least Angelica doesn't
spend so much time in the shops, and money is saved. And Angel is
cheered up: Lady Rice gives Angel some opportunity to take over
from time to time: but with Jelly so upset they're making a dreadful
mess of the typing. Brian Moss asks if it's the time of the month and
they say yes. Though it isn't.

Ram's back! But Lady Rice won't let him stop off at the car-park.
"I'm in the middle of a divorce," she says. "I have to keep my nose

clean," and won't let the others get a "well, perhaps," or "I daresay I'm being neurotic," in at all. None of the usual changes of mind. Ram seems hurt: the back of his neck is rigid with upset. Lady Rice feels apologetic: she had not quite understood that Ram, too, had feelings—those have become things that women have and men don't—but she won't relent. Ram says to his friends he doesn't understand women one bit: they lack consistency.

(21)
Lady Rice on Her Alter Egos

Lady Rice is getting better. She can think about other things than her distress. She is no longer suicidal. She considers the part of her that is Jelly, and comes to the following conclusion:

"It is not that I dislike Jelly: she just doesn't inspire me. It's she who makes me the boring company I think I sometimes am. Edwin certainly thought so, or he wouldn't have preferred Anthea to me. It's Jelly's fault."

And it's true that Jelly is the kind of woman who has few friends: who gets up in the morning, enjoys a solitary breakfast, feels the satisfaction of a good day's work, buys the cat food and goes home on public transport. She is not a compulsive telephone talker; she does not like sharing and caring with just anyone; she enjoys a flirtation because she can see that sooner or later she will need to get married and have children, and anyone likes to be admired and to be in control. But Jelly does not particularly need or enjoy the running commentary on life that friends require and provide: the oohs and ahs and guess what she said, and he didn't, did he, the bastard; how could she, the bitch! that others seem to enjoy: she is not, frankly, interested in very much or curious about others. She likes to look neat and sweet, and she is certainly not above spying and prying because this too gives her power: she likes to have secrets, she is secretive; she likes to know secrets, to have them in her possession but not pass them on. But she has learned her lesson about friends. They can and will betray you, and though you offer loyalty, loyalty is not necessarily offered in return. Judas Iscariot didn't care about the money: he just wanted Jesus up there on the cross. The closer you nurture the worm to your bosom, the more likely it is to bite.

Seek solitude, thinks Jelly. Jelly doesn't feel all that much: she prefers to think. Lady Rice finds her insensitive.

As for Angelica—well, Angelica always had friends. After she became Lady Rice, she gathered around her all the bohemians in the area; such writers, painters, sculptors, weavers, cookery experts, TV directors there were to be found. All she needed, after her years as a pop star amongst people whose favorite phrase was "know what I mean"—because passion and puzzlement so outstripped their command of the language—was a dinner table. Over eleven years these bohemians became her old friends. Even Edwin found them lively, and would come home saying "Who's coming to dinner tonight? Well? Well?" rather than just "What's for dinner?" The talk would be about books, films, reviews, politics, the world of the imagination: not horses, dogs, weather and crops, and required more keeping up with, but Edwin did not at the time complain. Edwin read books, he read poems—though he found his legs too long for theater seats, and his knees twitched at the cinema.

Edwin was to revert later, of course, to type, to his original state; was to put the Jaguar behind him to go back to the Range Rover: to the wuff-wuffing insolence of the hunt, the tearing to pieces of hungry beasts: the pop-popping of shotguns, the bringing of the soaring spirit dead or dying back to earth, if only to show who's who round here. We, the hunting/shooting/landowning gentry.

Imagination hurt: that was why sensible people discouraged it. Speculation unsettled: certainty helped you sleep at night. If you shot wild creatures, you were less likely to shoot your wife, less likely to lose her in the first place. For these changes in Edwin, this regression, Lady Rice blamed Susan and Lambert almost more than she blamed Anthea. Anthea at least acknowledged herself as an enemy; Susan posed as a friend.

Angelica had only by accident been a pop star, Edwin would explain to everyone, trustingly, in the warm bright days when others were still to be trusted. A teenage girl of wit and temperament which far exceeded that of her parents, a rarity, a talent; her father dying, herself led astray—not sexually, of course; she wasn't like that; discrimination was Angelica's middle name. "Discrimination is Angie's middle name," he'd say, and Susan would nod her ever so slightly patronizing head, with its bell of heavy blonde hair: or turn her bright bird eyes on Angelica and smile sweetly and say, "oh me, I'm hopeless; anything at all makes me happy" and all the men around would wish they'd be the anyone to make her happy, their things the anything; and sometimes Angelica wondered if Edwin should be included in "all the men," but surely not, Susan was her best friend. Best friends were not like that.

Angelica, in The Claremont, deciding that too much discrimination had been her downfall, refrained from calling room service to say her club sandwich was horrid, would they take it away and replace the smoked bacon with unsmoked. She controlled herself.

(22)
A Curse from the Past

"Verbal assault," Edwin had claimed. That she had verbally assaulted him. What can he have meant? Lady Rice thought and thought. She was, truth to tell, no longer so much concerned with the matter of alimony as she had been. For all her fine words, for all the apparent finality of her opinions on the subject—as if she had reached some mountain peak of truth and there was no going down again; you were obliged to spin forever around your conclusions— the subject had ceased to be obsessional. She would leave all that legal stuff for Jelly to get on with; she would leave Angelica with the burden of looking up old friends, and the attempt to restore the integrity of the self before marriage—a silly slip of a girl in a leather jacket with rings in her nose—and get on with the task of considering her guilt, her possible contribution to the breakup of the marriage: not that she believes she can have had any part in that: no, it is just that remorse, or the appearance of remorse, might win her husband back—not that she wants that either, no, never—

In the Velcro Club, where the hearts and souls of those sundered or about to be put asunder, are understood, it is well known that obsessions are as changeable as the weather: and that the change is as painful as if the Velcro were alive, a million nerve endings twanging, and the shift from one obsession to the next hurts terribly as the stuff goes *skew-whiff*, and a screaming fills the air, too high-pitched to be quite heard, but there, there—verbal assault. Was she ever rude to Edwin? Did she ever berate him, insult him? Surely not. "Flop and wobble," she'd once said to him, and he'd taken that amiss. Flop and wobble.

"Flop and wobble," Angelica's mother would say, surveying the jellies her little daughter loved so much. Mrs. Lavender White, née Lamb, would often make such a hopeless dessert, incompetently if devotedly, for Saturday tea—alternately soft red, acid green. "Flop and wobble," she'd complain. "How does it happen?" A rhetorical question her little daughter saw fit to answer one day:

"You don't put enough of the packet in," Angelica said. "It's obvious, silly."

She was her father's little girl and had his casual habit of diminishing her mother—not that Lavender ever seemed to mind.

"I follow the instructions exactly," said Angelica's mother. "It would be a wicked waste to do otherwise. One half packet to one pint of water—as I am instructed, so I do."

Stephen White, coming back from choir practice, would survey the shaky structure of the family dessert and say, "Flop and wobble again, my dear," in kind affection and jump up and down to shake the room and make the confection collapse totally. Of such detail, it seemed to Angelica, good marriages were made. Those were the days when Angelica was called Jelly, her given name proving too long a word for easy saying.

But even blessings can turn out to be curses; land mines laid in a long forgotten war. "Flop and wobble," Lady Rice had said aloud one early morning as she lay in her marriage bed beside Sir Edwin Rice. "Flop and wobble," and indeed she was thinking of nothing but family tea and happy times, pre-adolescence, but Edwin took it as a slight, turned abruptly away from her, removing his enfolding arm, lay with his back to her for a little and then climbed out of bed and dressed. They had been married for ten years: the days of misunderstandings and makings-up were long past. Lady Rice could not think why he chose to take offense. Later she realized her husband was at this time "seeing" his cousin Anthea.

Unfaithful husbands divide into two kinds: the one feels guilty, brings flowers, baths babies, tries not to hurt: though later spoils things by confessing all. The other feels guilty but looks for justification in his wife's behavior: see, everyone, how she fails to look after me properly, has grown fat, or undermines my self-esteem, whatever, wherever her weakness lies: but when the affair has ended — should it ever end — he keeps the secret to himself: refrains from burdening his wife with it: she has paid in advance, as it were, for his blow against the marriage politic.

This particular morning Lady Rice did what she could to explain: "flop and wobble," she pleaded, was not a slur upon her husband's prowess. How could he think such a thing? But indeed he had not lately been as moved by his wife as once he was, but Lady Rice supposed that to be a normal fluctuation in his sexual energies. Worries at work, perhaps. But Edwin would have none of her excuses, though Lady Rice prattled on. Edwin, usually so easily entertained, so happy to hear tales of his wife's childhood, remained for once obdurate, unfascinated, profoundly offended.

"It's no use," said Edwin, when finally he spoke, "trying to deny your own words. What is spoken is what is meant, consciously or not. What you were doing is wishing impotence upon me. You're trying to undermine my confidence again."
"You just want to take offense," she had wept. "Why are we having this dreadful time? What is the matter with you?"
He gave her no clue. And being, as Edwin would have it, unobservant, or, as she would say, innocent, Lady Rice failed to connect her husband's claim to martyrdom at her hands with his guilt. She was to be blamed for the crime against her. To put it bluntly, Edwin had fallen out of love with his wife and was inclined to blame her for this loss. He felt it, oddly enough, keenly, and the more keenly he felt it, the more he blamed her. What a mess!

Flop and wobble, verbal assault. Lady Rice could see what Edwin meant. No such thing as an accident; no unmeant, casual remark, was without meaning: no matter how unconscious the impulse to deride, it still existed.

"Come off it!" said Jelly. "Stop blaming yourself. You're hopeless!"

(23)
Being Right

Angelica is in charge. Her determination to occupy the moral high ground allows no argument. If the ticket machines on the way home from the office are out of order, she will seek out an official and pay him, to his annoyance. The more she services Brian Moss the more self-righteous she becomes. She points out discrepancies in his petty cash: or a piece of spinach stuck between his front teeth: she raises her eyebrows if he comes back from lunch late. She insists on talking about his wife and his children even as her head goes down on his member.

The others can see the unwisdom of it, but there is no holding Angelica in this mood. She won't even let the others laugh. Everything is too serious: she's rigid with correctness. She takes them shopping at thrift shops and signs all available petitions: she saves the whale and sacrifices tuna in the interests of dolphins. She accosts a woman, a total stranger, and reproaches her at length for wearing a fur coat. She has become a vegetarian. Jelly believes she is in control but there Angelica will suddenly be, using Jelly's mouth to speak with. It is dangerous. This unit only works by consensus.

"Brian," Jelly finds herself saying one morning, "would you like me to put an ad in the *Times*, enquiring about the whereabouts of Una Musgrave, Tully Toffener's mother-in-law?"
She was on her knees in front of Brian Moss. Nothing further had been said about Jelly joining the permanent staff and all agreed that in the interests of job security her boss should be kept happy.

Her mouth needed a rest; the muscles had begun to ache from overwork.

"But why?" asked Brian, startled.

"Because it's right," said Jelly/Angelica, bleakly.

Brian Moss's erection faltered and Jelly gave up altogether. She rose and went back to her desk to write out the advertisement. He scowled and fidgeted.

"Why should you care about Tully Toffener, anyway?" asked Brian Moss. "The man's a total freak." He could see the transition from occasional sexual engagement to the normal master/servant relationship becoming more and more of a problem. If the intimacy went on for too long, Jelly would feel entitled to take over his conscience entirely. Wives were expected to look after that, and be damned as wet blankets, but not passing girls at the office.

"Freak or not," his secretary replied, "Tully Toffener's your client and you are obliged to look after his interests."

> "For God's sake," said Jelly, "shut up."
> "It's my duty to speak out," said Angelica.
> "We'll lose this job if you go on," said Angel. "Not that I mind. There are more ways than one of earning a living."
> "Angelica is right," said Lady Rice. "Tully and Sara Toffener sat at my dining table."

On the same principle that some cultures believe that if you save another's life you are then responsible for all the bad deeds they may go on to commit, so Lady Rice felt she owed Tully and Sara at least this much—that Sara's right to inherit did not go by total default; either because Brian simply couldn't be bothered, or because she, Jelly, sapped his strength and his interest in his work.

> "And another thing," said Angelica, "sex with a married man is totally wrong. You have to stop, Jelly."

"Blow-jobs don't count," said Jelly. "Everyone knows that."

"It's disgusting," said Lady Rice. "It's sheer torture. I hate you doing it."

"If it's the taste you're complaining about, put cinnamon in his coffee," says Angel.

"Angel," asks Lady Rice, "how do you *know* these things?"

Angel says that everything Lady Rice knows, she knows; it's just she, Angel, will admit it and Lady Rice won't.

"I'm not going to stop it," says Jelly. "I don't care what any of you say. I like the feeling of power; I like to have him helpless. Anyway, I want to ask him for a rise."

"Do that," says Angelica, "and we'll get fired. Things are touch and go anyway. You just wait and see."

Ajax suddenly says, "We Heroes of Troy were at it all the time. I loved Ulysses, and so died on my own sword. I could not bear the humiliation of betrayal."

"Get that man out of here," Jelly, Lady Rice and Angel shrieked at Angelica. "This is girl talk."

"Why blame me?" asked Angelica, and they all listened carefully, but Ajax had gone.

"Anyway," added Angelica, "that's just gender prejudice."

The next day Jelly, anxious to prove Angelica wrong, asked Brian Moss for a rise.

"It would be sordid," said Brian Moss, with that pomposity which so often accompanies financial discussions. "Sleazy, even, to raise your wages in the light of this new relationship of ours. It could only reduce you to the status of a whore. Presumably you'll want to get married one day, Jelly: I'm sure you wouldn't want to have any such blot upon your reputation. Such a bore living with secrets from the past; time bombs waiting to explode. I have one or two myself. No, better no secrets at all. Sex must never be exchanged for money: it reflects badly upon all involved. I'll keep it to our lunch hour, if you like, so there's no suggestion of sexual harassment in the office. You are working by the hour, after all. And presumably these intimacies of ours give you as much pleasure as they do me or you wouldn't be doing it in the first place."

"He must be joking," said Angel. "Blow-jobs are all take and no give, ask any woman."

"Well, I like it," said Jelly. "That is to say I don't want to stop it. Office life can get boring."

"Next thing," said Angelica, "it won't be no rise because you're doing it, it will be do it or I'll fire you. And then you'll have to do it, because upon this job depends our future prosperity, in more ways than anyone could imagine. You'll have no choice."

"Then I'll do it," says Jelly, her mouth being by this time again occupied with Brian Moss's engorged and twitching member, which mention of money always cheered up.

"I don't care. No problem."

"She is a heroine," says Lady Rice. "She really is."

Brian Moss stopped mid-blow and bore Jelly down upon the sofa and lifted her skirt; desire finally overcame guilt.

"I'm so tired of second best," he says.

"He loves me!" cries Lady Rice.

"Oh, oh, oh," cries Angel in ecstasy, entwining her legs round the small of Brian Moss's back; there is no sealing her lips or steadying her breath: the others give in and think of alimony.

(24)

Angel Out on the Town

Angel remonstrated with Lady Rice. If they all submitted thus to Brian Moss, why was she being stand-offish with Ram? She, Angel, had really enjoyed the rides to work. Even in the back seat of a Volvo in a car-park Ram had been a better lover than Brian, who was okay but not really connecting. He was worrying too much about his betrayal of Oriole, or whether the forever locked office door would attract comment, to be open to much real passion. It was all lust, no love, and lacked aspiration. Time and privacy might well improve her boss's performance, but when was that ever going to be available?

"He shouldn't worry about discretion," said Jelly. "It's too late. The whole office is buzzing. Nothing like this has happened, so Holly in Accounts told me, who's ninety if she's a day, since old Gerald Catterwall got off with Una Musgrave before she disappeared."

"We can't possibly go with Ram now," said Lady Rice, "even if it was a possibility before. Surely one can only have one man at a time?"

Angel hooted with laughter, and Lady Rice sulked.

"Holly in Accounts can't see a thing, thank God," said Angelica. "That's why The Claremont's bills get paid. Supposing she gets new glasses? What then?" Embracing Brian Moss so totally had set all her anxieties off again. She was biting their fingernails. Angel took offense.

"Well, I'm going with Ram tomorrow," said Angel. "I'm going

to ask him to drive down to the car-park, and none of you can stop me. Jelly, what do you say?"

"I say," said Jelly, "let's do it. A girl can get quite an appetite for this kind of thing: I feel so lively and peculiar and restless. I wish Brian and I had had a proper bed, not an office sofa; he didn't really have a chance. But I don't want to be hurt; I don't want too many eggs in one basket; yes, let's take Ram down to the car-park. Let's spread the load. Angelica?"

Angelica said, "Okay. I feel bad about biting my nails. Perhaps it'll make me feel less anxious."

Lady Rice said, "No, no, no. It isn't right. Sex with a chauffeur! It's humiliating. If anyone finds out, they'll say I'm promiscuous. All those years of virtue for nothing! I can't give in now."

But Angel said, "Sorry, Lady Rice, that's three against one. You lose. I really can't stand another evening cooped up in this fucking hotel: I'm going out and you lot are coming with me."

"Where?" Lady Rice, Jelly and Angelica asked nervously, but Angel just laughed and fastened her net stockings to the little bobbles which hung from the thongs of her lacy suspender belt.

"I like the grip of the fabric round my waist," she said, "and the stretch of elastic down my thighs. I can't stand the way you girls wear tights, just because they're practical."

Angelica and Jelly fell silent; they had no option but to let their wilful and drastic other self her head. There was no holding her: she, Angel, had taken over the senses: it was she who moved the limbs, used the mouth, turned the eyes. They were intimidated. Later, instead of sleeping or watching television, they all, including Lady Rice, accompanied Angel down to the bar and allowed her a triple gin, and a wink or two at an Italian couple, man and wife, glossy and worldly, who, being on holiday, seemed anxious for a third to join them in the bed. Angel had the knack of knowing whom to wink at, and whose smiles best to respond to. Angel responded in the manner the couple hoped, and they paid her two hundred pounds in cash, in advance.

"I'm a realist," said Angel to the others by way of apology, accepting the notes.
"We're on our own. We can't go on in Brian Moss's office for ever. He's going to find out sooner or later. We'll be fired. Then what? We have to have another career up our sleeve."
"Slut, whore, bitch!" ranted the others, but Angel took no notice. And they feared she never would again. They were finished. The "cash on completion" was not, as it happened, forthcoming. Angel was lucky to get out of it alive.

There was hell to pay the next day. Lady Rice was so furious, miserable and suicidal that Angel, subdued and pathetic, declared she would never do such a thing again, on pain of Lady Rice taking an overdose of sleeping pills and putting an end to the lot of them. She had learned her lesson. She would never mix sex and money again. Then Jelly had to take a day off to recover from the excesses of the night, so they didn't get to the car-park with Ram: she felt too shaken to call Brian Moss to say she would not be in that day. He'd think she'd walked out on him: Angelica claimed he wouldn't be sorry, and Jelly accused her of gross cynicism, but not for long: she was too depleted.

By evening they felt better. Angelica observed that the world of forbidden sex was too full of euphemisms to be safe. You could get killed, suffocated, or whipped to death, and then be disposed of, and who would know? "Joining a couple in bed," sounded cosy, white-sheeted, yawny and warm, but in fact turned out to be cold, unhygienic, and a matter of strippings, whips and manacles as the wife took her symbolic revenge on a decade of the husband's mistresses, with his consent, and the husband reasserted his right to have them as, when and how he chose. There was a kind of masochistic pleasure, she could see, in being a victim and without choice, but there was a difference between being a Bad Girl and a Whore, and in the end, if they survived at all, whores lost their heart of gold, coming up as they did all the time against too much evil and despair; they ended up with hard, cold eyes, and a hard false smile which frightened children. She'd go along with Angel as a Bad Girl but not as a whore. People got altogether too romantic about the latter.

"Okay, okay, okay," said Angel. "I get the message."

"I was so frightened," said Angelica.

"So was I," said Angel, "actually," and began to cry, and they all cried softly together.

"I have to have a holiday," said Angelica, when the pillow was thoroughly wet with tears. "I simply have to. I want out."

"So do I," said Lady Rice.

"And me," said Angel.

"Oh no, you're not, Angel," said Jelly. "If I have to hold the fort here, if I'm to keep Brian Moss happy, if I'm to have a good time with Ram, if I'm going to keep an eye on our divorce, I need you, Angel."

"Ram!" said Angel, perking up. "I'd forgotten about Ram."

(25)

A Gust of Chilly Wind

Una Musgrave answered the advertisement in the *Times*. Like an answer to Tully Toffener's prayer, like the wild gust of chilly wind which accompanies the gods on their travels, she appeared in Catterwall & Moss's downstairs reception. Jelly just happened to be sitting behind the desk: she was helping Lois out. Lois, a born again Christian, had handed in her notice: she was going at the end of the week, to, everyone said, an office where there was less scandal and intrigue. Though Brian Moss had said to Jelly, "The problem is she's in love with me. She's jealous of you. Remember once when I thought I'd locked the door but I hadn't, and she pushed the door open—?"

To which Jelly replied, "Oh phooey, she's underpaid and overworked, like the rest of us—"

He had not taken offense. Nothing seemed to make him take offense, just as nothing would make him pay her more. He liked her to be tart, anyway. The sharper her tongue the more pleasure there was in silencing it, the more intimate its flavor. They had reverted from full intercourse to its lesser form: Oriole had won in her absence. Everyone knew blow-jobs didn't count.

But here was Una Musgrave, sitting on Jelly's desk, looking at her hard and speculatively, as if she knew very well what went on behind the scenes. Jelly felt that she had met her fate, her comeuppance; that her soul was known. She was in her mid-sixties, Jelly supposed: one of those women who is born unstoppable and impossible; a face handsome from good cosmetic surgery, hair thin from

bleaching but glossy from care, a figure skinny from Pritikin, large
kittenish eyes, high silicone breasts, long polished nails on liver-
spotted, always moving, energetic hands. Jelly thought—or was it
Angel?—no matter how liver-spotted the long sharp scarlet talons: a
danger and a challenge to the cosseted dick. And Angel thought—
or was it Jelly?—yes, but he'd have to pay for it somehow. Lots.

"You have something for me to hear to my advantage," said Una
Musgrave. "I read it in the *Times*, so it must be true."
And Jelly stood up, pale and demure with a triple set of pearls from
Fenwicks and a nice pale pink cashmere sweater, half-price because
of a single pulled thread which Lady Rice came out of retirement to
attend to, a red pleated skirt, shoes a trifle battered but well polished
(The Claremont's overnight service) and sturdy tights; hair neat, an
exceptionally clear complexion (Brian Moss swore that was his
doing) and a buttery little mouth, and led Una Musgrave to Brian
Moss's outer office. She was very conscious of Una's eyes upon her.

"What does she want?" asked Angel. "Our heart, or our body
or both? For herself, or for the White Slave traffic?"
"Don't be so absurd and old fashioned," said Jelly. "She's just
come for her inheritance."

Una Musgrave wore shiny black leather boots up to her thighs, short
red skirt, white sweater and a wide patent belt with a buckle which
looked like solid silver to Jelly. Brian Moss came out of his office,
blinked, and asked her in. Jelly felt displaced and unable to com-
pete, and even Angel blenched.

Once a week the management of The Claremont provided a bowl
of complimentary fruit, each apple so perfect and red, each pear so
well-formed and greenly glossy, each plum so unblemished and free
from wasp invasion, as to make the contrast to the fruit from the

Rice Court orchards more remarkable. The Rice Court fruit trees were ancient, gnarled and beautiful: the fruit they produced was meager and misshapen by commercial standards, but full of flavor so long as you could find a pest-free scrap, and were prepared to bite and trust.

The hotel fruit—and the bowl had been refilled that day—was without flavor: all perfection and irradiation. Jelly found herself crying; she had thought tears were Lady Rice's province, but no. She too could be brought down by the misery of remembrance. She missed the orchard: brilliant white and pink with blossom in early spring: she missed the annual vain endeavor to keep the birds away from the cherries: see, see, Edwin! They've taken every one. It can't be true!—but always was. She missed the bleak winter branches of the trellised plums against the Elizabethan wall; she missed the walled vegetable garden, and the ancient asparagus beds which should have been replaced and never were, and the way thistle would disguise itself as artichoke: in her mind she could place everything exactly: move in her head between the gooseberry and the black currant bushes, knowing how much to the inch she had to spare, frowning at nettles, smiling encouragement at bold plump orange pumpkins, reclusive dark green courgettes. All this she had lost; all this had been stolen: the human part of the loss was possible to forget. But all this garden history Anthea had robbed her of: Anthea and Edwin, together, had deprived her not just of future, and present, but of the past. She hoped the rose bushes she had pruned over the years would prick, and wound, and make anyone who dared touch the blooms bleed to death. She was getting a headache.

"Take an aspirin," said Angel.
"It isn't that kind of headache," said Jelly.
"You're missing the others," said Angel. "They're better at coping with misery than you. And it's mad to be jealous of Una

Musgrave. Good God, she must be sixty-five if she's a day.
Brian Moss won't look at her for a moment. And she's a client.
He wouldn't be so stupid."

"I'm staff," said Jelly, "and that's pretty stupid, too."

"Anyway, there's always Ram," said Angel. "Good old Ram.
Did you know his name was Rameses? His parents were cruis-
ing down the Nile when his mother went into labor, five weeks
early."

Angel was trying to distract Jelly. She didn't like the way Jelly was
staring at the fruit knife which went with The Claremont's fruit
bowl.

"I think I'll slash my wrists," said Jelly. "I can't go on."

"The knife's too feeble," said Angel, "even to cut through our
skin."

"Then I'll order a steak from Room Service," said Jelly, "and
they'll bring a good strong knife with a serrated edge."

Jelly picked up the phone. Angel slammed it down. Jelly picked up
the fruit knife and started to saw away at her wrist. She reddened the
skin but could not draw blood.

"Told you so," said Angel.

Angel hitched up her skirt to see how her legs were doing. They
were furry with unshaven hair.

"My God," said Angel, "how any of you ever got on without
me? I'm the most important part of you and all any of you ever
do is insult me!"

She made them go round the corner to the all-night beautician in
Bond Street, and had her legs waxed in the old-fashioned way, with

hot beeswax, smeared over the skin with a spatula, allowed to cool, and then ripped off. The process produced a smoother and more enduring finish than the lighter, less painful, quicker drying synthetic waxes now available. Jelly felt better.

(26)

A Sniff of Skin

Jelly had gone to work with not just her legs but her crotch shaved, and invited Brian Moss to put his hand up her skirt, feel and admire. Brian Moss was reluctant so to do.

"I don't want this thing between us to get too personal," he said. "You know that. I love Oriole very much. If she isn't enthusiastic about sex it's because she's too tired, poor thing. Two children under five are a handful for anyone. We bring them up in the modern way, trying to develop their personalities, so they don't sleep much. I'm in charge by night. Elsie has nightmares, Annie gets colic. I get back into bed with Oriole: I may be cold but I'm loving, yet even in her sleep my wife rolls away from me. I seem to disgust her. She says my feet smell, and she doesn't like the texture of my skin. She claims it's clammy. But I do love her. I expect she's right about me and I'm just a hopeless sort of person."

"Feel my skin where I've shaved it," was all his secretary said. "You'll find it interesting. Smooth, but with a kind of prickle just beneath the surface; a very white skin there because, when you come to think of it, between the legs very seldom meets the light of day."

But Brian Moss was not to be tempted: not by words, descriptions, nor open invitation as she led his hand upward, rubbed his finger against the shaven skin, tried to guide it inward into the soft damp warmth of the split.

"I don't know what's got into you," said Brian Moss. "You never used to be like this. Oh God, is it all my fault?"

And he lit a cigarette, finding a packet in an open drawer.

"You see!" he said. "You've started me smoking again. Oriole made me give it up when she was pregnant. Passive smoking can do untold damage to unborn babies."

"And to you, too," said Angel. "But I don't suppose your wife mentions that."

"You don't seem to think well of wives," said Brian Moss nervously. It seemed to him his secretary was behaving oddly. He would have to get rid of her; he had let himself get involved with a seriously disturbed young woman. He would miss her but that couldn't be helped. She was not, after all, as stunningly attractive as he had supposed. He preferred, at any rate outside marriage, the kind of blatancy Una Musgrave and her kind provided. Give Jelly twins and she'd end up like Oriole anyway.

"No," said Angel, "I don't think well of wives." She was sitting on the edge of the desk, removing her little lace-up boots Jelly had bought at Marks & Spencer. She let them fall. First the right, then the left. She kept her eyes on Brian Moss. "Especially not cat wives."

"What's a cat wife?" he asked, though who knew where such conversation might lead.

"A cat wife wants a home and a man to pay for it, and someone to father her children and when she's got it, she snarls and drives him away."

She was unbuttoning her sweater, undoing her bra, wriggling out of her skirt.

"Don't do this," he begged. "Someone might come in."

His secretary ran over to the door, neat bosom bouncing, locked it, took the key and threw it from the open window. He heard the faint dry sound of its landing two floors below.

"Oh yes, I know your wife's kind well," said Angel, undoing his belt, unfastening buttons, unzipping his zip. "And thank God for her. One man's misfortune is any whore's good fortune."

"Don't do this," he begged. "You're not well. You've been working too hard. Get dressed. Get Lois to go down and get the key and let us out of here."

"Not till I've had my fun," said Angel. "I deserve some too. It's my lunch hour. You'll have to do as I say, or I'll tell Oriole about you and me."

"There is nothing to say about you and me," said Brian Moss, "that I won't deny at once. I'm not afraid of blackmail."

"I'll tell her about the mole on your thing," said Angel, giggling. "Sometimes it seems little and sometimes it seems big. It's a matter of proportion."

"I'll say you saw it by accident," said Brian Moss but, since he was by now naked to the waist and leaning against the wall, his statement lacked conviction. His belt fastened one hand to the handle of a drawer above his head; his tie fastened the other to its fellow; his penis was slowly and powerfully rising.

"What have you done to me?" he demanded. "I'm completely helpless."

He saw the expression on his secretary's face alter: the wildness faded from her eyes. She simply looked aghast.

"For God's sake, somebody," Jelly squealed. "Come and rescue me! Angel is totally out of control. After all she promised—"

"Told you so!" said Angelica.

"Not again," said Lady Rice.

They were back. Jelly breathed again.

"Good lord," said Lady Rice, backing away from the trussed-up Brian Moss, "I am really so sorry! I don't know what came over me. I'm not really your secretary at all, I'm Barney Evans' client, Lady Rice. I do have excellent secretarial skills, though, so I don't feel too much of a fraudster. And it might be thought by some that you deserved this."

Mad, thought Brian Moss, trying to slip his hands from their bonds, and failing. Entirely mad!

The door handle was rattling. It was Lois.

"I can't open the door, Mr. Moss," called Lois through the door. "It seems to be locked."

"The key's on the ground outside the window," called Angelica. "Angel threw it out. Go and get it!"

"No, no!" cried Brian Moss, but he was too late. Lois had gone.

"This is professional suicide," said Jelly. "You realize that?"

"You can't go on pretending any more," said Angelica.

"Let's face it," said Lady Rice, "we need treatment."

At which Angel ran round the room of the mind shrieking and squealing she didn't want to be cured: she didn't want to be locked up. Angelica caught her and quietened her.

"Let me out of here," pleaded Brian Moss, but his secretary was making coffee, setting out his cup and saucer, the powdered milk, the sachet of sweetener, and didn't seem able to hear him.

"Lady Musgrave's here," called Lois through the door. "What shall I say to her?"

"Tell her to come in," called Jelly.

"No, no," cried Brian Moss again, struggling to get free. At least his penis was lying quiet and still. "Ms. White, you are fired!"

"Thank God," his secretary replied, in the attractive timbred voice she had lately taken to using. Brian Moss had taken credit for that. "Thank God!"

(27)
Official Business

Una walked in through the door as Lois opened it and Jelly walked out. Una looked after Jelly, not without admiration, and moved to undo Brian Moss's bonds.

"I can't thank you enough," said Brian Moss, re-establishing his circulation, re-arranging his clothing. "My secretary has had some kind of fugue. A *crise*. Perhaps we should postpone this meeting?"

"On no account," said Una. She still had Brian Moss's tie in her hand. She smoothed it out and tied it for him, pulling up the knot just a little savagely around his neck. The tie was yellow, with a pink and red pattern but did little to give the impression he hoped to achieve—that of a wild man falsely imprisoned in a grey suit.

"I think it would be better if we did," begged Brian Moss. "This has been a most upsetting incident," but Una was persistent, saying in her experience men always made the best decisions immediately after sex. She wanted Brian Moss's enthusiasm: she wanted him to help her raise the capital necessary to restore Lodestar House as a private hotel. She had never wanted anything from her family. She was not a family kind of person, but this windfall having fallen into her lap, she would extend her business interests into London. Brian Moss said he would do anything she wanted.

Brian Moss could see Jelly packing her desk in the outer office. She was slamming and stamping about. He tried to concentrate on what Una Musgrave was saying, which was about her early family history. Sara Toffener appeared to be Una's daughter by her stepfather,

Wendy Musgrave's husband. Una herself had been born out of wed-
lock: Sara had been born when Una was fifteen.

"A victim of child abuse!" he said. "How dreadful."

But he'd said the wrong thing. Una snorted.

"I was an abusing child," she said. "I hated my mother and wanted
my stepfather just to spite her. And I got him. Once I'd got him I
was tired of him. Always my problem. Sara was such a plain little
girl too, and I was lumbered with her. I gave her away as soon as
possible; I was far too young to cope. I'm glad she grew up to find
Tully Toffener. People find their own equivalent in the other sex,
I've noticed, and can end up perfectly happy."

Brian Moss thought it was probably safe to invest in anything Una
Musgrave thought workable. She would not be diverted from profit
by sentiment or proper feeling.

Brian Moss could see Lois as she bent over to help Jelly with the
lower drawers. Perhaps he could persuade her to stay. It was only by
comparison to Jelly that Lois appeared plain. Plain girls, in any case,
were more stable, less neurotic, than the pretty ones.

"No one's drama," said Una Musgrave, "I can see, is of any real
consequence to anyone else. You're not even listening. As it happens, Lodestar House turning up in my life again is a fine example
of the synchronicity which has accompanied my path through life.
Ever read Jung?"

"No," said Brian Moss.

"If you don't think a little more about me and a little less about your
dick," said Una Musgrave, "I won't pay you for this session."

Brian Moss paid attention.

"A house with many rooms is a wonderful thing," said Una. "In the
house of our dreams each room represents a different aspect of the
self. Did you know that?"

"I don't dream much," said Brian Moss, "nowadays. I'm far too tired. I have two children under five."

On her way out of Brian Moss's office, Una stopped in her booted stride at Jelly White's desk.

"If ever you want a job," she said, "get in touch with me. You're just the type I like."

"What type is that?" asked Jelly.

"Demure and devious," said Una, "and not what you seem. Mind you, what woman is? I see you as someone with a past that you roll up as you go, so you hardly remember what happened yesterday, let alone last night."

"It can be a problem," said Jelly, "and getting worse."

"It's always darkest before dawn. Your lipstick's smudged," said Una, taking out a little frilled cotton handkerchief from her pocket and dabbing at the corner of Jelly's mouth. "But it's a useful little mouth, I can tell."

Part Four

Going Home

(1)
Angel Goes Home

"I've never seen Rice Court," says Angel. "All you others have. You forget how recent I am."

These days Angel would play for their sympathy. She felt guilty that Jelly now had no job, that the divorce would have to get on without useful intervention, and that Lady Rice's satisfactory alimony was now less likely than ever.

Barney Evans wrote to Lady Rice that further delays were bound to ensue, since apparently Brian Moss's computer files had been maliciously wiped by an employee with a grievance. It was an Act of God, and his client must see it for what it was, nothing more: Lady Rice should not expect the case to be settled within the next twelve months: eighteen was more likely. However, Sir Edwin, the circumstances being what they were, had agreed—without prejudice, of course—to allow Lady Rice an interim payment of £400 the month.

Angel had been disappointed when the letter from Barney Evans arrived with news of financial reprieve: she had hoped that sheer necessity would oblige the others to consent to her going to work for Una Musgrave at Lodestar House. As it was, they could continue to live free and respectably at The Claremont, use the credit card at the stores and to pay Ram, and the £400 a month for cinemas and the occasional meal out, to preserve them from the tedium of Room Service.

"I expect Anthea spends four hundred pounds a month on dog food," said Angelica. "Mean bastard."

"Even more," said Jelly.
Lady Rice just sighed.

Rest and absence of strain were good for them. They felt physically
well. They swam in the hotel pool; used the hotel's beauty parlor.
They had each other for company. Ram would call them up occasionally, if he was free; they never asked him in, but he'd found a
fresher, airier car-park behind Harrods somewhere, and the Volvo
was comfortable and familiar and the darkened windows meant the
degree of illicitness and of danger worked to their sexual advantage.
Just an ordinary parked corporation limo, rather rocking about.
Nothing unusual.

Angel was growing more mature; Angelica was cured of anxiety;
Lady Rice's spirit no longer flew here or there in search of its monster; Jelly got on with her book on, of all things, the Servant through
the Painter's Eye, which took them all to art galleries, and, they
hoped, expanded their cultural awareness: a field in which they all
felt they were lacking. Not a word from Ajax. All was well, so long as
no one stirred too deep.

But here was Angel asking in apparent innocence if she could go
down and see Rice Court. Why? What was the point of confronting
the past? There had been too many shocks, too much trauma. It was
best forgotten. If once they had had an ambition to be one person,
that was long over. They were, they reckoned, what most women
were anyway—divisible into parts, but had, unusually, become conscious of those parts. At first it had caused trouble: no longer.

Or so in their folly they thought.

"Why not?" asked Angel. "Ram can take us down. It will be an
outing. Other people go to Heritage Parks, why not us?"

"I'll tell you why not," said Lady Rice. "Because it would break my heart. Because I'm still humiliated and ashamed; I just prefer not to think about it. I am a discarded woman; I was mistress of Rice Court, now you want me to go to the Funfair as a punter. Never."

"I think it would be okay to go," said Angelica. "I could visit my mother. It's time I did. We wouldn't try and see Edwin, or anything like that."

"Oh no," said Jelly, with heavy sarcasm. "Of course not!"

"Because that's all behind us," said Angelica.

"If we wore a wig," said Jelly, "we could see him and he wouldn't recognize us. I reckon we should go, but in disguise."

"He wouldn't recognize us anyway," said Lady Rice, and burst into tears, which she hadn't done for ages. Nor did she any longer sit on the edge of the bed for hours, just staring into space, too preoccupied with her woes even to be bored. As the shocked, the bereaved, and the betrayed so often do sit, arms and hands limp, mouth slightly open, as if they were in a trance.

"T'rific!" cried Angel. "Three against one! We're going! Next time Ram calls—"

And the very next Saturday there was Angel, lounging on a street corner, waiting for Ram, wearing grunge: that is to say layers of dark-ish fabric alternating with snatches of lace: men's socks and heavy boots, the latter bought second-hand on a market stall. A tight satin vest beneath a torn leather jacket compressed and raised her breasts.

Ram's sleek Volvo turned into Davis Street: there was his client, leaning into a lamp-post, blowing smoke into the air, like Marlene Dietrich. The car slowed, drew in on a no-parking line.

"Is that fashion?" he asked her. "Or disguise?"

"Neither," said Angel.

He held the door open for her. He was not wearing his uniform.
Passers-by stared.

"I like a woman of many moods," he said, as they set off for the
North. "Anyone else and I wouldn't have done it. I like to play football on Saturdays."

"Women tend to be more than one person," said Angel, "at the best
of times. Men get just to be the one."

"I like all of yours," he ventured, but she did not encourage such
intimacies. It was his body she cared for. He contented himself with
saying that if he were her he wouldn't go and see an ex-husband
dressed like that and she said it was fortunate then he wasn't her,
and they fell silent. And when, at a service station, Angel invited
him to join her in the back of the car, he refused, politely. She was
clearly under considerable stress. He'd caught sight of her from
time to time, reflected in his mirror, gesticulating, mouthing, and
murmuring to herself, sometimes slapping her own wrist, though
that, these days, happened less often than it used to. She would
speak to him in different voices, offering contradictory instructions.
He had worked out, but only recently—until then these encounters
had quite upset him—that there were four of them. Angel had
started things off: now he preferred Angelica: she allowed him more
time, in which he could develop and demonstrate simple affection.
Though Angel's instant enthusiasm, instant response, was certainly
useful when time was at a premium, and privacy doubtful. He
didn't like leaving his women unsatisfied: the fact was that Angelica
frequently was, though she swore she didn't mind. Jelly induced a
kind of guilty, heady excitement which could keep him awake at
night thinking about her. Lady Rice required words of love, and
he'd oblige, falsely, but then she was being false too. "I love you,"
she'd say dreamily and obsessively, but it would only become true,
he felt, if he mistreated her in some way. Offer a quarter of the self
and you could hardly expect a whole self offered in return. His client could have his body and that was that, and not even that if she

looked like freaking out. But he considered them his girlfriend, and had no other. He had developed a taste for the multi-layered. Often girls seemed absurdly single.

Sometimes he felt like some sea creature which had been washed up by a high tide and now lay beached and helpless. The water had receded and left him behind. It would flicker into his awareness that he lived in a state of suspended animation, waiting to be reclaimed. Then he'd tell himself he was having an identity crisis, that was all, and go out and polish the Volvo, put on his chauffeur's cap and say, "this is me, this is me."

For once the Rice Quartet seemed interested in something other than his body. He could see it was good to thwart them, sometimes.

"Where do you live?" the sad, posh one asked.

He explained that he lived on a houseboat on the Thames, at Chelsea, and garaged the Volvo on Cheyne Walk. An aunt had given the car to him, when he'd been thrown out of the Royal College of Music for insolence. Since then he'd used the vehicle to earn a living while he worked out what to do next.

"How long has that been?" she asked.

"When I come to think of it," said Ram, shaken, "ten years. I thought it had only just happened."

She said that once she too had been offered a place at the Royal College. But who could settle down to sing Handel when they could have a recording contract, stardom, and rock and roll? Not she, certainly. Not then. What had his instrument been? He said give him anything and he could play it: he'd been on the conducting course. She was impressed.

"If they threw everyone out for attitude," she said, consolingly, "they wouldn't have a pupil left."

He acknowledged they'd merely suspended him for a week and he'd been offended, said he'd never return, and hadn't.

"We're nearly there," he said, annoyed at having revealed so much about himself, "I only hope you know what you're doing."

Lady Rice hoped to see desolation and to hear lamentation as the Volvo approached the house, but she did not. The grounds were in good order, dreaming in the summer sun, the horses grazed tranquilly in the fields; nature itself conspired against her, to say "see how well we all get on without you!" Signposts—well painted and placed—now pointed to Rice Stables, Kennels and Cattery, as well as to the Funfair, The Manor House, The Restoration Gardens, The Maze, Gift Shop, Pottery, Theme Park, Exhibition and Toilets. Oh yes, there had been progress, and very fast progress, without her.

Visiting families wandered around the outside of the house; well-behaved children finished their ice creams before entering, and there were enough bins everywhere to take their debris. The glaziers had been called in; cracked panes of fine, crisp glass, saved in Angelica's day because of their rarity—some being over two hundred years old—had been brutally replaced with young, thick, tough, even glass, but otherwise Lady Rice could find no fault with what had been done to the place, if you liked that kind of thing. She didn't, and the success of those who did was the more bitter.

Lady Rice introduced herself to the unknown woman at the ticket desk—there had been further staff changes—and noticed that entry prices had doubled. She murmured that she was a friend of the family: could she see Sir Edwin?

"This wasn't why we came," said Angelica.
"We can't possibly see him dressed like this," said Jelly.
"He'll see through it to the person beneath," said Lady Rice, hopefully.

"It just seems the sensible thing to do," said Angel. "Now we're here."

Their heart beat loud, thumping, and raced all over the place.

The receptionist looked doubtful, but lifted the telephone and got through to the private wing and said to whoever answered, "Sir Edwin has a visitor, Lady Anthea," and Angel thought that is not fair: anyone who didn't know better would assume that Anthea was Edwin's wife, and took the title from him. She felt even that singularity had been taken from her.

Lady Rice waited. Visitors looked at her curiously. Lady Rice noticed that the price asked for cream teas had risen, too. The oak floorboards which she had hand-waxed to a deep sheen were now covered with a practical polymer sealant; a little notice even said "Floors at Rice Court sealed by the Polyserve Company"—no doubt the price for the job had been reduced on account of it. Anthea, she had to admit, saved money where she could, spent it where she should.

It was not Sir Edwin who came through the green baize door that separated family quarters from public space, but Anthea. She seemed older than Lady Rice remembered: perhaps the effort of domestic life with Edwin, the intrusions of Mrs. MacArthur, the role of *châtelaine* mixed with bursar had taken its toll over the last year: or perhaps Lady Rice saw more clearly now. Anthea's complexion, which had seemed so attractively wind-blown, was now riven by a network of fine, tiny wrinkles; the skin stretched over cheekbones was red and blotchy from, Lady Rice assumed, too much alcohol.

"Jesus!" said Angel. "What a mess! Bet she washes her face with soap and water."

"Look at yourself," said Jelly. "What do you think we look like?"

"Oh God," said Lady Rice. "I don't want her seeing us like this. Can't we just get out of here?"

"She's pregnant!" cried Angelica.

And so Anthea was. A clearly defined football-shaped bump, which she carried as if it was nothing to do with her whatsoever, could be seen just below waist level. Unprepared for this, Lady Rice turned to flee. But Anthea caught her arm.

"It's you, isn't it?" said Anthea. "What are you doing? You've no business here. I'll call the guards. Leave Edwin alone, you little bitch. He doesn't want you; why don't you just go? You're quite mad. Look at you! If you were a horse I'd shoot you. Put you out of your misery."

Lady Rice saw herself as others must see her. The broken, contorted face, the peculiar clothes, the lack of inner substance or definition. She tried to wrest herself out of Anthea's grasp but the other woman's hands were bony and very strong. Anthea rode to hounds: she knew how to grip on for dear life. Anthea breathed whisky fumes in her face. Lady Rice was scared. So were the others. There wasn't a sound from them. Anthea's nails were digging into her arm.

"Security!" called Anthea, in clipped and authoritative tones, as if she were the one under attack.

Lady Rice could see Edwin approaching: he was too fleshy, he looked ill; he was a man no longer charming: just another disgruntled heir bent on self-destruct.

"Edwin, help me!" she called, but he just stood and stared. Anthea seemed beside herself.

"Kinky Virgin," Anthea sneered. "Kinky Virgin! Edwin told me what kind of virgin you were. Famous for it, every which way but normal. A slut, a whore, a disgrace. If I saw a dog doing it, I'd kick it.

Kill it. He pitied you, more fool him. You and your unperforated hymen!"

"If we have to talk," said Edwin, "can't it be in private?"

"I want the whole world to hear," shrieked Angel.

"I am falsely accused," yelled Lady Rice.

"He took my life and sucked me dry and spat me out," snarled Jelly.

"I hate him; he is despicable. He betrayed me and insulted me," spoke Angelica, in loud but level tones.

"No it can't!" yelled Lady Rice.

"It's all behind us now," said Edwin. "Surely?" He seemed craven, and hardly worth getting excited about.

"Get the crazy bitch out of here," snapped Anthea, but the male security men just stood by, not wanting to intervene in the drama.

"I want my rights, Edwin," said Lady Rice calmly. "I want a proper divorce settlement and I want it within the week."

"She has no rights," said Anthea.

Lady Rice spat at Anthea. Anthea drew back, appalled.

"She can have whatsoever she wants," said Edwin. "Christ, Angelica, I'm so sorry. Why did you just back off like that? What was happening to you? We could have sorted it out somehow. Lambert told me everything."

"You bastard," shrieked Anthea at Edwin. "You only ever cared about her. You've delayed and delayed and delayed this divorce. You've no intention of marrying me: you never had. I'm going home. You and that prick Jellico used me to get this place in order. You never loved me. You won't even marry me. You love the gutter, and everything that crawls in it. This woman spat at me!"

Edwin looked baffled and confused. He wasn't listening to a word Anthea said. He didn't care. The visitors crept nearer. Was it some kind of pageant put on for their benefit? But they didn't like the language.

"Angelica?" asked Edwin.

"Too late," said Angelica.

> "Are you sure?" begged Lady Rice.
> "Completely sure," said Angelica. "Shut up."
> Lady Rice shut up.

"I'll write to you," said Angelica firmly. "We'll by-pass solicitors. I'll let you know my terms. And I want my eight hundred thousand pounds back."

"I'll put more pressure on Jellico," said Edwin, "though it's out of my hands. I hate talking about money. Can we be friends?" He was almost in tears.

"No," said Angelica.

> "Are you sure?" asked Jelly.
> "Quite sure," said Angelica.

"Christ, I miss you," said Edwin. "Couldn't we even meet?"

"No," said Angelica.

> "Aw, come on!" said Angel.
> "Just shut up," said Angelica.
> Angel did.

"It's been such a mistake," said Edwin. "We were happy together."

Anthea, in her bitterness, lifted her hand to strike Lady Rice's face. A security guard—a woman, in smart white shirt with braids here and there and a stiff navy skirt—held back the hand. Another propelled Lady Rice to the door. Visitors lining up for admittance stared. Lady Rice half-tumbled, half-stumbled down the steps. Back in the Great Hall Anthea pummelled Edwin with her fists, while he looked distracted and bored.

Lady Rice sat shocked, bruised and triumphant in the back of Ram's car. It is easy to leave a man who wants you, almost impossible to leave a man who doesn't.

"Where to?" he asked.

"The local superstore, where else?" said Lady Rice bleakly.

And there, in spite of Angel's protests, she bought cheap shoes, the plainest of underclothes, the least fragile tights available, a striped little skirt and a black sweater.

Ram followed her directions—a right here, a left there—and eventually drove the Volvo down a track into the fastnesses of the Barley woods.

They left the car: he carried the bags of shopping. Lady Rice led Ram down sun-dappled paths, where the pine needles lay thick and reddy-green, and their softness silenced the noise of their steps, to a stream, which fell down rocks and formed a pool before rippling off through the woods, rush-fringed.

"I used to come here when I was a child," she said. She took off all her clothes piece by piece, looking at them with distaste.

She removed what he now realized was a wig, and hurled it into the bushes. The hair below was fair and cropped.

"Sorry," she said to him.

"That's okay," he said. She looked fine to him. Her body was firm and slender, boyish. He realized he'd seen bits of her naked, never the whole, entire. Just this bit or that bit: this persona or that.

He left her alone, not trying to help her in any way, seeing himself as a permitting presence, nothing more, because it seemed to him she was going through some kind of ritual, and it was better for him not to interfere. She splashed water on the arm where Anthea had bruised the flesh. Then she crouched down and washed her face, rubbing and scrubbing the make-up away, and waited until the water was clear again, free of powdery, pinky, greeny swirls. Then she immersed herself completely; the water was cold: she shivered.
"What are you doing?" he asked her. "Are you being re-born?"
She nodded.
"Do you know why you're doing it?"
She shook her head, seeming alarmed by the question, and clambered out of the water. Ram looked around for something to dry her with, and picked up her discarded T-shirt, but she shook her head violently. He realized she saw her old clothes as polluted.

"I feel very faint," said Angelica. "So cold!"
"I can't see very well," said Jelly. "I have water in my eyes."
"We'll die of pneumonia," said Angel. "I feel so strange!"

Ram offered her his folded cotton handkerchief, and she used that to dry herself, though it was soon sodden. She dressed, damply.
"You look about ten," he said. "Now where are we going?"
"To my mother's," she said.

(2)

A Short Visit to Mrs. White

"You're looking good," said Lavender to Lady Rice. "It quite reminds me of when you were little."

"The trouble is, Mum," said Lady Rice, "I can't remember much about myself as a girl."

"I'm not surprised," said Mrs. White. "All those drugs, all that drink, and all that sex. I wouldn't want to remember if it I were you. Until the day you got married and became your husband's responsibility, you were a nightmare for all of us."

"Why didn't you tell me?" asked Jelly.

"I didn't know I was meant to," said the new Mrs. Hatherley, puzzled. "You seemed happy enough, up there in the Big House, looking down on the rest of us. You never even came to visit me. You were ashamed. Everyone knew it. Shouldn't you bring that young man in? The one who's driving the big car?"

"It's not his place," said her daughter, grandly, with a flicker of her former style. "He's the chauffeur. When I need him I'll bleep him."

"First and only time you brought Edwin to see us," said Lavender, "you were in a little MG. He was much too big for it. Pretty stupid, if you ask me. Perhaps you'd better not ask him in. It might be unlucky."

The second Mrs. Hatherley had moved house. She lived now in the home the first Mrs. Hatherley had created, over twenty-seven years of marriage. The first Mrs. Hatherley, Audrey, had died of a stroke shortly after she had divorced Gerald, but before the property settlement had been made final. The house had passed automatically into Gerald's possession. Gerald and Audrey's daughter, Mary, still unmarried and proud of it, was happy to live where she had always lived, although with a different mother. Friends said there was really very little difference between Audrey and Lavender: why had Gerald gone to all that bother? Mary had given up any thought of protest and now just enjoyed the ex–Mrs. White's cooking, and the habit she had of ironing and folding clothes before putting them into drawers, which her real mother had seldom done. Audrey would pick up dirty clothes from the floor and wash and dry them, but left them for the family to pick out of the laundry basket. Sometimes they would need washing again before this happened. Dust and damp would get into them.

"Don't you feel peculiar living here?" Jelly asked her mother. "Using Audrey's teapot? In Audrey's bed? Doesn't she haunt you?" But apparently not.

"It's really nice living in another woman's home," said the new Mrs. Hatherley. "Other people manage to have the light switches in all the right places, and enough sockets to go round. Audrey didn't stint herself, I must say. Nearly drove poor Gerald to bankruptcy, but what did she care?"

Angelica hurt her teeth on a rock cake that had stayed in the oven for too long.

"Shit!" she said, and her mother raised her eyebrows and said, "If you don't like them, don't eat them. A good rock cake's always hard."

"Mum," asked Angelica, "did I talk to myself a lot when I was a child?"

"All the time," said Mrs. White. "Used to drive your father mad. We'd be woken in the morning by the sound of children playing. Different voices and all. But there'd only ever be you in there."

"Boys' voices too?"

"Oh yes," said Mrs. Hatherley. "Boys and girls. All in there together! That was rather a worry."

Lavender served as good a scone and as bad a jelly as ever. She was an uneven cook. But with her change of name, as it happened, she no longer seemed to Angelica to be her mother at all: Angelica saw herself as orphaned. Mrs. White had transmuted into Mrs. Hatherley, and in the sea-change lost maternal status. She had become just another of the older generation of Barley housewives, varicose-veined and stout-waisted.

"Yes, boys as well," said Mrs. Hatherley. "Boys and girls all in that little body together. What a marvel!"

"You didn't say anything to anybody?"

"No. It kept you quiet while we lay in of a morning. You all seemed to get on well enough. Your dad and I would joke about it. 'No only-child problems for Jelly,' Stephen would say. And I'd say, 'But when she gets to teenage, will it be decent? Supposing they get off with one another?' But by the time teenage came the voices had stopped. There was just the one of you, and not a particularly nice one either, I'm sorry to say."

"Mum," asked Lady Rice, "I'm getting the picture. When you talk about all those drugs, all that drink, and all that sex, what do you mean? I can't remember."

"That's what I mean," said her mother. "You burned your brain right out. I told you you would at the time. All that kinky virgin stuff. That disgusting band of yours. It was practically fornication on stage. And not the kind any of us had ever known about, either. We didn't know where to put ourselves. I'd sacrificed myself for you, given away my life for yours, and here were you throwing your life away. What price virtue now, I thought."

"I'm sorry, Mum," said Angel.

Lavender looked at her quite softly and embraced her.

"I forgive you," she said. "You're back sane and sweet, that's the main thing."

"That's all right then," said Lady Rice to Angelica. "She's sorry and she forgives me. I'm off. Say good-bye to Ram. Bye, Angel. Bye, Jelly. It was a short life, but I can't say it was a sweet one. All I ever did was moan and groan."

Angelica put a hand to her head.

"You haven't got any proper sandwiches?" she asked her mother. "I'm just so hungry all of a sudden."

Lavender sent Mary off to make fish paste sandwiches. Mary went unwillingly, as if she was often told what to do, and put up with it, and didn't like it.

"Mum," said Jelly, though the word came with difficulty to her lips, "another thing. Put your mind back to when Dad died. How did it happen? What was I like when it did? Because I seem to have forgotten that too."

"I'd rather not say," said Mrs. Hatherley, and at that moment Mr. Hatherley let himself cheerfully into the hall and joined them for tea. He ate all the paste sandwiches, leaving none for Jelly. He ate with his right hand, while his left encompassed one of his wife's sturdy legs. Mary came in and out of the room, sent on this task or that, feeding dogs, tropical fish and guinea pigs, all already more than fat enough. Mary wore a diamond engagement ring. Jelly had vague memories of standing next to Mary at Choral Society concerts. They'd been best friends, or Mary had claimed her as such. Mary always sung off-key.

"Do let me get on, dear," said Mrs. Hatherley, trapped by the leg, but her new husband felt disinclined so to do, so she stayed where she was.

"Are you engaged, Mary?" asked Jelly, to distract attention from the sight of her mother and her stepfather in this erotic communication, but Mary said no, it was just a ring her father had given her on her thirtieth birthday.

"Be an angel and play us a tune, Jelly," said Mrs. Hatherley from her imprisonment. "I've still got your father's piano. It takes up a lot of room and I was going to burn it but something stopped me."

Jelly obliged. She played the opening of "Jesu Joy of Man's Desiring." The piano was so out of tune it was funny. Her fingers stumbled dreadfully over the keys but no-one seemed to notice. Whatever she did, these nice people wanted to approve of her. Aspiration bounced up to the ceiling and back down again, deadened. There was no way the notes she played could ever get up and out to join the music of the spheres, which was their natural place. She could see that she had failed in her life. On the other hand it was hardly her fault.

"Your father used to play us such lovely tunes from the *Beggar Prince*," said Mary, "when we were little."

"Why don't you tell your girl the truth about everything, Lavender," said Gerald Hatherley. Now he had finished his sandwich, his right arm shot out and he trapped his daughter's legs as well as his wife's. They all squealed happily.

"Might as well," said Mrs. Hatherley. "What's the harm now? Once you stopped being little, Jelly, you seemed to take no notice of your father; whether he was there in the room or not what did you care? He'd got you into the Royal College, but you didn't go, you cut that record instead. 'Kinky Virgin.' He could just about get used to the music but then someone sent him the lyrics. I'm sorry to say he died in minutes, sitting in that very chair, over there."

"Are you saying I murdered my father?" asked Angel.

"Oh no dear," said her mother, "whoever sent him the lyrics did that. I think it was Gerald's first wife. She could be so spiteful."

"I remember now," said Angel. "I remember you telling me my father was dead and me saying to you 'but how could you tell the difference?' and I laughed and you hit me, saying I was a monster. And you were right: I killed him and then I made a joke of it."

"Well, dear," said Mrs. Hatherley, "I must admit it wasn't very nice of you," and she squealed and laughed as Mr. Hatherley started tickling her up and down her leg and Mary squealed, "Me, me!" and got even closer.

"But then again," her mother said to Angel, "when I thought about it, I could see what you meant about not telling the difference. After the choir was disbanded—no one wants to hear proper singing any more—your father just sat in that chair for years and stared into space. I was always a lively girl. It wasn't right for me. I only married him because of you. He was very good to you considering you weren't his child. I'm sure he's in heaven smiling down at me and glad for my happiness."

The girls took a little time to re-group.

"Oh, well," said Angel. "If he wasn't my father I don't have to go round feeling so bad. I'm not a patricide after all. You can get on without me, Jelly. How's your memory, Angelica?"

"It's okay," said Angelica. "Getting better by the moment. I can even remember the lyrics of 'Kinky Virgin.' I wish I couldn't but I can."

"Then I'm off," said Angel. "Self-destruct. For God's sake girls, keep your legs shaved, and never, never, wash your face with soap and water. Sorry I lost you your job, Jelly."

"That's okay," said Jelly, but she was talking to no-one. Angel simply wasn't there.

"The poor girl's quite stunned," said Gerald Hatherley. "She's gone white as a sheet."

"I'm not surprised," said Mary, with some sympathy. "I wouldn't like to get to our age and find I wasn't my own father's daughter."

Jelly remembered why she had liked Mary. Cigarettes behind the bicycle shed, bicycle rides in the woods.

The cottage window opened directly on to the street. Ram drew up the limousine just outside, so he could look directly through to where Jelly stood, and at the family scene within.

"But then you knew that, didn't you, Jelly?" said Mrs. Hatherley. "In your heart? You must have!"

"Well, no, I didn't," said Jelly, "because nobody told me."

She shook her head at Ram, and he drove on.

"Are you all right, dear?" asked her mother.

"I think I've eaten too much," said Angelica. "I feel so full! Who was my father, then?"

Lavender continued to be evasive.

"I wasn't the sort to claim Welfare, so I had to marry someone, and Stephen turned up. He was very kind. We weren't unhappy; don't think that; but he was a lot older than me. That's what we'd end up doing in those days: unmarried mothers like us. We'd marry someone much older, to have somewhere to live and bring up baby. Forget the sex. All that sex had ever done, so far as we could see, was get us into trouble. Or so we thought. Of course the world's a different place now. The State takes the place of the older man when it comes to support."

"You never told me," said Angelica. "You should have told me."

"I thought you would have guessed," said Lavender. "Leave it at that, Angelica dear. You don't want to know anything more."

"I do. You must tell me. Who was my real father?"

"At least it wasn't someone from a sperm bank," said her mother. "That I would be ashamed of. I was very young. I was quite the tomboy. A football fan. There was a little group of us. Groupies, they call them now. We used to try and have the whole football team. None of us ever managed the lot."

"You're telling me you don't know who my father was?"

"They were all good-looking lads. I don't know how these things work. Perhaps you got a little bit from all of them?"

"No, Mother, that is not how things work," said Angelica. "How many?"

"About six, Jelly," said Lavender.

"Don't call me Jelly," said Angelica.

"It was your father's idea to call you Angelica. I never liked it. When you started talking to yourself I said to him, are you surprised? That name could split into a dozen different nicknames. I told him but he always knew best."

"Don't call him my father."

"He was a good man, and a good father to you. Don't deny him, don't insult him."

"What was the football match, Mum?" asked Mary. "My God, Jelly might be anyone's!"

"Don't call her your mum; she isn't," said Angelica. "She's mine."

"Don't be spiteful, Mary: sometimes you're so like Audrey," said Mrs. Hatherley. "You can tell poor Angelica's upset. I was right not to tell her before. Some things are better left in the closet."

"Whatever you do is right by me, sweetheart," said Gerald Hatherley, once prime mover at the PTA, now a man enjoying his prime, his hand moving so far up his wife's skirt that she squealed and Mary said mildly, "Oh Dad, not so far, you'll shock poor Jelly. Fancy not knowing who your father is at all!"

Jelly White felt wholly illegitimized, as if someone with no existence at all had worked for Brian Moss, wrapped a wraithful tongue around his member: no, not even that kept her in this world, not even mouthfuls of his seed could keep her nourished; she was going, she was almost gone.

"Good-bye, good-bye," Jelly called to Angelica, as she felt herself going, "you'll be okay now, won't you?" but it was too late,

Angelica could not even hear. Thus Jelly slipped back into Angelica, and was incorporated.

Angelica stood up and looked at herself long and hard in the mirror, and liked what she saw: half a dozen possible fathers but one result, however chancy.

"I'm ever so sleepy," Angelica said. "So tired!" She lay down on the sofa and her mother covered her with a rug. Angelica slept like a baby.

"That's what she used to look like," said her mother, "when she was very little. I wonder if she's feverish? So much life-news in so short a time!"

She took her daughter's wrist and placed her finger on the pulse; she thought for a moment it faltered, as if it had decided not to go on. Then it started up again, firm and strong. The mother was reassured, and left her to sleep.

Ram made larger and larger circles as he waited for Angelica to bleep him. The visit had taken longer than anyone had expected. The sun had set; crowds were beginning to leave Rice Court; the main road was busy, the smaller roads unaffected. First the Volvo circled the estate, with its sensible little houses, all more or less new, with their thin, practical walls between inside and out. Then Ram widened the circle, including the village of Barley, with its duck pond, its village green, its English country gardens, its quaint, well-preserved gentility. Here at least the stone walls were thick and solid. Then he included Rice Court in the circle and its theme park, where the new and the old mixed so strangely, and he could just see over the tops of the trees to the ruined castellated tower of Cowarth Castle and thought he would widen the circle further when the phone bleeped. It was Angelica.

"You okay?" he asked.

"Just fine," she said. "Single-minded." And he didn't complete the circle—but reversed, swung the car round, and went back to pick her up.

Angelica waved good-bye to the smiling, loving faces.

"Where to?" asked Ram.

"I suppose the Royal College of Music might have us back," she said.

"Us?" he enquired.

"You and me," she said. "Starting over. Let's get out of here quick."

"Jesus!" he said, but he accelerated hard and they went.